IDENTITY:

LARRY CUMMINS, BUSHRANGER

PETER LONG

HAWKEYE
PUBLISHING

First published in Australia in 2023 by Hawkeye Publishing.

Cover Design by Kate Doroshenko

A catalogue record of this book is available from the National Library of Australia.

ISBN 9781923105072

Proudly printed in Australia.

Hawkeye Publishing would like to acknowledge the Turrbal people who are the traditional owners of the land on which our publishing house is located in Brisbane. The Turrbal people are the original storytellers of our region.

www.hawkeyepublishing.com.au
www.hawkeyebooks.com.au

Praise for
IDENTITY: LARRY CUMMINS, BUSHRANGER

'The recreation of the everyday lives of the characters is absolutely convincing – as is the presentation of their emotional and psychological lives. Peter Long's ability to render the fine details of life in this period with historical authenticity is on a level equal to Hilary Mantel's writing about Cromwell and the 17th Century in England. Larry's first-person accounts of the physical and psychological trauma of incarceration by the colonial authorities are intensely affective and disturbing. The descriptions of the brutal attempts to break prisoners' resistance and annihilate their identity would stand up against similar narratives of personal degradation in world literature – Primo Levi's *If This is A Man* and Solzhenitsyn's *Gulag* books come to mind. While readers gain an intensely affective insight into Larry Cummins' personality, in the final chapter where the dramatic personae of the novel are gathered for a wake/inquisition into Larry's life, they all give contradictory accounts of him. When it is noted that even his grave can't be located, it is concluded 'He's as hard to locate in death, as he is in life.' This is a clever twist in this narratively sophisticated novel.'
Professor Stephen S. Torres

'Larry was a larger-than-life character whose voice captures the very essence of Australian outback living. Despite the hardship he suffers, and the results of his own bad decisions, he maintains a sharp sense of humour and moral compass. Both sides of Larry are held up for closer inspection – the loving family man and introspective thinker, and the impulsive, poverty-hardened opportunist who lived by his wits and belief in his own streak of luck. *Identity* is a fascinating, fictional take on historical events, especially for Australian readers who grew up on stories of wild colonial boys. The main character is likeable and thought-provoking.'
K. M. Steele, Author of Hunt for the Virgin Rainbow

Praise for *IDENTITY: LARRY CUMMINS, BUSHRANGER*

'A vivid tale of a bushranger's life and an animated insight into the motives, consequences, and the ultimate price of living as an outlaw. A page turner.'

Edita Mukic, Author of Between Before and After

'A wonderful follow up to *Steve Hart – The last Kelly Standing*. The way in which Peter Long has authentically recreated the essence of 1860s colonial Australia, told through the eyes of various characters, is nothing short of masterful. Colloquial dialogue, visceral descriptions and impeccable research, all weave together to form a vivid story, a time capsule to the past. The plight of Larry Cummins' colourful life of adventure, heartache, resolve, and risk taking, has been beautifully recreated by an author whose family connections make the story heartfelt and real. You'll peer down Larry's rifle sights, smell the gunpowder, gallop astride a colt pursued by an unrelenting trooper. You'll laugh, cry and suffer with him, you'll smell the sweetness of freedom, rebuild a life, find love again, endure hard times, take a chance. And you never know who might make an appearance in this metaphoric retelling of history. An intriguing and reflective ending.'

Jack Roney, Author of the Detective Jarrod O'Connor Series: The Angels Wept, The Demons Woke, The Shadows Watch

'Peter Long's literary style compels thought and reflection. In my view, an under-rated author adding compelling and important works to the Australian historical fiction genre. A few pages into *Identity* and I was swept along. I read this in a weekend – you will too. Masterful.'

Cate Sawyer, Co-author, Winning Short Story Competitions: Essential tools for the serious writer

This novel is dedicated to my parents, Red and Betty Long, and to the members of the Long family descended from Larry Cummins' son, Sidney Long. I remember with fondness the warmth of their embrace.

PREFACE

I wrote this work to record my reaction to discovering late in life, and via an incredible moment of fate (Chapter 1), that my great grandfather was Larry Cummins, a notorious 1860's bushranger in the Upper Lachlan area of New South Wales.

Maurice Cummins, the author of the Cummins' family history, *A Long Way to Tipperary*, had contacted our family to ascertain if Larry was, in fact, James Long our great grandfather. Subsequent DNA testing has confirmed the fact.

Having been a writer since my teens I could not believe my luck that such a rich subject had landed in my lap, but then, the enormity of the responsibility hit me. When I read the history, family voices echoed in my mind. I'd read numerous histories of other bushrangers, like the Keniffe or Kelly gangs and, while touched, was not disturbed. In contrast, I had a visceral reaction to the events featured in the family's journey.

I realised truth is stranger, and in this case, more dramatic, than fiction. I didn't want my novel to be a pale shadow of Larry's story, already told wonderfully by Maurice.

I began to write about the topics that had touched me emotionally from Larry's point of view. That approach appeared straightforward but as I wrote, family voices continually interrupted. As one often guided by intuition, I decided to include them – create a domestic history.

This is a deconstructed novel. The chapters, roughly, roll out in chronological order as depicted in their title.

LARRY'S LUCK
1996

THERE is nothing more final than a funeral. The person is dead. You'll never see or speak with them again. When the deceased was the sole remaining parent, there is no room for delusional beliefs about life carrying on as usual for those surviving. Hard decisions must be made. What will happen to the family home? Who should get what furniture and artefacts? What memorabilia will you keep?

Brother and sister had organised the funeral. A simple matter on the face of it. It involved estimating how many people might attend, picking the deceased's favourite music, finding snapshots that might accurately represent them, determining who will speak and have an involvement in the service, who will not be allowed to speak, and ensuring provision of appropriate food. Then there was the business of tracking down a preacher who, although not knowing the deceased, would feign a familiarity without aggrandising their own life over the deceased's.

The brother and sister now know all this, but didn't before.

Guests from far and wide had attended.

The Returned Services League had done its bit for an involved member. Its representative had shared the deceased's active World War II service record. The deceased was a member of the regiment who stopped the Japs at Milne Bay – the Japs' first ever defeat. He was one of the family's four boys, all who had seen active service: two in the same campaign but on different violent jungle tracks; two at sea.

There were very few veterans alive with whom to share the stories and, with time's passing, even fewer to attend funerals, to support the bereaved. A chapter in family history closed: pages in the national parchment of our identity, closed.

Family had attended the funeral.

The eldest and sole surviving brother of the deceased's generation attended.

The only remaining widow attended.

It's strange how longevity appears to rely on random factors: age, health, genes, circumstance, environment.

The deceased's son was not expected to outlive the father to learn and pass on secrets. As a teen, the son was struck down with the bends diving the war wrecks off New Guinea, where his father and uncles had fought the Japanese.

There was a brief time when the son was not expected to live. An Air Force plane's mercy dash, intensive care, weeks in a hyperbaric chamber, assisted breathing, massage.

All the while, his girlfriend, at his side, stubbornly refused to be daunted by the prospect of disability.

In weeks, he gained some consciousness and learned that he would never walk again.

Over time, the son did walk – if you could call his tortuous gait a walk – and functioned fully in the community: travelling, living abroad, building a family, gaining a pilot's licence.

Just days after the father's funeral, the son's sister watches her brother move furniture, pack the trailer and clean the house, with each step at the end of the day taken as deliberately as the day's first.

The son walks by swinging his hips to extend a leg. The signals to tendons and ligaments are erratic and the toe drags for a moment, then locks in and places itself, awkwardly, on the flat. He is determined to work unassisted, very determined. Pig-headed in some ways, like other family members, but the sister reminds herself that his stubbornness had been required to pull himself back from the brink.

The sister smiles at him as he wobbles over with a glass of water to where she sits on the kitchen bench, and true to type, he returns her smile.

The electric light above the Laminex bench highlights the sister's excellent facial bone structure, and the starkness of the empty house, devoid not only of furniture, artefacts, and colour, but also, of people.

Absent are the parents pottering about; the kids running through the now bare halls. There were so many family celebrations. Her twenty-first birthday was held right there where the massive pine table had stood. She'd cut the cake and blown out the candles, looked into the faces of those who loved her. The mark over there, where the grandchild, her son, ran his scooter and ripped an ungainly hole in the wall, was never fully repaired. Even the electric light would not function tomorrow – she had organised for the electricity and the telephone to be cancelled. Final acts for a final curtain.

Do we ever recover? Do we carry on but not recover; papered over like a pocked wall? Each loss leaving a hole into which all information about that individual – all acts, insane or noble, pertaining to that person – are sucked into it by the failure of others to hold tightly onto the history, to listen to those on the edge, and appreciate the secrets they're passing on.

Secrets and mysteries about identity, about sacred byways, about uncoupled language, mystical lands once populated by the ancestors and abandoned when family explorers, or refugees, headed out in animal-skinned coracle, log canoe, wooden sailing ship.

Silence.

They will have to decide soon: move on, say good night, switch the light off, lock the house. Once the door closes there will no longer be a "home" to visit. They will be cast adrift to psychically cope by themselves, to provide their own sanctuary; a "home" to their offspring.

The phone rings like an electric saw cutting the silence in jagged pieces. Brother and sister flinch; stare at each other, mouths open. She lifts an upturned hand as if to message "go figure".

'The phone was supposed to be disconnected days ago.'

He nods, understanding.

'Don't answer it. It's probably a phone technician testing the line or disengaging it.'

The phone rings again, echoes around the vacant house; mesmerises. They watch it vibrate on the floor like a squat plastic toad. The sister straightens.

'Maybe I should answer it.'

'No, I will,' the brother says. 'It will ring out before I get it, given the speed I travel.'

They chuckle and he slides from the benchtop and marks time a moment as he winds up his gait.

She knows there is no point arguing.

'Suit yourself.'

Another ring rattles around the empty house.

Yet another, as he wends his way towards it.

He reaches it; lifts the receiver mid-ring.

'Hello?'

The sound of the caller's voice buzzes in the handset. The son shakes his head slowly.

'Yes, this is Mr Long, but a case of mistaken identity, maybe not the Mr Long you are hoping for.'

A pause, while he listens.

'No, I'm sorry, he can't come to the phone. I'm afraid he has passed away. Died!'

Silence. The sister hears the extended mumble of a voice from the handpiece.

'Oh, did he? Yes, I think he may have, some time back. I think I remember him saying he was trying to track down some family history... An advertisement? Oh yes. Yeah, it could have been... in

The Australasian Post you say? He was looking to learn about the fate of a rocking horse and a sword belonging to his family. Yeah. Ah!'

Further murmurs from the mouthpiece. The sister, Carolyn, watches her brother's face as he listens. The caller has him captivated; what was once slight irritation is now transfixed attention.

'Oh, is there? Another ad? Wanting to contact descendants of James Long?... Never heard of him.'

The voice in the earpiece buzzes on. The son inhales, expels air loudly.

'Yes, I think Dad's family did come from the Albury-Wodonga area.'

The voice in the earpiece.

'And he wants to get in touch with descendants?... Wait a moment and I'll see if we have a pencil. You were lucky to catch us. We've just cleared and packed their belongings, ready to walk out the door and lock up. We thought the phone had been disconnected.'

Phillip places the handset onto the stained wooden floor. Carolyn's eyes seek an explanation.

He shuffles towards her.

'A pencil. Do we have a pencil?'

'Here, in my purse.'

She rifles through the purse on the bare kitchen bench, finds and offers a pencil.

'Here!'

'Thanks.'

He shuffles to the abandoned phone.

'Right, fire away!'

The voice in the earpiece is less frantic.

'Morris...' Phillip spells it into the mouthpiece. 'M O R R I S. Oh Maurice, M A U R, right. Sorry. Cummins. C UM M I N S... good, got it. Number?... Okay, we'll contact him. Thank you... Bye.'

Phillip bends; cradles the handset.

Carolyn is all ears.

'Who was that?'

'A fellow who lives in Warwick. He saw an ad that Dad ran in the *Australasian Post* seeking information regarding a family rocking horse and a sword. Remember when Dad was obsessed with family history? Apparently, the fellow then read an advertisement in their local paper placed by a Maurice Cummins in Canberra, researching his family history. Cummins is looking for the descendants of James Long from Albury. He must have listed Sidney as a sibling, and the children of this James Long are known to have moved to Queensland. The caller wondered if we were the same family. Made the call.'

'It's Larry's luck we're still here in the house, eh?'

'Exactly! That's what I told him. Another few minutes and he would have missed us.'

'Larry's luck that he put two and two together, if both ads are related. It's like a decayed, worm-eaten hand reaching from the grave and grasping us around the ankle to deliver a message from two generations earlier.'

Carolyn draws her shirt tighter in response to the cold chill that ruffles her shoulders.

They sit for a moment in silence while the incredulity of the moment sinks in.

'Yeah, another five minutes and it would have passed unknown.'

Phillip shakes his head.

'Dad submitted that ad, maybe… twelve months ago. The bloke sat on it for that long. I wonder what prompted him to phone at this precise moment?'

'Yeah, true. Why not give this Maurice a call? It's not too late. Could be more Larry's luck and we may be about to inherit a fortune, or a family castle.' Carolyn smiles. 'Or a debt, or a serial killer.'

Phillip nods, scratches the back of his head.

'Anyway, what's this 'Larry's luck'? I haven't heard it used since we were children.'

'Dad has been saying it since he's been unwell. The kids and I have adopted it while looking after him. Dad told us it's an old family saying of his father's – can mean both good and bad luck.'

'Oh?'

'Yeah, say, like Uncle Ken, you've had two fingers chopped off at the woodheap by your brother, poor luck; but gee... lucky it wasn't your whole hand.'

Phillip laughs.

'Ha ha. That's all the sympathy you'd get in our family, anyway!'

'Yeah, what was Dad's saying? 'We don't grieve for the dead, we let others do it'?'

ROBBERY UNDER ARMS: A CRIMINAL STORY 1863

THE Mudgee mail coach pulled around the corner below the Big Hill, on the Blue Mountains' western slopes, and made its way two-hundred yards up the hill before it stopped and discharged its passengers. The six horses, already breathing heavy, tossed their manes and stamped their hooves before trudging on. The passengers followed on foot to avoid "blowing" the horses on the steep incline.

From above, Fred Lowry watched the coach resume, then glanced across at the two fancily attired gentlemen beside him.

'This is it chaps. Quiet and friendly. We'll have five minutes to complete our work. Any longer and we'll be interrupted. As you've observed, this is a busy road.'

'You're not wrong about that,' agreed the youngest, Larry Cummins, already concerned about the travellers who had passed while they waited for the coach, and who, despite their distance from the roadside, may have recognised them.

John Foley, often short of a word, added, 'I seen so many trap patrols the past few days while I staked out the Hill. We can't dilly dally.'

Dressed as local gentlemen in tight Bedford-cord riding breeches, polished wellington boots, ornamented brown sweaters with cuffs, and breasts overlaid with dark waistcoats with blue flashings and silver buttons, they gambled on avoiding undue suspicion from the coach guards. They'd stolen the clothes the day before, but Larry's hung loose, he being smaller, slighter, and fairer of complexion than the others. Thankfully, from a distance, he managed to look reasonable.

The plan was to approach the mail coach while it slowed. It was an easier and less obvious place to bail it, than to fell a tree to halt its progress elsewhere. It would be a profitable bail, with a bank manager riding in the coach.

So far, the costume ploy had worked, and as they drew abreast of the coach, Lowry rode slightly ahead to cover the walking passengers, while Foley delayed a little to call on the guards riding atop the coach to bail-up, as soon as Lowry signalled "all clear".

'Bail-up!'

A guard reached for his rifle.

Larry discharged his pistol over the guard's head in warning.

Coach and bushrangers' horses shied and reared upon hearing the sound.

The guard raised his hands, fast.

All was controlled.

Now to lift the valuables.

~

Mrs Smith stood so very, very still in the mid-morning sunlight. She refused to open her eyes. Even if the tall rider on the sleek bay was to beg her, she would refuse.

The sweat from climbing the Big Hill mounted between the dam walls of her compressed breasts and marked out an island of damp across her blouse's back panel. Fear now prompted perspiration and added further to her distress. The horseman had addressed her. *Was she also to lose her valuables; a hundred pounds of the King's legal tender hidden in her crinoline?* Her shoulders slumped as if the package grew heavier and far bulkier than it did a moment ago. *Was it more obvious to these animals?* She could feel Bank Manager Kater's fear radiating off him as he stood close by.

She knew she must be brave.

~

'There's no need to fear us, madam,' bushranger Lowry asserted from behind his foaming black beard, '… for we are gentlemen and would not harm a lady… But, as for this fine specimen of manhood here,' the bushranger pointed his pistol at a small, bandy-legged, well-dressed man, his fair hair slicked down, standing in the line of coach passengers, '… it's a different matter, altogether.'

The bank manager's eyes followed Lowry's pistol barrel.

'Please, don't harm me… I've never done anything to harm you.'

Knowing Kater from earlier reconnaissance and reputation, Lowry smirked.

'A representative of a bank and you've never harmed me?… Have you ever given me money out of the generosity of your heart? Eh? Have you not always refused to give ma kin money when they've come to borrow it? In fact, humiliated them in front of your staff and customers as you sent them on their way?'

The banker squirmed, answered in a hurry.

'It was my job, nothing personal.'

Lowry bent his head level with the bank manager's.

'Nothing personal? Well, this is my job, nothing personal. Don't expect me to be generous if you fail to assist us.'

Kater's face reddened, his eyes flared.

'Sir?'

Lowry threw his head back in mock surprise.

'Oh, sir is it now?… Shut up and hand over the bank's money.'

'I don't have it.'

'You don't have it?'

Lowry dismounted, tapped his pistol barrel on the banker's gold watch-chain draped across his waist.

The banker glanced at the exposed chain.

'Oh, er, yes, take my watch, if you must, and then set me free.'

The bushranger pulled the chain, and the watch followed. He slipped his find into his own fob-pocket; tapped the banker firmly on the forehead with the point of the barrel.

'We know you have the money, so don't lie.'

John Foley, leaning inside the coach, let out a 'hoy' and threw a carpet bag at Lowry's feet.

'Here, mate. It's locked.'

'Oh, what have we here?'

Lowry collected the bag and handed it to Kater.

'Open it and don't delay.'

'I'm not sure I… I…'

'Open it. We haven't got all day.'

Time was running out and the bail, so slow.

'The money will be of no use to you. They're used notes, taken out of circulation, and I'm returning them to head office for disposal.'

Kater's voice broke as he'd spoken, exuded a squeaking note and a trembling end to the sentence, exposing his fear.

Lowry shook his head.

'Let me be the judge of that. I'll start my own currency – "Lowry money" – if I must.'

~

Larry Cummins' horse bumped the lady as he rode through the crowd and further up the hill. He was concerned, as the banker resisted, that the bail was not running to time. The hill was steep, and a lookout was needed to warn the two bushrangers working at the coach below, should someone suddenly appear over the horizon.

This robbery was a big deal. If the rumours were true that the Stock Bank cache was in the haul, the lift would be in the league of their mates, Frank Gardiner and Ben Hall's, deeds – many thousands of pounds – a king's ransom, and would make the harsh bushranging life worth it.

He could do a lot with that money, but there was a risk.

The first time he had bailed someone, Larry had watched the fellow, a hawker, for hours, hence knew he was unarmed and relatively safe. He'd approached him masked, and with gun drawn.

'Bail-up or I'll shoot.'

The fellow nearly shat himself, and handed over a few quid, some coins, and some of the cure-all medicines made from goanna fat, that he hawked as medicine. A pittance.

But there was something powerful in being another identity behind the mask, in the feel of the gun, in the obedience of the older man to the armed teenager's commands. The wiser, worldly man obeying the country boy who had never seen the city, knew little of a world more complex than the sparse community within which he roamed. He was in control.

There had been many more incidents since then and all rolled out as planned. Hopefully, this bail would too, but here, he was not in control.

Feeling weary and eye-drooping tired, the coach scene below rolled out like a hazy dream. The occasional angry tones floated up, but he relied on reading hand movements and body language to interpret what was happening. It seemed fine, if slow. Weeks on the run from the police with Gilbert, Gardiner, and Hall, hundreds of miles from home, had driven him dog-weary. He wanted to get home, be with family.

Chased by Pottinger's men, they'd made fools of the traps by using their stolen racehorses to outrun them on every occasion, but it was relentless. One gang member, barely weeks before, had been tracked for 260 miles by black-trackers, and killed at his family's home, where he believed he was secure, far outside the goldfields and surrounds.

Drinking wildly, eating irregularly, sleeping rough after long nights, Larry felt far older and more dissipated than his nineteen years.

If this was the bushrangers' life: he was wearying of it.

This haul may allow him to relax for a while, to work on the farm and to get to know his child, and spend time with his childhood sweetheart, Bridget. The money pilfered, to date, was barely worth the risk of bailing up a traveller. A couple of pounds here, some shillings there. It would have been better were he to stick to his dead father, Irish Joseph's, cattle and horse duffing business. Lift the odd horse from the arrogant squatter, remain anonymous, and slowly grow rich. But he'd craved for the recognition of the gangs, for bedazzling the traps, performing brave deeds, riding fast horses, and shouting drinks for all at his favourite shanties.

Despite all his lifting, he remained barely a candle-flicker on the trap's landscape, overcrowded with well-known villains, but this may be about to change once news of this hold-up spread.

Larry was surprised, Foley and Lowry didn't wear masks as they pillaged. He and his brother, Jack, always did, although one morning when Jack bailed a couple on their way to town, the woman said, 'I know you, Jack Cummins, by your voice, and by the two missing fingers on your gun hand.'

Larry had chopped Jack's fingers off with an axe in a childhood dare.

'You must be mistaken madam,' Jack had said, deliberately, as he pushed his face up against hers and stared fiercely into her eyes from above his mask. '...because I would kill anybody who mistook me for that lout.'

He'd watched the message sneak in. Watched perspiration bead along her brow.

'So, are you mistaken?'

She'd hesitated, then, without a blink, said, 'I am, indeed, good sir.'

'I thought you were. Now, hand over that brooch.'

Being recognised rattled young Jack.

It also put them on the police list of suspects for this type of crime.

'She bloody recognised me from that one wee fault – two missing fingers. I'd forgotten I'd lost them meself, and that's me identity – somethin' missin'?' he'd raved.

'Covering our faces with a mask is a waste of time for us now,' Foley explained, with Lowry nodding in agreement, when Larry challenged them. 'Everybody knows us and we're a begging scalp for any police trapper, it's not worth the effort to mask up. Besides, in this case, if we approach the coach, masked, the guards will shoot us before we get close enough to bail them.'

Larry saw the merit in it from that point of view, but was pleased young Jack was not here, exposed. Jack was safe should this bail go askew and their identities be revealed.

In fact, he believed Foley and Lowry enjoyed the notoriety. At night, with too much grog on board, and dice flashing, the pair recounted the exploits of other, more notorious bushrangers: John Peisley, Ben Hall, Frank Gardiner, to name a few. The latter's Lachlan Gold Escort robbery of thousands of pounds, a pinnacle of the trade worth emulating. It was as if the couple, while resentful of, were enchanted by these characters, hoping the news of their own adventures and misdeeds would spread to boost their stakes.

'I think they'd enjoy being captured just to boast to the newspapers the extent of their liftin',' Larry revealed to young Jack one night, while drinking alone in McAllister's Inn. 'They're shameless and daring but set for a short life.'

Jack had screwed his face with disdain.

'Well, why do ya run with them?'

'They're mates. Sometimes you get caught up with the idea. You make promises when you're shickered, and a man's word is a man's word, ain't it? I'd hate to be shamed by them, called a Nancy boy, I would, Jack. You know… Be more than I could stand. Me word's me word – it's who I am.'

Jack didn't appear convinced.

'Be careful, then.'

A noise, below, claimed Larry's attention. He watched the bushrangers negotiate with the coach party. Foley dragged a man's head by the ear, inches above ground, this way and that, like hypnotising a chook. Then he stopped, released the ear, dropped to his knees, and fiddled with the valise before him.

~

Mrs Smith remained frozen. Her shock at how gentlemen could stoop so low as to rob other people's belongings prevented her coming to grips with the reality that these were not gentlemen, but dingoes in lamb's clothing.

She'd made the mistake of attracting the tall, dark rider's attention, the one with the laughing eyes, and closed her eyes tight, perhaps to avoid a repeat. *Oh, his look was hungry. It was as if he'd peered through a straw deep within her and seen something she knew was there but lay hidden from all, especially her husband.* It raised a flush in private places. *What if they tore off her clothes and, in turns, ravaged her, here in the dust, like the wild beasts they were? Like highwaymen had done to the poor lady at Cherry Tree Hill during a bail only weeks before?* She trembled, sweated even more.

A voice, so close. Her body jumped as if a spring uncoiled. She'd not heard him approach. The message fingered through the trance's veil, intruded where it wasn't invited.

'Yes... you, my lady.'

Which lady? She was the only lady.

Someone's breath brushed her delicate neck and spittle bounced off her powdered cheek, and the odour of mutton fat, from their foul breath, invaded her. A finger poked her ribs just below her bounteous breast, penetrated deep.

'Yes… you. What are you hiding under all this?'

He shook her bulging skirt.

Despite her commitment to ignore any intrusion, Mrs Smith, eyes still closed, stepped back. Crinoline rustled and the shammy containing the hundred pounds she was taking to the bank in Sydney pressed reassuringly against her over-soft flesh.

'I'm a lady,' she whispered.

'Are you now?… A lady?… and a beautiful one at that,' he added.

A beautiful one at that. No one except her silly father had ever proposed that she was beautiful, and perhaps even he lied. Comely, attractive maybe, and she may have imagined the latter, but never beautiful. Her body glowed as she replayed the words.

'A lady has nothing to fear from John Foley, ma'am. I told you that.'

And with that, his footsteps retreated. She heard the rattle of coach livery, brass buckles, and the flap of leather harness, the odd swear word, commands to a horse to 'stand still', to 'move its hoof', and to 'back up'.

The sweat… moisture, enveloped her inside and out. She swooned, might faint, but refused, still, to open her eyes.

~

Come on boyos, hurry it up, Larry urged in his mind. Being idle with nothing to occupy his time made him twitchy. At any moment travellers, perhaps traps, could appear along the ridge.

Below, Lowry had re-mounted, a soft bag slung across the pommel of his saddle, carried like you would a day-old calf when duffing breeding stock. *Was it full of loot?*

Larry watched as Foley uncoupled the horses from the coach, removed their harnesses and set them free. They galloped tails high, ducked their heads and kicked free with exuberance. Without horses, news about the robbery would be delayed until the hapless travellers walked the sixteen miles to the nearest town, or were lucky enough to meet a police patrol moving around the territory attempting to deter such crimes. A delay provided time for the bushrangers to cross into another county.

Larry peered further along the road above and noticed dust. *Riders. It could be a troop of traps.* A spring curled tight within his stomach, contracted. *Shit.* He released a long whistle to alert the men below to hurry. *Would they escape in time? Had the bail borne fruit?*

~

Lowry heard the whistle, peered up at Larry. Understood the danger in his wild signals. Scanned the sorry passengers.

'Well, that's our work done for today, folks.'

He turned to Foley.

'Grab the rifles and mount up.'

He tipped his cabbage-tree hat to the sorry passengers.

'Bye, Mr Kater… Ma'am.'

~

Mrs Smith opened her eyes in the voice's direction. She stared at Lowrey's face, only to be blinded by the sun flashing behind as he moved his head. That most beautiful smile. She cast her eyes downward to avoid the glare and as his horse spun, she counted beneath his coat five revolvers embedded in his belt, saw the silver of polished steel on his knightly steed's hooves, and stared at his retreating back as he and his mate cantered up the hill. With a hand gesture to the rider on the hilltop, all three riders turned north into the roadside scrub and disappeared.

Later, Mrs Smith would report that she recognised Larry Cummins as the rider on the hilltop, having seen him at the Limerick races some months earlier. *Had she been mistaken, merely responded to the power of suggestion, when police listed names of known accomplices?*

~

Larry, loaded with bank notes from the nearly six thousand pounds they'd bailed, split from the others after an hour's hard riding. Rode to the Bolong, to be with his little family. He hid much of his booty on their block, protection against lean times.

The following Sunday, after a day on shanty rum, he rode home with brother Jack past Richlands, the large squatter's run that founded the district. They continued to nearby McKinnon's farm – people known to them.

It may have been the drink, but out of the blue, Larry approached the homestead. He noticed Jack's enquiring eyes.

'I need some saddle gear for the new horse, now that I've returned Hogan's horse to him, and this monster is too large for my gear.'

Larry flashed his pistols at Norman McKinnon the moment the poor fellow moved onto the veranda to meet them.

'Bail up, if you value your life.'

Jack looked surprised, perhaps imagined Larry would pay. Larry's hands were unsteady as a result of drink. The pistol as steady as a willie wagtail's tail. McKinnon's hands lifted shoulder high. Larry flashed a friendly, if lopsided, smile.

'Top of the evening to you, Norman. Give us any money ya have and we'll be on our way.'

'No money here, boys, it's months since the pay's came through and we are all on wee rations.'

'Tobacco? Ya must have tobacco.'

McKinnon rifled his pockets and handed over tobacco.

'Here, take a fig.'

Larry took it, dismounted, and attempted to roll a fag with shaking hands, spilling tobacco as he tottered towards the shed's rear.

'We need bridles… and saddles, also.'

Norman twisted his head, followed Larry with his eyes, but remained silent.

Larry rattled about searching the shelves.

'Ah. We're in luck… saddlebags.'

He grabbed two bags, along with a girth, yet didn't collect bridles or other gear as he'd threatened. He stumbled back and remounted, waved with a sweep of a limp arm.

'Goodbye to you, sir. We'll be on our way… Hopefully, we've not troubled you too much.'

Norman stood still as a fence-post. He didn't smile as they cantered away.

Out of sight of the homestead, Larry, face earnest, turned to Jack.

'That was easy. Like borrowing from a friend.'

Jack's brow was cross.

'My oath. Too easy. Didn't we talk just last week about the need to use masks, disguise our identities?'

Larry heard the criticism in Jack's question, realised the sense of it.

'It's only Norman, Jack… McKinnon won't cause trouble. One of his daughters is practically ridin' with me mate, Ben Hall, and his boys, or they're ridin' her.'

He spurred his horse, which grunted in surprise then broke into a fast canter.

Jack had no choice but to follow his retreating back.

'I hope you're right, ya stupid bastard.'

The boys returned to the Bolong, and young Jack further on, to Myanga Creek, and the safety of his Ma's hut.

AN INVITATION TO A DANCE: BRIDGET'S STORY

COME one, come all,
Dance and supper at the Crookwell Hall,
Belle of the ball.

I don't recall Lawrence ever laughing out loud.

He would arrive at our farm late afternoons, accompanying his father and uncle, and sit wordless upon his horse while the older men chatted. Father would be readying himself – strapping on leather leggings above his boots, tightening his horse's surcingle, looking for hobbles – before joining the visitors on their way to the Richland's back paddocks to "moonlight" scrubbers. I could not take my eyes off the lad. My father would refuse to be ready before they arrived. It was one of his many, nasty habits and it was all about making them wait – to be in control. They didn't appear to notice, those Cummins' folk.

One afternoon I caught him, the youth, staring at me as I sat on the stool on our cottage's front porch. Yes, staring. He wasn't looking at me as if I were a child, nor looking at my pimples, but at me, Bridget. As if I was a grown person – an interesting person. I shivered; a chill of excitement passed through me as his eyes peered deep inside.

'Ha, ha, ha, ha.'

Listen to him. Laughing with his mates. One of the lads is telling a story about his father's notion of dancing, and Lawrence finds it hilarious.

'Dancen's easy, my pa says. You just step out with your sandal and stamp down with your blucher.'

'But what about the music? Don't ya have to do it in time to the music?' asks Larry.

'Not as far as Pa is concerned.'

Larry laughs.

'That's why Mum no longer dances.'

Larry's face contracts, puzzled.

'Why? Does he embarrass her?'

'No, once he stomped down with his blucher at the Laggan Ball, and stomped on her foot and broke it, and it has never healed.'

'Healed "heel",' bellows Larry.

I once thought he were a serious chap, and he is, but there is also a lightness to him. A quick wit to the point of sarcasm. Maybe with drink in him he finds that place inside himself. A softer, funnier place.

There he goes again; hilarious.

I love that place, his inner silly place, and it took a year with him visiting with his da, for him to find an opportunity – he said courage – to talk with me over the shaded water trough where the horses drink. Then we met up at a Saturday night dance and, between dance sets, we run outside, squeezed along the drays and sulkies and "four in hands" tied up along the fence line, and we kissed. I couldn't help it, but I pressed up close against him and I tell you, I couldn't stop pressing. I wanted to melt right into him.

My gosh we'd talked about it, my girlfriend, Ida, and I. What it would be like to kiss a boy. And, oh-h-h, it was far better. Maybe I was forward for my fifteen years, and I should have been more modest, but I was settled on him.

He was seventeen, maybe eighteen, after all.

He told me I was beautiful. More beautiful than the frilly dance-hall girls he'd seen at the Sofala goldfields. He would never say, but I think he'd more than looked at them, because he was very comfortable around a girl, and I didn't have to educate him much about making love. But that, too, was part of his appeal – he was far worldlier than any boy I knew.

For the wedding, I wore the veil Mum wore for her wedding over my red hair. It was beautiful and framed my freckled face in a manner to lighten it, pleasantly, Ma said. And Father Lanigan, the visiting priest, married us. He said some nice words from the Saints and joined us back at Mrs Cummins' place for drinks and dancing. I couldn't have been happier.

Da liked Lawrence and his younger brother, Jack, but Ma tried to warn me off Larry, as everyone called him.

'He's wild, Bridget. He doesn't seem to know when to step back, or to think through his moves.'

'That's what I like about him, Ma. He's not boring. He wants to break out of here. Not like the other boys happy to sit about waiting for their chooks to grow eggs.'

My words had a slight hiss, which makes those who don't know me ask if I am coming down with the cold by any chance? It's annoying. The hiss that is. I avoided boys after being teased about it at school. Larry hadn't noticed it.

'But he's already up to no good.'

'Like what?'

'Like lifting horses, fighting, grogging. What will he be like in ten years' time? All broken, all sodden. Look at your father.'

'Exactly. You married a man just like him, and you're happy… He loves me, Ma.'

'I'd be happier if it was Jack. At least he's your age and friendly.'

'Well, it ain't Jack!'

I hear Larry laugh. He's off again. How could she say he's not friendly?

We've been married for longer than two years now, and a child. *How did that happen?* I thought we might have had some adventures before children came, before Lawrence could grow a beard. We built the slab hut and rather than bark the roof, Lawrence cut shingles from the farm's ironbark, like he's seen on a house over at Bathurst, to make it posh. It looks a treat. The Cummins' owned a couple of blocks, so we built on a separate block to Lawrence's Ma, and we have our own little world.

Lately, he's never home. Travels with his da and my da; or is off with his mates – local cornstalks like his self – and he has made some money. But it doesn't seem right, me and the children being on our own so much. You might have heard me talking about hiding the dice from him and wonder why I am so against it? Well, even when he's home, he'll spend nights at the grog shanties playing dice and drinking. They all play it. Stops 'em feeling bored and, if they win, it appears like money-for-nothing.

I hear Lawrence cackle again.

I cut in on him and his mates hanging around the door of the dancing barn, where most of the men stand, arms crossed, while we women sit around the hall's walls, like frogs on a log, hoping someone will ask us to dance.

'Come on dear, let's dance,' I say.

He pretends to argue, acts as if I'm a nagging wife, then takes my hand with a fuss, and we circle up for one of the new bush dances, made popular by us young people, as we sashay doe and turnabout. The Irish jig our parents danced to, now has a local flavour, with a slower rhythm and a changing of dance partners, spins, and slides along the mud floors, with weaving in and out on a human chain. It's fun and social.

I like being held by the other men, to listen to their innuendos and to feel, and smell, their differences, but my heart still races when I see him return next to me in the line, and it is my turn to dance with my husband. He's handsome and strong, and braver than anyone I know.

The tea-chest with a single-string base, the little accordion, the fiddle, the tin whistle, the drum, the dance-caller for some of the dances, creates a music as local and familiar as the wallabies nibbling the grass outside. It feels good to be alive and blessed to be in the countryside.

He knows everyone in the hall, my Lawrence, although they live across the district. There's barely a minute that passes where he's not talking to or recognising someone as we dance.

Not long after we danced that first night and kissed under the stars, Lawrence took me across to the Tuena goldfields. It was my first visit, even though my da often visited. I rode Lawrence's black mare and he rode his new and recently broke grey colt. We looked a handsome couple.

It took a lot of arguing to get my parents to agree. We set off early and by mid-afternoon we rode into Tuena along its main street and I saw a world I could never have imagined. The area was covered with tents and people spilled about like coloured marbles in all the spaces where there was not a building. We rode along blue-metal side streets and into a cobbled-stone main street, lined with log edges, and in places, wooden pathways rose along the shopfronts to keep the strollers' boots dry.

I laughed when I saw camels and donkeys, and strange contraptions breathing steam.

'Somewhere,' said Lawrence, examining the machine from a distance, 'with so much smoke, an Irish dragon must be lurking.'

The buildings along the main street were huge, and many sported gaily painted signs. One of every five buildings was a grog shop, and the tinkling sounds of a piano would leak out their doorway as we passed. Some were two stories high and on the top floor veranda of one, young women with bright red lips and scanty blouses that bared their cleavage, wearing dresses short enough to expose their delicate ankles, whistled and urged Lawrence to park me and join them. I'd never seen painted lips before and it made these ladies appear so fragile, yet dangerous.

Strange, petite-boned, yellow-fleshed men, wearing baggy shirts and trousers, with peaked bamboo-woven coolie hats, shuffled along the road in teams of three or four, often holding hands, some with goods perched on the ends of a pole draped across their necks. We passed several, what I later learned, were Chinese Joss houses, with walls painted red topped by strange-shaped roofs like native bark canoes. That night, when we walked home, we could see many Chinamen, as they were called, lying on stretchers and smoking long pipes, in a tent beside the house. Lawrence said it was opium tobacco that they smoked, and they appeared oblivious to all and anything around them. Apparently, many other miners also smoked it in the hours when not digging, and soon lost their claims and goods as a consequence. There were rumblings of unrest, Lawrence told me, as some believed the little foreign devils were out to poison all.

We ate at a store whose sole purpose was to serve meals at tables adorned with fine, Irish-linen cloth. The owners made a fuss of Lawrence and, of course, now me, because they were customers who purchased cattle from his da, and they had often met. They also paid attention to me but I found I had nothing to say, so sat there smiling like a village idjit. It was all so wonderful.

I could have cried with joy later that night when Lawrence led me into a wooden hall packed with chairs facing a raised stage. This was my surprise. We sat and a large crowd soon joined us and we crammed in tight. The lights dimmed. The music commenced, and to howls from the crowd, the handsomest man I'd ever seen walked on stage, and sang a song I'd never heard, but wish I had. It was the entertainer, Charles Thatcher, and his voice was like warm treacle to my senses. Whenever there were riots on the goldfield, I believe the government should roll Mr Thatcher in, to quell it. I'm sure not one person drew a breath until after he'd left the stage. One song – *The Wandering Gold Digger's Lament* – he was urged to sing numerous times. When he sang it for his encore, there wasn't a dry eye in the house. Oh, you should have been there. You really should.

Even today, I recall how delicious he looked and how shiny were his shoes. I'd never seen boots so shiny as those, ever, not even Frank

Gardiner's boots were so fine. Oh yes, I met the famous bushranger several times. He and Lawrence are friends.

Later that night, when lying across our bed, and I'd recounted the day's events and what captured my attention at the theatre, Lawrence asked me to marry him.

Was I fifteen? Maybe? But I agreed; didn't hesitate. I decided to make love, then and there.

He was so eager – like an excited puppy – he was all over the place. It felt so good to have him settled. We'd snuggled up fully dressed after that and, while Lawrence snored, I never slept a wink, being so excited, and so cold.

The next day I was plagued with guilt. Catholic girls should not shame themselves so. I couldn't blame Lawrence, although I wanted to. He said not to worry, he would marry me. We just shouldn't say anything to nobody. We married, but I'm sure locals counted the days back from young Joseph's birth. You know what they are like.

I hear him laughing.

He's returned. The boys have been outside for grog. He appears to have spare cash, and my girlfriend says he has paid for most of the grog. Someone, it may have been Maggie from the store, mentioned a robbery-under-arms, a mail stagecoach, out at the *Big Hill.* I wonder if he were involved? I don't dare question him. It's best I don't know nothing, he says.

His brother, Jack, isn't here tonight. He stayed home, at his ma's. Now, that is unusual, because the two of them, usually, are inseparable. And they do liven a dance up with their malarkey. Apparently, Jack is upset about something Lawrence's done. Word is that the police seek the brothers for lifting saddlebags from the McKinnon's. Traps visited my da's place looking for them. Now, that's the difference between the two. Jack will lie low and make his ma happy. Lawrence refuses to lie low. Insists, instead, that he's innocent, so why worry? Maybe he is? He's cut me out of that part of his life.

Perhaps he's become too arrogant? He hates it when I say that.

Talking about police, I'd hate to lose Lawrence, for, as I tell him, I can't imagine a life without him should he be nabbed for a crime. He is my light. Of course, there's also our child, Joseph, who needs a da. Do I sound like a nag? Sound like my ma?

I see and hear him laugh.

He looks my way. Must have caught the concern on my face because the smile has washed from his.

'Let's go home Lawrence, it's a long ride and a cold night.'

It takes a moment for my words to register.

'Okay darlin', let's go.'

There you are, see? When he's with me he's tame as a cowshed cat. He never looks to fight me. Yeah, he drinks, but he's not melancholic, and he's great with Joseph. Maybe he's a different person when he's alone, when he's away, when he's messing with his mates?

We head outside, into the darkness, grab the sulky, tighten the harness, and Lawrence lifts me into the seat, covers my legs with a rug. He springs aboard and we ride directly into the largest moon I have ever seen. It hovers on the skyline: a large yellow pumpkin of a thing, fills so much of the horizon, and backlights the trees on the ridgeline as jagged black teeth, as black as can be. If there were hob goblins, they'd be out tonight doing all sorts of mischief and pulling the stockings off many a sleeping child. I wonder what the fates have in store for us, our little family? I do.

I lean against him, and I say nothing. Just happy to have him to myself for a moment. I have a lot to say – I just never know how to say it to him.

'Don't worry darlin' Bridget, nothin' bad's ever going to happen to me, lucky Larry… Nothin'.'

Despite myself, I smile. I believe him. I do. I really do! Why shouldn't I?

TO KILL SENIOR CONSTABLE MURPHY:
BROTHER JACK'S STORY TOLD BY LARRY
6TH AUGUST, 1863

SENIOR Constable Murphy has nabbed my brother, Jack. I'm stalkin' the constable and he'll hand Jack over to me when I find him, or he'll pay the fuckin' price. That I can wager.

Although it's not a manly thing, I can say without a moment's hesitation that I love that lad, that big-boned, smilin' lad – my young brother, Jack. I love him for his pluck, his slow burn, his ready laugh, and his soppy eyes that tear up when Ma gets all sentimental. Oh, we've had our barneys, like all brothers, but they were short lived snips, which I chose to pursue in the hope of stirring a blue, or getting his attention, or killing the boredom.

In Laggan, boredom is not rare, especially here, along Myanga Creek. There's not much honest work to do and what adventure there is, you must make for yourself. Been like that since ever I remember. The gold discovered over the range – well, that livened it up, somewhat, with the travellers passing through; the town hall meetings trumpeting false progress; the prospectors seeking to unearth a whisper of gold in our creek to make their fortunes. Then there was the odd trip to the diggings with our pa, to provide horses to the rich and meat to the miners, with long boozy nights in their wild hotels witnessing the strangest collection of folks, costumes, and strange ideas to distract us.

That were exciting, but, in between, there's boredom. Grinding, weary boredom only a bush lad would know, as to provoke him to wildness and a lass to run away to a life of service, the arms of a no-hope traveller, or to another town somewhere, anywhere, to avoid the boredom, the prying eyes of all who have known you since birth, and the fear of it being all there is in store for ya. Failing that, either we drink, or we fight. Often, we do both, Jack and I, as do most young fellas in the area, and that, yes that, may have been our downfall.

Joseph, 'Irish Joseph', our pa, a Tipperary lad, son of a battling *Whiteboy*, hated our fighting, unless of course it were against someone else, then you'd see his chest puff out and his shoulders round over. He, too, was quite a "goer", handy with his fists in his younger days, our pa, we hear. But he never says nothing about that now. Ma says they left Tipperary in Ireland to avoid the grip of the wild rural gangs and the terrorist stoush with stick or bat that could leave Pa crippled, or, maybe, Ma without a man. Fighting had become a way of life for him and like a man fresh sworn off the grog, he hated to see others caught in its grip, and lost no time in tellin' us kids off it, like he were a roving bush evangelist.

'T'ere's enough hate in ta world for ya to go fightin' someone else and not ya family, not ya brother. Now cut it out or I'll bash ya both.'

Ma, God bless her, Ma loves us fighting… so long as it's not near her.

'Go up the yard and do it,' she screams.

She was raised with brothers and they was always fighting, and she knows a fat lip and a bloody nose are not the end of the world, though to listen to some who live up nearer Laggan, our town, you'd think it was the end. Fighting – boys being boys – would have them screaming blue-murder for the traps to tame us.

Having said that, I don't provoke young Jack no more – he's got forearms as large as some men's thighs.

'We'll bet two shillings on Johnnycake,' sang one shanty regular, face all florid with the drink one evening when a fight broke out involving young Jack.

'Six-pence on Jack,' bet another.

'Two-and-six on young Jack, please Morrie,' our neighbour requested.

In case ya haven't guessed, Morrie is the bookie at the shanty. He squizzed his face.

'How come ya bettin so big on Jack? He's only a boy after all… Wouldn't have hair on his cods yet, would he?'

The neighbour shook his head.

'He's a big lad and I saw him take on someone at Crookwell last week. He can hit.'

'Stand back folks. Bareknuckle rules.'

With a nod, the blue was on. Johnnycake Smith skipped across the space and whacked Jack before he'd raised his hands. The neighbour shook his finger at the pair, but Morrie, seated and too busy sorting the bets, missed it.

'See, Jack can take a blow too, my God. Johnnycake must be two foot taller than him.'

There was an exclamation from the crowd. The thump of fist on flesh echoed around the room. Morrie raised his head in concern, a lot of his money riding on Johnnycake.

'Jesus, what just happened?'

'Jack put one direct over Johnnycake's heart.'

Morrie stood to see over the crowd.

'The Cake is down! I don't think he's gonna get up.'

Jack had leant over Johnnycake with finger pointed.

'You going to apologise, now?'

'What for?'

'You know what for. For shaming my ma. Do you want more?'

Johnnycake, teeth clenched and bloodied, shook his head.

'No, I apologise. Sorry for what I said about ya ma.'

Three or four hits in the whole fight.

Angry, Jack punched a mickey-bull once and you could hear its breath escape from the impact. Johnnycake confessed, later, to my Uncle John.

'Mate, I've been kicked by a horse often enough, but it was nothing compared to being punched by that Jack.'

His reputation grew. Recently, at the races, one local knuckle-man, Jim Connors, full of grog, offered to fight anyone in the bar brave enough to stand on the jacket he'd dragged on the ground behind him. You should'a seen him, Connors… sashayin' past all the men like a temptress with her dress hitched high, bare legs flashing.

'Come on you miserable lot, I'll fight any one of ya, who's game enough.'

But when young Jack had stepped on the coat, Connors added, 'That doesn't include you, young fella,' and refused to fight him.

Jack has the respect proper, of even the best.

But how can ya fight something ya can't see? And, how hard do ya fight when ya can see, but your opponents – the troopers – arrive with law on their side? No matter how good he were with his fists, our Jack, it weren't just a man he was fightin', he were fighting something much bigger: the law, the government. It's like fightin' a Bolong River mist, ain't it? Impossible to make a dent.

I can't abide the way the traps just arrive, unannounced, and because they have law on their side, can remove a person as if he was shit on a stick they was takin' outside to bury. Like when Tom Hogan, a local mate, got took. Says he asked, 'What ya here for, Trooper?'

'We've been sent to arrest you,' said the trap.

'What's ya jumped-up charge?'

'We hear ya been poddy dodge'n', Tom.'

'Who said? What evidence?'

'Ya neighbour told us.'

'Bloody squatter. Show me the calf?' said Tom.

'You're nabbed.'

He reckons his wife saw the injustice; protested.

'But he's innocent. He hasn't left the house block all week. Look at the shed he's been building.'

But they took him anyway.

It's not right, and Pa says it's the same here, as Ireland: church, the law and power, holdin' each other by the cods. Tenant farmer over there, poor settler farmer here and protestant landlords there, rich protestant squatters here.

The Goldfields were close by and rumours of the riches to be had were hot on everyone's lips in our area. Our pa had seen the benefits of feeding the miners with livestock at bloated prices as being a surer way to make a fortune than washing the sparkling sand. That the stock he supplied were not always home-grown, but duffed, was neither here-nor-there, and as the miners flooded in he had to supply by any means. Local squatters' stations like *Richlands*, next door, had absentee owners and many unaccounted cattle and horses 'ripe for the liftin'', as our pa would say.

Many a night at the shanties we would take our fill of grog and relish travellers' tales as they passed to and from the diggings. Our local shanty was quite small, with a canvas lean-to out the back for busy nights or when the coaches stayed over. Inside, the cooking and tobacco smoke clung to the low bark-lined ceiling and joined the stench of sweaty, unwashed bodies. The oil lamps flickered light upon the table.

'You good elks think the gold will last forever,' boomed a voice with an American accent. 'In California we thought the same thing. But, believe me, gold dries up... Those who have the main vein can last longer, but for the rest, the golden dribbles soon fail.'

Ah, you could smell the whiskey as stringent as their implied warning.

'You think the bushrangers here are a problem. Why, y'all, we had the same troubles with outlaws we sometimes called bushwhackers. Now, the James' brothers, Jesse and Frank, you'll all like this story…

they robbed banks and trains and were Southern Guerrillas, durin' our civil war, who didn't deserve to be jailed. Them good ole boys was cheated, all because they fought on the losin' side. I can assure ya of that.'

It had happened in another continent, but sentiments know no boundaries if our reactions were any guide. The miners was always complaining about the Legislature, or the Mine Inspectors, not respecting their rights. They understood the US South's sense of injustice.

'The civil war. Man… I don't ever want to hear another cannon-blast again. We lined up, thousands of us, across a small corn field, as did them Unionists, and in line-abreast, marched, until our muskets were in range, would shoot, then kneel and load while those in the line behind would fire, then, in turn, do this until there were no one in our line left to do the shootin'… Their artillery cut us to pieces from point-blank range.'

'You survived though, right? Not too bad.'

The traveller lifted his shirt; displayed an horrific scar.

'See there, young fella, no ribs. A shot had to be wrenched from there. It's why I can't dig at the mines… can only ride the coach.'

'But you killed someone, right?'

'Yeah, I hope I gave as good as I got. I was close enough to see the whiskers on their chins, so I knew when I'd dropped someone.'

'How exciting. I reckon I'd go okay. Especially if the stupid bastards had to stand still. Even roos run and I knock them.'

And when there were no foreign travellers, we revelled in the local news.

'Hey, you fellows, the traps were chasing Ben Hall up north and he pulled a bank job, right in their own puddle. Says so here in the *Bathurst News*.

'Read it to us,' we'd demand of the only fellow who could read. And, when he did, it was such a story. The newspapers wrote it as if the journalist was riding with the gang.

'And the constables rode in only minutes after the gang had left the town…'

'Hooray Ben! Good one!' we'd cheer.

Our news reader would continue.

'The Constables had seen the Hall gang waiting in the bush, as they had ridden in, but believed it to be a timber-cutting gang. *By hook or by crook, I'll get those braggards*, the senior constable had thought to himself.'

'Boo,' we'd scream, and laugh, and order another drink.

Same for stories read about brave Johnny Piesley. We'd love it when he'd outsmart the traps, his Majesty's best, and lead them on a merry chase. What adventure! What pluck! What excitement! Several of us had met Frank Gardiner, and such was his style that Jack and I were mesmerised and would enact scenes of dash and daring to replicate his.

In the moonlight, we duffed stock with Pa, our uncle, and other close acquaintances, and lifted the odd horse or two if we ventured upon them. In the daylight, we had our own adventures, Jack and I, lifting watches and wallets from the travelling public. Inevitably, we came to the attention of the traps, and it's why I'm fuming now.

That bloody Murphy, that jumped-up constable. It's gettin' personal between him an' me. It is, I tell ya. Had I been there at Ma's, when they visited to arrest us over some missing saddlery, it would have been different: I would have got right up him.

Two against two. Jack and me, against traps, Murphy and Molloy. No contest. We would have sat them on their fat arses, scarpered and laid low until the fuss settled.

But I wasn't there.

When I arrived, tired, after days of running with Ben Hall and me mates, Ma met me all het-up.

'The traps was just here. They've taken Jack.'

'What?'

Ma said they'd just turned up, like a piece of dried cow shit that bobs up as a surprise in the milk bucket during milking. Murphy at the front door and Molloy at the back. Poor Jack inside, half-dressed, mindin' his own business, had no warning, and nowhere to run. Just a loud parade-ground voice coming outta the blue.

'Larry and Jack Cummins, it's the Binda police. Give yourselves up. We're here to arrest you on account of the robbery at Richlands; The McKinnon's farm.'

What robbery? We borrowed two saddlebags and were right polite about it.

Well, our family shat themselves, didn't they? Apparently, Ma screamed. Sent Jack up into the loft with his pistols, where Murphy sighted him.

'He's up in the roof… He's armed. Fire.'

The Trap's pistols caused a right racket. Jack's bullets missed, Ma said; raised dust in spurts beside the constable. The police contingent returned fire. Bullets ricocheted around the hut, pieces of wattle and mud from the walls flew everywhere, but Jack had Ma and his brother and sisters to worry about, didn't he? He had to surrender. What else could the boy do?

The kids said Ma gave the traps a gob-full. Tried to pull Jack free.

'He's innocent, I tell you… You're trussin' him worse than you would were he a Myall black. Loosen the chains for stuff's sake.'

'Back off, Mary.'

Ma said he wasn't wounded, though a bullet hole through his trouser leg showed how close he came to a wounding. You never think ya might be hurt in this game, you just don't. You believe you'll get away with it. What could ever go wrong? The thought of that hole makes me panic a bit, I can tell you.

I riled up like a steam kettle. That was my little brother they'd trapped. I ran and bridled the bay horse from the horse paddock, swapped the saddle off the grey I'd just rode in on. I set out, like an insect-crazed bull, after them. But when I reached the slip-rails, I heard

Ma shouting and glanced back. She was waving an object in the air with one hand and signalling me to return with the other.

I turned the bay's nose and swearing a high note about the detour, returned to the hut.

'Jesus, Ma, what ya doin'? Them bastards have a half-hour on me, at least. I can't be waitin' for a shoppin' list from ya! What do ya want?'

I was out of control, I tell ya.

Ma handed me the old brass rifle which hung over the fireplace, but I'm not sure what she expected me to do with it. Bail 'em up and drag young Jack away? Up to that point, I planned to just bash into 'em and punch him free, if I'd thought that far.

'Don't let 'em take our Jack,' she said and slapped my horse on the arse, sending me on me way, but nearly on my date, such was the pigrooting the horse puts in after the slap, and me with one hand swinging this blunderbuss of a rifle and the other caught on a loose rein.

~

It were a desperate ride cross-country, but now I'm in a wattle patch and on a small ridge overlooking the wagon track.

At this time of the year the golden wattle splashes bright yellow across the field like scattered coins upon a rug. It loves disturbed ground, and displays along tracks and roads; paves them with gold.

I don't know why but my eyes run, and I sneeze and sneeze. Why did I pick this place? The road below is where they should pass – the gutless bastards. It's a few hundred metres from hide to road, and an easy enough shot were you wanting to drop a 'roo. Different matter wanting to wing a 'roo, wing somebody, wing a fuckin' policeman, but that's now the plan.

It's like running brumbies. You must think ahead, predict where they'll race, and be there before them, sometimes travelling at an angle to their flow, to run them on the haze-rails to yard them. After a while you begin to think like a brumby. Jack and I was raised running brumbies for Pa and his brother, John, so using the landscape comes natural. But will the traps be so smart? Will they follow the road, or push cross-country, like we do? My pick is they are too lazy to forge a shortcut. They have their man. They're usually dumb city folk who don't think like this landscape. They just don't. If I'm correct, I've beaten them here.

Whew, what luck, I guessed right. From the distance, three men, line astern, appear. The big chap in the middle must be Jack, led by Murphy, in his stupid toy-soldier uniform, followed by Molloy, another toy-soldier, in the rear. Perfect for the purpose. Like a row of wood ducks on a creek bank, ready for the plucking.

I have it sorted. I wriggle my body into the ground to remove discomfort; sight. Then, bejesus, out-of-the-blue Murphy drops back to ride beside young Jack. For hours they've probably ridden in single-file, one after the bloody other, why the fuck choose now to chat? Why for chrissake? Young Jack's shoulders are stooped. He looks a beaten man and not up for the chat.

I have the rifle aimed. It's funny... you have a gun, it's like... stupid, not to use it. It's not as if you'll put it down and throw a rock. If you didn't have the gun, you'd try something else, like I'd earlier planned. You hear fellows in our line of business say it all the time: 'I had the pistol I had to use it. People take notice.' It's heavy, it's cool, solid and soothing; doesn't tremble or sweat with fear like you. Its power over you swells and you learn that, with it, you can own others; a real treat, I assure you. It'll be nice to get the drop on these bastards. If only Murphy gets out of the way.

Come on now, constable, "senior" constable, move aside. Move ya fat arse. Lead out like you did before. You've had your chat. Oh, bejesus it's too late now for an upfront shot, to stall them enough to storm out and bail 'em to release Jack.

Look at him, Murphy, the big fat-gutted trap, he's in line with Jack. The constable is closest to the scrub patch and his pud, his big body, like a slaughtered beast hanging in the miners' meat hut, shelters Jack. They now are dead opposite the wattle patch. No... too tight a shot to wing – disable – the sergeant. Not a lot of him free of Jack's large frame behind him, to wing. Too risky.

A little forward of the blind now, the senior constable's stopped jabbering and his horse has moved a pace ahead of Jack, isolating Murphy for a moment.

Come on Larry, punch a bullet into his shoulder; a graze to distract him and put the fear of bejeezus into Molloy so young Jack can dash free.

Rifle to the cheek, peer along the sights. Breathe out, out... out... slow in... sight Murphy and as the rifle rises with your breath, gently squeeze the trigger at its peak... That's it, like you was squeezing warm water … Squeeze … There ya go!

Crack!!

I focus after the recoil. Oh… bejesus, Mary, mother-of-God, the Constable's horse has stumbled, exposed young Jack.

The horrible crack of my rifle discharging in the still, bush morning, booms like a cannon; a thunder-wave roaring through the silence. White cockatoos squawk, explode skywards like white/yellow, sulphur-hot shrapnel against the green hills; their anxiety, catching.

The smell of gunpowder penetrates my senses.

Young Jack's hat spins in the air and his body follows the same trajectory, as if attempting to bite it: a dog snapping at a pesky fly to stop it, the hat, falling, falling, falling forwards.

I… Christ… I have hit him, our Jack, my Jack, my brother. I want to gag. My bullet has struck him in the head with the sickening impact of a horse's hoof; has dug deep. Deep enough to knock him off his horse. The torn artery sprays blood over Murphy. Young Jack's blood covers Murphy like a red shadow. I think a miracle has happened and it's Murphy who's been struck, but no! Young Jack continues cartwheeling over the horse's shoulder. Cartwheeling, exuberantly, spinning like his hat.

The hat lands with a flutter. Jack lands with a flop, a bag of butcher's bones.

Mary, mother of mercy, what have I done?

Jack's horse rears back in fear, drags young Jack after it until his death-locked fingers separate. Murphy and Molloy gallop away to avoid the ambush; gutless bastards.

I can't believe it's Jack, flat-out there in the dust.

'Ma… Ma!' he calls.

I want to recall my decision… the moment just unrolled. Wipe it from reality. Put Jack back on the horse. But he lies there now, lifeless, not a sound.

I want to rush out, kiss his pale lips, comfort him, but I see Murphy and Molloy on the overlooking ridge, pistols at the ready. If I had guts, I'd sit with him. But I don't. I mount and gallop away through the scrub.

~

I take an age to return home. How will I tell Ma?

I needn't have worried.

A neighbour was sent to get Ma. He says she kicked up a right shite at the police station, saying, 'What have ya done ta ma boy, my beautiful boy? What have ya done, ya mongrel bastards. You've shot him. You've shot a mere boy! Sixteen.'

Her forehead is streaked with dried blood, as if the-crown-of-thorns once rested there.

'What have ya done to ya forehead?'

She examines it with her fingers as if she'd been unaware of the injury.

'Bashed it on the window lintel beside where the Senior Sergeant stood, again and again, until he told me what he implied by sayin': "Someone else, maybe Larry, shot Jack?" The bastard just waggled his head as if to say, *I'm a senseless woman and wouldn't understand.* I asked him how you'd even know your brother was captured, because you weren't there when he was taken.'

'What'd he say?'

'Nothin'. The idjit just stood there like a log, with stupid Molloy nodding, agreeing with me, makin' a fool a Murphy.'

Does Ma know it were me?

She doesn't ask, but she knows. She looks deeply into my eyes; holds my stare but doesn't ask. I don't say a word. How can I? I just cry with her. Cry, along with sister Catherine, her the keening, Celtic-wailing banshee of a woman. It frightens me more 'an a charging bull, or the dirty traps – me ma, wailing. She never done so when Irish Joseph, her husband – Pa – died earlier in the month. She acted like she were angry at him. She threw clods into the grave then. Not tears.

We cried for our young Jack. That big boofhead with the giant hands. That big boofhead with the giant smile. I loved him, I did. I still do, but we don't talk of such things up here in the Abercrombie. We let others do the grieving.

THE AVENGING TROOPER, JOHN CHALKER: A HORSE-RIDING STORY

BE Jeesus, thinks Larry, *this new guy can ride.*

He had a ten-minute start on Trooper Chalker but the trooper has made up so much distance he's now only three-quarter of a mile behind.

Larry and mate, Johnson, had left the shanty after a melee. They'd drunk too much, waved their pistols about, threatened people. McAllister, the affable but rat-smart publican, settled things. Larry believed it was all sorted, so he and young Johnson had ridden off without further thought.

McAllister must have lagged them, because within an hour, they hear horses approach, surprised to learn it's traps, when moments later, bullets whistle past and shatter pieces of granite from roadside boulders beside them.

'Shit, mate, let's ride.'

Larry drives the spurs, as does Johnson. Both horses stretch for the gallop. Another volley from behind. He watches Johnson's horse nose into the dirt, and Johnson spill forward to join it. Both bodies mix as they roll, and Johnson's doesn't move. The next moment: pain as a bullet punches into Larry's shoulder and nearly knocks him off his mount. The sound he makes surprises him. A sound a woman might make as her pelt is torn in childbirth. Despite the impact Larry manages to stay astride, but barely. The trooper doesn't pause; follows

Larry while others tend to the fallen Johnson. The trooper's not to be distracted.

Larry sticks to the river-flat, believing the speed of his horse, a progeny of the famous racehorse, Whistle, will prevail. The trooper is not snared into a flat-out race. Instead, he rides jockey-style, up on his stirrups, forward on his horse's neck, with short rein. He canters, and speeds up only when Larry disappears over a knoll, eyes locked like a black-tracker on the leading horse's imprint. When Larry walks his horse, the constable jogs his; man and horse marathon fit; in for the long haul. The constable wagers on average speed and funnelling terrain to apprehend his man.

Hour upon long hour the pair traverse the soft plains, neither yielding; locked in a deadly game. In the lead, Larry is never sure if he can pause, or if he does, how long he should delay. Twice he drops down to a waterhole to swill water into his hat and long draughts down his aching throat. The horse can drink but how much water to allow the poor beast? If Larry disappears on the plains the trooper might panic for a moment but risks it will not be long until the vista allows his prey to reappear. Larry can't believe the trooper doesn't stop, to take his legitimate designated work-breaks, to boil the billy like most employed officials, but chooses, instead, to apply relentless pressure.

Having crested a lengthy ridge with a slight incline, Larry smiles when he realises the range, once a pale, purple backdrop, is now a towering rock-strewn wall, converging like a funnel towards the river. The granite boulders, scattered along its wind-worn face, reflect sunlight in patches within the scrub. Even the horse relaxes as the landscape alters from pasture into light forest, and canters as if enjoying a second wind. There is room to disappear from the trooper's sight for more than a few minutes, room to imagine alternatives. Here, one can hide to avoid either capture, or the gruesome task of ambush, or double-back on one's tracks if given enough space, time, and terrain. But the trooper closes.

Another hour and Larry steers, with his near-side leg, to edge his mount further up the ridge until it breaks into the tightly packed, heavily scented, softwood scrub. In the past, this technique had worked a treat against other traps, reasonable riders in the open but hopeless in the scrub's maze of turkey bush, hook-pricked 'wait-awhile', fallen timber, and barely penetrable, wattle, and oak. The average policeman, or trooper, is city-bred, put into the service by a family member, or in it for the uniform and steady pay. A thick-lipped, broad-browed, stumble-footed mob is how Larry describes them. They struggle with rural ways, and bush skills; those elements familiar to the Abercrombie's Irish cornstalks.

High in the scrub, the novice over rides, pulls the horse's head this way and that, steers a course, believing they are smarter than the animal. But old hands like Larry, used to chasing scrub-cattle and brumbies, let the horse have its head. They stay low and tight, rise on the stirrups when the horse bounds over debris underfoot, use arms and shoulders to parry branches and brush.

Having its head, the horse, even more familiar with rough passage than the cornstalks, develops a rhythm in harmony with its surrounds. Trust allows the horse to compensate for the rider, adjust the rider's frame within its personal space, and choose gaps between trees and beneath branches. They travel fast and often get ahead of a wild bush mob, or arrive at a destination well ahead of estimated, fair-weather travel times.

Today, speed, distance and failing light, should brush the trooper off his tail. Leave the bushranger to his flight. Leave him time to stem the wound's blood-gush which has reddened an entire side; dress it; survive – return to his darling Bridget.

But the trooper doesn't take the bait to join him high in the scrub. Instead, he remains along the lower scrub-line, where the density is lighter. Probably gambling that the bushranger will not cross vertically over the mountain range above him. The trooper will use it, the cliff face, like a Gaelic footballer might use the sideline to haze his adversary's prospects of a side-step to avoid the tackle. After a mile, and with the darkness encroaching, he does curve into the dense scrub above, where he can hear Larry crash through and where, in the failing light, he can join him in a universe where the ear is more efficient than the eye.

Larry halts, as was his way when being chased in scrub: a ploy he'd learned as a young boy being chased by brother Jack. His heart races. Panic. He hears the constable crash through underbrush, nearby; closer than when Larry entered. Jesus this guy can ride.

Larry is a local legend with a horse. His mother tells any who will listen how, barely five years of age, when his da had left early for an extended duffing trip without bidding him farewell, Larry had woken, and riding bareback, tracked him for twenty miles across isolated mountain country: an amazing feat for man, or boy.

Irish Joseph, once aware of the boy, stopped, twisted on his saddle, looked behind, watched the little fellow bridge the gap.

'Jazus Larry, what ya be up to, follurin' me like dis?'

'You never said goodbye, Da!'

'Is dat right, me boy?'

'You always say goodbye, and I always wait to hear it.'

'Aye, dat I do. I t'ought you was asleep,' says the father, reaching for a lie.

'Even if I am, ya must wake me, Da.'

'Okay, I will. I will... Bye me boy.'

'Bye, Da!'

Then the child spun the horse about and made the return journey. Arrived home at dusk.

History, the past, is not necessarily a talisman to ward off the future. Those who live by the gun are only as good as the moment. No matter how fine a rider you are, there may be riders better, or luckier, hunting you.

So, get the hell out of here. Spur to rib and with horse's neck stretched, Larry picks up pace, until the swishing branches blur, and the horse's breath labours. His main chance is to put distance between the trooper and he. Once the darkness falls, dash down into the distant mullock heaps glowing golden from miners' fires and lamps in the valley below. Pray the trooper loses his nerve, or his footing, or both, and is removed from the race. Or, at worst, pray that should the trap capture him, witnesses working the shafts will restrain the trooper from murdering him in cold blood. Poor Bridget, fresh with child, would never cope, were he killed.

The ridge's scented scrub soil is soft underfoot, and the breakaway gullies and washouts beneath the bushes place pressure on the horse's step, pressure on the rider's skill. For it is easy to fall; to stumble at speed. Easy for rider to mistime his step, misjudge his leap of faith onto the safety of the washout's far side.

In shadier, denser scrub, the saplings stand upright, parallel, rigid like prison bars; bump horse and man. The Lawyer-vine grabs a hat, rips a shirt, manacles the bushranger, threatens his freedom, pulls the horizon down to barely an eyebrow's width, compared to the wild hills and floodplains he has roiled over for two decades. It would not do to be trapped here, to be taken like a wild beast trophy. No. He doesn't need to be buried here to belong to this landscape. He was born into it.

Take him by stealth, take him in the doily-primped cottage of a local shanty. Take him while he is drunk and half out of his wits with bootleg whisky. Take him while he has his pants down in the juices of his loved one. But Jeesus, not here. Not here in his element, where, like a wild colt, he should reign free.

The fading sun disappears, sporadically, behind a cloud. It allows patches of darkness to invade the cloying scrub, then it appears again, flashes amidst the trees like a bright lantern, a Min-Min light, blinding him until his eyes adjust. Flitting, enticing him deeper, faster. He and horse churn through the underbrush to chase those golden moments, as if the holy father were lighting the boy's path.

He stops. Listens. Dark, thick silence captures him. The cicadas click, the branches creak, the wind sweeps lightly above, but pure silence! Phew!

Thank Christ he's lost the big clumper. Wishes never again to face him. He's good. No mean compliment coming from one of the region's best.

The trooper had followed Larry like a sprite. Had planned, ridden hard. Had managed his horse's health and endurance. Yet, in the game of cat-and-mouse, Larry once again had beaten the cat, thank Christ. Silence! It was a silence only the immersion within thousands of acres of bush can bring. But his complacency had been shaken as never before. It was one-on-one dangerous, a deadly game with gunpowder and shot for the loser. But he, Larry, had come through: wounded, weak, trembling from loss of blood, but God bless – delivered alive.

But then, ah Jesus, it couldn't be?

He hears the trooper move. He must have frozen at the same time as Larry, the bastard. How did he do that? He must have St. Pat, the traveller's saint, in the saddle with him.

Away! The fat albatross of being the "chased", the prey; of finding his way while evading the bloody perilous trap, swings more heavily around his neck. It could have been worse. Worse if the black-trackers were against him too. Even if he shook off the trooper in the dark, a black-tracker would be at him again by daylight. Mile after relentless mile, over stone and rock, across open country, or scrub, the tracker would follow. Sometimes walking a circle, sometimes looking into the distance as if they'd lost interest, the tracker would pick up the trail, note drops of blood on fern, mark of imperialists' knife-hard hoof amid an island of soft-footed inhabitants, a disturbed stone. The tracker was no friend of the man on the run.

Larry's next move, he must judge to a second. It might now be dark in the scrub, but twilight in the forest country. It would be night-black by the time he hits the mining leases. So, he steers the horse on a descending angle to aim for the lower forest country. But, Jesus, it is dark up here.

Along with Irish Joseph and Jack, he would "moonlight" wild cattle at night, to capture them unawares, and to avoid capture themselves. On those occasions, there was a moon to ease the passage, to highlight a branch before it smashed you, a rock before the horse swerved. But now, the moon is absent. The bushes swack like cat-o-nine. The branches beat upon him like police batons on Tipperary lads. He is at the horse's behest and compensates himself only by thinking the trooper is just as uncomfortable, and his motivation lower. His liberty is not at stake. He, the trooper, does it for professional pride, for King and country. *WHY SACRIFICE YOURSELF?*

Twenty more bruising, frustrating minutes before Larry and horse break free of the scrub country. They have bashed and crashed their way adroitly, like clumsy bats, through the complexity of the darkness and the bush. While the colt has been amazing in the scrub, it senses the freedom of the forest country and extends its thoroughbred racing-stride. Larry leans forward over the bridged reins and steals a look behind. No sign of the trooper, thank Christ. He can slow down to save the horse for the final dash. Far enough ahead, he may be able to hide, or ambush the bastard trooper. His steel pistol hangs selfconsciously on his hip.

He'd rather hide. Since the incident with his brother, Jack, he was gun-shy. His victim was no longer an inanimate object, a target, or a silent, toothless marsupial, but flesh and blood like those who loved them. Regardless of what love you got yourself, whether you got some or none, you now understand its manifestation in others. You saw it in the victim's loved ones, their children, their mothers. You saw their grief and understood the link between the comforting revolver and the hate spat out its rusty barrel. You saw it with Fred Lowey, who "died game", resisting arrest right beside you, after you lay all night in the same bed. Watched his pulse ink his jacket, spell his life out like a whimper for those at the shanty to see.

Fred's loved ones had wept, not seeing the poverty in his *noblesse oblige*, of shooting-it-out and not surrendering. A brutish plea for independence, a cry for honour where none is required, a quest for identity, where all are branded scum from birth.

Larry hears a crash parallel with his path but further up the incline. There will be no hiding tonight. It's the trooper, leaning back and low in his saddle, glued to the seat, his long legs extended forward, stuck to the rhythm of the horse. He's two-hundred-yards above Larry, like an eagle spearing out of the sun at an unsuspecting pigeon. He has the high ground and the tactical advantage to swoop at will if Larry maintains that entry-angle to the gold diggings below.

Even though the sweat flies from the colt and the poor thing is white with lather around shoulder and flanks, Larry spurs it to gallop. Its terrified eyes bulge like a bullfighter's bull, aware a predator is about to pounce. Exhausted after days on the run, its initial burst of energy fades like a boomerang out of wind. Larry corrects direction, heads vertically down the ridge. He lifts the horse, with leg pressure, or with touch of stolen spur, as it slides, sometimes leans splay-footed on its haunches amid the scree and dusty rubble at the ridge's base.

His mood lightens. He glimpses the digging's outer mullock heaps in the dusk. Makes out shacks, or tents, illuminated by campfire, or oil-lamp. He aims for them, while the trooper's horse gains ground. It clatters and crashes through the light underbrush behind, like a herd of horses, not one. The trooper shouts, curses at Larry to "bail up or I'll shoot", or to "halt right there, you're under arrest."

Larry waits for the bullet's whack to thump, again, into his back; the sound of discharge to verify the pain. Will Larry's luck hold?

He swings his horse around the scattered heaps; some mud-coloured, some sunset-golden. The trooper and he, in a deadly race, jump hidden shafts, and dark sluice-gutters cutting deep into the landscape, swear at each other like emotion-drunk children, like banshees in the wind. Still, the trooper comes.

At one sweep, the trooper reaches across and grabs Larry's bloodied shirt and pulls. Larry, despite his pain and frozen shoulder, leans lower, grabs the trooper's boot, and lifts it from the stirrup as if to dislodge him. It forces the horses to diverge and swerve different sides of a rubble pile.

The trooper releases his grip from the bushranger's shirt. Larry senses it is either him, or the trooper, and reaches for his pistol, to do what he hoped he would never have to do; kill the bastard. Then he hears the sliding horse, the damning curse, the sound of falling bodies, as the constable and horse slither down a shallow shaft. Larry lets the pistol slide back in its holster, and wishes the trooper ill harm, but doesn't look back. Gallops like a luck-filled demon into the flooding darkness. Free, but for how long?

GAGGED:
LARRY'S PRISON STORY
1863 - 1867

DRIP…

Every story starts with a sentence. Some you control, others you don't. Is fifteen years a sentence long enough to learn a difficult lesson? Fifteen years he said. Yes, fifteen hard fuckin' years labour on His Majesty's roads. Year one in chains.

Drip… Drip…

You don't want to hear that sentence ever again. You obviously believe there is no hope in restitution, or you wouldn't break out, or believe your bush skills can keep you out of here for your remaining lifetime, or fail to recognise how long a day, a week, a year is, in order to be able to sustain yourself, either inside, or out. You've not lived long enough to, realistically, estimate. After all, you're only twenty-three years' young.

Drip… Drip… Drip.

When you find yourself in a hole, in a jam, you at first can't believe you're in it. Then, in your own mind, you rely heavily on luck to save you, or you pray to some Hebrew or Celtic God for smoke-and-mirror answers. You believe something outside yourself did it and that the same is going to rescue you. That's right, luck, bad luck, got you in the hole and you think luck will pluck you from it.

Nothing, nobody, arrives to rescue you and you can't reconcile it. You rant, curse, swear, and blame other men... and the grog, but most of all, you rail against bad luck. Agh, that bitch, Lady Luck.

It's only later, with age, that you realise what luck, or timing, actually has bought you. An inch more to the right and the bullet that ripped your collar would have removed your smart-arse head. How, if the bullet didn't, the hangman would have, had they charged you for killing Jack. How the bullet that struck your jaw may have exploded your brain were it an inch higher. Had your horse taken another half a step, then the shot that ploughed into your shoulder may have ripped into and stopped your heart. How it could have been you, and not Constable Chalker, who fell down the mineshaft.

But you don't think that at first. Ya stew in your misery.

Drip… Drip… Drip… Drip.

You wonder how you could have ended up here, trapped like a skulking dingo when it all started simply enough: a few mates, a few grogs, a bit of a wild romp. Some of us is born wild after all, so there should be a few allowances made. You think the police are going to make a case to excuse you; that the magistrate will dismiss it as a big mistake; that the priest will explain how you're a good lad from a good, Catholic family; where the grog ambushed your brain for a moment, and they'll release you. It was a bit of a game, really. A chance taken, a moment of fame.

Oh, ya got fame all right.

'Okay Cummins, I hear you're lucky.'

'Why's that, sir?'

'You was with the great bushranger, Lowry, when he were shot? Right?'

'Not so lucky. I was nabbed and tried.'

'Lucky you wasn't killed, as the traps were hoping.'

'I got tough justice.'

'Lucky they never found ya, till later, when witnesses was around. They'd have shot ya like the mongrel dingo ya are.'

Everyone in here knows you're the genuine article; a regular bushranger, but so what? A loser amongst losers. Your value? The meagre price they put upon your ugly head. Wanted alive or dead. Any stranger could have claimed your scalp – no questions asked.

Drip… Drip… Drip… Drip… Drip away…

The story reaches its climax at twenty-three years of age. The dramatic bits, mere poetic pieces to liven-up your monotonous epic, when ya examine it. Years and years and years on your bed staring at a point on your wall, rolling the blank sheets out one after the monotonous other, in a Dickensian mawkish yarn, if anyone could hear you.

Listen.

Drip… drip... drip... drip, drip away.

Chip, chip, chip, chip, chip away.

That is a sound you hear in your cell in the middle of the night, the deep, dark night. The only sound, that of trickling water returning to the water table, like a trapped soul searching for home. You should be sleeping like an innocent soul, but you're not. You're awake, listening for something, anything.

Sometimes, it whispers to you.

Slip... slip... slip... slip… slip away!

Get the fuck outta here!

And when you lie there, night after night, year after year, with not a soul to talk to, you wonder how it works and how you could slip away?

How does water get there just outside your window? A leaking drain, a crooked tile, a moss-covered gutter? How does it maintain itself in a constant rhythm? Listen again.

Drip.... drip... drip... drip. Then, within that rhythm – another rhythm – a skip – 'drip away', after each set of five constants.

It doesn't play early in the night, nor during the day. Yet, in the darkness, the night gods beat the tattoo just for you.

Ah, thank God, you've been informed, like a pygmy in deep jungle is informed by ritual drums; you're still alive! The luck remains with you. Funny, how the fuck small symbols like this – a dripping drainpipe – become important; desperately important.

This poetic message doesn't tell the life-story, directly, but offers more. You might read the meaning as offered, or create a unique meaning; glean an insight into the importance of the poem's subject through absorption of the writer's entire effort. This may change your life in a manner more significant than first imagined, or not imagined.

The poet records it in compulsive detail in order to capture even the rhythm of the real, or imagined, world. The reader might see it as haughtiness on the writer's part, as an arrogance they can dismiss or diminish but, surely, by so doing they demonstrate that they have never sipped the wretched poison of creative desire, never been forced to point out the unfamiliar features, the grotesques, of a familiar world.

It was your loutish arrogance, your peaked hat, your long leather boots, that drew the authorities' attention. It is here, the rehabilitation commences – when your narrative is measured against others; tested, controlled, constrained, to strip it of its personal importance. In order to survive, your storyline must disappear into your imagination.

Not all can hack it. Not all can hack the solitariness of the creative task. They lack imagination. They lack the succour of memory. The imagined flight of the fastest horse with you plastered upon it as it bounds loose across field, salt-bush, dusty track, and vacant valley. The imagined flesh (say) of dear wife Bridget, in particular, the sweet wet flesh. Those prisoners, who have never experienced such stored memory, or cannot manifest it in imagined memory, can never escape. They're trapped.

If you retain the ability to escape into your imagination even after many years, you might find the drip requiem can change again.

Hip, hip, hip, hip, hip hooray.

Put the emphasis on the 'hoo': 'Hooray'.

Hip, hip, hip, hip, hip hooray.

But you rush. That's enough for today: we have time. We have all the time in the world; fifteen years.

Each day, every day, is like this. You start the day with blank skin, in a dim cell, wondering what your mind will bring forth to tattoo upon it. Sometimes, if you're lucky, it will bring something new, something fresh, something exciting like a prison cat can bring you a plucky mouse to maul and tease, and do with it what you please but, mainly, it's a boring remnant of yesterday, or an offering of a well-chewed theme from which you've sucked the marrow and exposed the inner fibres to a point no longer serviceable.

That's the test, because you come to it due to a lack of understanding, a lack of comprehension. Despite the rumination, despite the thousands of words gang-pressed for explanation, you come to it without satisfaction. The ruling has not been made, or the magistrate has not explained it, in terms that make it fair, or reasonable, or distinctive enough to capture the reader's sympathy, to ensure they would understand and align themselves with your point of view.

'The prisoner has shown no remorse?'

'He denies he was ever there, your honour.'

'No one has come forward to represent him, or to speak in his favour?'

'No, your honour.'

'I sentence you to fifteen years, not to mix with other prisoners, or provision for education.'

Solitary confinement – years of it driven by a Court ruling to prevent you conspiring with others to do mischief, to lead insurrection, mutiny, or to escape. That is the punishment. Barely a hole in the bottom of the door to receive the food, bread and water, a morsel poked through while you are forced to look away, denied even the benefit of a stolen glance, of shared emotion, of recognising a compassionate glance from the other; or of receiving some learning. You're not allowed the satisfaction of having the disgust carried in your cur-coloured eyes, or written across your scummy face, registering in their pea-brain. Locked away, you have lost your voice and you cannot reflect your identity.

No point in your family – if you've never learned to read or write – writing to you. Unable to scribe even your name into the sandstone wall, there's absolutely no point their corresponding.

Thank heaven for the visiting priest, Lanigan, who by dint of God, or as a victim of fate, crosses your path too many times to be coincidence.

'What is it that you need, Lawrence?'

'Word from home, Father.'

'I don't see your family at Mass anymore. Not one member. Not even your ma.'

'They're ashamed to be in company – to get judged for my sins.'

'Only God can judge, Lawrence.'

'Tell that to neighbours, Father.'

'You could write.'

'None of us can read or write.'

'You went to school?'

'Aye, but I didn't learn nothin'; nothin' of any use that is.'

'Well, I'll bring you some books, and see if I can get you started.'

He organises for books to be delivered into the jail. You, the prisoner, get them only after every literate, scab gaoler has read them, and thank God, there aren't many literate. Each Sunday, the old priest spends an hour with you to help you learn the meaning of words and use a dictionary. Words leak slow, at first, then drip with comprehension, a tattoo of meaning, a small flood of knowledge. The world opens, although by that time, when you can read, the family never writes, if indeed, they ever had written.

The imagination, that palace of dreams once lost in the fog of your memory, now flows from your brain, through your hand, through the quill, to smoke in thick trails like rope to rest, released upon the page. It is out there, then; visible. Inked for all to see. A part of your growing identity.

But, once you have a voice, as feeble as it might be, there are those at large who would restrain it. You panic. You want to scream to embed its importance, to protect the capacity to use it, to alert the broader company of man that there are those who would silence you.

So strong is the gaoler's need to silence your voice, that Warden Small has invented an instrument – the gag. The bastard of a thing is applied for insubordination and can replace the cat-o-nine when the screws wish to avoid a record of their intimidation.

It's a humble enough instrument: a bridle with an eight-inch-timber bit, one-inch-square, with a strip hollowed-out along its length (to enable you to breathe). Reins of rope tied to its ends. The apparatus is forced between your yellowed teeth, the rope around your head, tightened by a winding mechanism to pull the gag tight. The winding can cause you to scream pain's violin notes, as harmonious as the cat-o-nine, but it's a silent scream, and doesn't offend them conniving screws.

It is easier to be unempathetic when you, the pained object, are out of sight, out of hearing. It is easier to be immune to an object's suffering if you can't identify with it: if you can treat the victim – their pain – as an inanimate object, or an animal without human needs. The gag meets all those requirements. You get to learn that fact.

'Get Cummins. Stop him wriggling. Well, stop 'im.'

'This'll shut ya up you smart-arse. Twist the back-winder Athol, then I'll let the head go.'

The greatest insult to you, trying wilfully to scratch your feeble narrative in a different direction, is to be gagged.

Therefore, you lead a type of life in here where, remarkably, despite their efforts to hide you, you learn to be visible because you are nobody, nothing. You continually are told so, if anyone bothers to notice you, but your being is defined by an impression rather than substance. You're society's marginal shadow flitting faintly like a fruit bat across the unpainted walls of the big house, outside the pulpit's comforting reach.

'Who do you think you are, Cummins?' they call. 'Get back into line.'

You attempt, even by your round-shouldered walk, to remain invisible, to avoid notice, to prevent drawing attention unto yourself, and soon accomplish it without trying. There comes an occasion where you attempt to hide, yet stand out like dog's balls against the cowed crowd. It is then, upon such a misdemeanour, the cat's tongue, the cat'o'nine, will rudely startle you from hiding.

Its tongue has a rough edge, slides itself along the cracks of your persona, leaving pain your only friend. It inscribes its message upon your rounded shoulders, your bowed back, the unyielding, crocodile-skinned, cracked-leather back, like the binding of your favourite volume. It's a message for all who meet and care enough about you, and who, like the blind, can rub their fingers across your flesh to know you.

This transgression, this institution, this belief, this insurrection, this small defiance of self-hood, this attempt at squirrelling away some private space from the public's penetrating gaze, it will break you, if you break cover too often.

Listen, the sun is not yet risen and the guards curse. Can you hear them further along the hall?

'Athol, I need your help. Cell nine.'

You love those panicked tones in this wing for its noise, excitement. Not only that, but it's human and, importantly, it's the frustrated sounds of the controlling screws. It wraps itself comfortingly around you, the lonely prisoner, like a black's possum-coat.

Listen again, the guards call each other like crows to the kill.

'Athol, are you there? Wake up, I tell you. I need you here.'

Perhaps someone has organised the final stage of invisibility and set themselves to swing in their lonely cell. Swing on a leather-thong stolen from transport cart or saddlery class, or on a native rope, woven from river-reed. Face bloated, feet bloated, a wet patch around the crotch, you can't mistake it when you see it; the blue but contented face of death.

Last week the traps reached one, who'd swung, in time to cut him down.

'It's a shame, I tell ya, chaps. I didn't want to return,' he'd said.

'Why?'

'I wanted out. I thought I was gone.'

'What's it like?'

'Hanging?… The rope draws tight around ya neck, because ya don't fall far enough to break it; ya neck. The air won't suck, regardless of ya tryin', for there is no vacuum. Ya suck and suck, but no air. You stare out, eyes-a-bulged but the world collapses, and your view increasingly darkens, until there is nothing but a speck of light; comforting voices.'

'Are you dead?'

'Maybe. Ya disappear down that hole as if sucked down a swirling drain. That's it. No pearly gate. No descent into hell. Nothing.'

'Shit. But you weren't dead?'

'No… but I'm no longer scared of the bitch.'

Isolation can cause that – a mental vacuum. Loneliness can. Lack of learning can do that: suffocate you. You suck and suck and, as a victim, are blamed for all the ills a lack of air can bring.

You listen; become more convinced that some poor bastard has swung. The uproar grows. Crows only call for big occasions.

'Athol. Get the clearance crew up to floor one.'

'Coming, boss.'

'Hurry, get ya finger out.'

The rattle and clatter of heavy boots on bluestone, on steel, on timber.

'Where are ya?'

'Cell nine, I said. Get in here.'

But no, gather your senses, there it is: that unmistakable smell of shit on the breathless breeze. Someone has written himself large by covering his body in his own excrement and bronzed his cage in the same decoration. He will have daubed everything, even his face, and be standing there, naked as a bush blackfella, with a huge, maniacal grin inviting the crows to claim him.

This is an identity you can adopt; take on all the shit offered until you believe it; become it.

They will have to touch him, wrestle his shit, hose the room, hose the artist, scrub the walls. The oppressed win because the oppressor must break the spell and enter the artist's cell. Must recognise the prisoner, break the isolation, the solitary confinement.

Reality is, if you don't break cover at some point in here, in even the most foolish of ways, then the danger is you merely sink into oblivion and succumb to the institution – the beast – to rot in its entrails: deep in the bowels of the damp, damp walls. Oh, mother Mary, the doors of complacency and brokenness will entrap you; have their unrelenting way with you – they will. Scan around.

Once the doors are shut and the court files locked away, you are at their mercy. You may have been sentenced to years of hard labour and no one would know if you did that labour, or if you rotted like a fox in a trap – no air to breath, no water to spare, no space to move within. Who is there to care? Do you think ya ma will care; will know the system enough to ask the right questions to rescue you?

You don't believe anyone will care. You take matters into your own hands. Look for an opportunity to break free. Tear like a drip from the fake security that holds you. Find that point, that minute spot where the walls are unable to contain you. Drip away!

'The prisoner had been located in a cell near the guardroom adjoining the condemned cells in order that he might be more securely watched and the fact of him doing so much in the cell without being heard may be counted for by the pattering of the rain which was very heavy during the storm on Saturday night." Sydney Mail

A FEBRILE FREEDOM: A BUSHRANGER'S STORY NOVEMBER 1866 - APRIL 1867

LARRY sits high on the ridge astride the stolen brown mare and scans the vast landscape before him. He's so happy to be back amid the granite of his birthplace beside the merry waters of Myanga Creek. Even the bush scents and the irritating smell of local timbers smouldering in his slab-hut's fireplace, below, comfort him.

Having stolen the mare on the day they escaped, he'd swung heavy John "Jack the Man" Southgate up over the mare's rump to "double" him out of Berrima. They were in the hills before the gaol's alarm had been raised.

Now he waits, his right leg across the horse's neck, arm propped on his knee, stubbly chin rested upon his fist. He'd been positioned here since well before daylight; knows that his family is awake because smoke now billows from their hut's rough, stone chimney. The occasional rattle of cookware floats up the ridge as Bridget prepares breakfast.

He'd dropped off Jack the Man to fend for himself at Fish River, about one hundred miles and three weeks ago.

If the police were alert, they would have staked out his hut. But chances are they had abandoned that idea after all this time. Perhaps they watch Larry's mother's house closer to town, mistaking it for his, further up the creek. They may even believe he has headed south to

Victoria, or north into Queensland. The reality is, without informants, the traps are helpless, and at this moment, there is nothing for an informant to report.

He'd helped Jack the Man find another horse. Larry didn't want the big fellow thinking he'd been abandoned. While on a work detail, the two of them had noticed a drain opening and, scared shitless, unsure where it would lead, had dropped into it and crawled the length of the escape-proof jail. Giant Jack was claustrophobic in the tight drain but hadn't complained. Had he struck a collar of bricks, restricting its diameter a mere few inches, he would have been stuck. Gutsy stuff! They'd crawled for ages in the sewer's greasy, smelly darkness at a frantic, but slow, pace in search of an exit.

Ahead might lie sunlight, fresh air, space, movement. Would it be worth it? Larry's mind had soared: an eagle hovering over hills and plains. The wind had whispered in his ear. His arms had ached to spread free as a dream, but while so close to freedom, he'd remained trapped.

Then, joy-of-joy, he'd reached the drain's outlet, sunlight, fresh air, the sound of running water: a river. After hours of using only brute strength and a small gardening tool, they'd removed the outflow grill, and despite being feeble swimmers, struck out across the river Wingecaribee. Its chilled current ran untrammelled, free; something the escapees appreciated.

Raised on the Bolong, Larry could swim, if poorly. He was unaware where Jack the Man had learned. The river deterred others from joining the escape, for, being country boys, they could not swim. To this extent he was grateful for Jack's support, but they had nothing in common, nor had contracted to stick together, once free.

Larry crossed but The Man had struggled. His stroke weakened: his head beneath the swirl more than above. Larry couldn't save him. The Man sank, as did Larry's heart. Then, downstream, The Man's big head had appeared above the surface. The giant could touch bottom. He'd bounced to shore. They'd made it.

That was weeks ago.

Now, the morning birds peg out their territories. The bush rhythm beats a normal pulse; warms with the rising sun, yet Larry remains hyper-vigilant. From his eyrie above the hut, he entertains a one-eighty-degree view across the valley's vast eucalypt stands stretching to the range's distant purple haze. Not one campfire is evident in the landscape. If the traps are hiding, then they're foregoing the luxury of a hot morning cuppa.

The horse relieves itself. Its movement shakes Larry, requires him to swing his leg back across its neck, sit upright to prevent being dislodged. The smell of horse piss is acrid and slightly overwhelming, before he's had a morning cuppa.

Come the evening, he will return and visit his family for the first time since the breakout. It is mid-December and he's been free since the twenty-seventh of November, travelled hundreds of miles off-road, often at night, backtracking and riding in long arcs to dislodge any real, or imagined, trackers. He's stolen clothes, saddlery, and food to survive, and managed to avoid other human beings in his quest to join his family. Yet still he hesitates. He'd imagined he would fly for home, rush into Bridget's arms, but he hasn't. He has business to attend, "cockatoos" to pay off, to learn the lay of the land, the movement of police, the exploits of mates.

Larry rides a mile or two east to the base of a large rock outcrop on the surrounding amphitheatre. He dismounts, and to avoid leaving a footprint for blacktrackers or treasure hunters, uses smaller stepping-stones to reach a distinctive rust-coloured rock. He pulls aside several covering stones, removes a leather saddlebag wrapped in oil-cloth and extracts a package of banknotes, similarly wrapped. From this he separates a wad of notes, part of his payout from the Mudgee Mail robbery, and distributes them across his pockets. He returns the remainder to the saddlebag and secretes it beneath the stones.

The money was not to be touched; kept to purchase a farm of their own. But prison, much to his chagrin, had busted that dream.

Cashed-up, he takes a leisurely cross-country ride to Strathaird, and upon enticement of a shilling, talks a doltish bush lad into purchasing on his behalf, canned food at the store, and grog from McAllister's public house: a flash slab-hut shanty of numerous rooms and a sweeping veranda.

'Was it busy? Was it full of customers?' he asks.

He'd been out of the business for five years.

'No... just a coupla regulars,' says the lad, as he kicks the toe of his oversized boots into the pebbly ground.

'Does it ever get busy?'

'Oh, Saturdee night she be busy, with all the locals and a Cobb & Co coach or two, requiring beds out the back. Oh, me gosh, yes. Busy.'

Larry notes this for another occasion. Uses a different but parallel track to return to his hut, in case he is being tracked. He wants to avoid Trooper Chalker, fresh from capturing Mad Dog Morgan, and any bounty hunters out for his hide, like scalpers after a mangy fox.

The brown mare is reluctant to return, and despite Larry's spurs, makes difficult work of the trip. Larry realises he must replace her with a faster mount if he is to outrun his pursuers. A fast horse is one of the secrets of his success. There is nothing more satisfying than having his pursuers fall further behind with each mile galloped.

He arrives home as the sunset bathes the far ridges in orange. Sits on a granite rock and swigs from an open whisky bottle; eyes peeled for movement across the vista. All remains peaceful as night falls.

The booze's warming glow comforts him and dulls his hunger. It is the first taste of real alcohol in five years, apart from the fermented fruit horse piss they occasionally make in the slammer. It's remarkable what tricks a man's brain can invent when it is swamped with alcohol, and how different the world appears free of its clasp. There's a man's dignity, but there's also family to protect. He knows the grog will have to go. One day!

Intermittent light spills through the hut's wind-tossed hessian curtains; the smell of mutton cooking wafts upwards with the smoke. It is time.

He places the mare on a long lead, to chase a green pick between the rocks. With saddlebags full of canned food and whisky, he manoeuvres the steep slope, edging towards the hut. As he closes the distance, Bridget's lilting voice and young Joseph's light tones drift across the space.

At the doorway he removes his cabbage-tree hat and places it behind his back, pauses, then pushes his head through the hessian curtain.

'Boo!'

Ladles and plates clatter as they hit the floor. Bridget, hands to mouth, shouts.

'Ah, Jesus and Mary, mother of God!'

Young Joseph screams. Bridget glares at Larry in the doorway; throws a wet dishcloth at him with force and accuracy.

'Ah Jesus. It's you. What in the Saint's name are ya doing that for, and scarin' us all?'

He smiles, wide as a barn door and as fake as a scarecrow.

'How else was I goin' ta let ya know?'

'We already know you is about. We get newspapers, you know. And the traps have been out to Ma's, so we do know you'd escaped. Ya could have left the cow-bell like we used to – instead a frightening us all.'

'I thought after all this time ya may have forgot.'

Bridget grabs the bawling child; comforts him. Speaks through tightened lips.

'Some things a person never forgets.'

As Larry crosses from the doorway his spurs jingle upon the swept-mud floor. He dumps the hessian sack on the bush-timber table with a clatter, removes a bottle of grog, throwing the wax stopper into the corner before he swigs. The smell of whisky swirls around the room. He points at the young lad clinging to Bridget's leg, head nestled into her fork.

'Who's this, then?'

'Don't ya even remember ya own child?'

'O' course I remember. I made 'im didn't I?'

Bridget's neck stiffens; she doesn't answer. He gazes at the boy.

'Hasn't he growed?… What, is he… six now?'

'Yes, I were fifteen when we had him. Our lives was well and truly before us.'

'Fifteen-years-old. My! It seems like a lifetime ago. I guess we had two years a bein' a family afore I was locked up.'

He passes her the bottle and she swigs deeply from its neck; winces at its bitter taste.

'Ya shoulda listened to me about gettin' caught up wif me father,' she says. 'Look where it's led ya. You could a had all that time with ya family… I hope you think it was worth it?'

'I was long gone before I threw me hand in with him. Me own da was no angel.'

He moves to the window, pulls the curtain aside and peers into the darkness. All that is visible are dark shapes, but the moon is rising and soon he'll see clear across the valley. He notices a mopoke on the limb of a neighbouring gum. Someone, it seems, always watches him – or is it prison that makes him feel that way? She addresses his sweat-stained back.

'You don't look sixteen no longer. What happened to ya teeth?'

'The chief gaoler knocked 'em out.'

'Why?'

'Because I tried to escape, and then gave back-chat when I was caught… He used a whip handle.'

'Pity… Ya lost ya smile.'

'It took more than busted teeth fa me to lose that,' he says, with a tone unusual for him. It sounded like bundled hurt, bottled anger, resignation.

He relieves her of the bottle.

'I bought some tinned food. It's all the go, now, I hear. It's okay, but I assume Ma's still providing ya with meat?'

'Yeah, and I also have me own milker, so I guess it ain't all bad. We get by.'

She fusses with the cooking; he swigs deep from the bottle.

'Here, boy,' he says, indicating with a swing of his arm for young Joseph to approach but despite even Bridget pushing him forward, he remains put. Larry attempts a welcoming smile.

'Don't ya want to meet ya da?'

He takes another swig, then answers himself.

'Nah, I guess not. I probably wouldn't wish ta associate with a no-hoper, a jailbird, either.'

He laughs at his own comment, glances around the cabin with its bush artifacts. He appears surprised he's not in his cell, but here, like a rabbit from a magician's hat. He watches the fireside scene: mother and child; domesticity.

'I've wished so often to be right here. In this room. I've taken every opportunity to gain my liberty through attempting to break out of gaol, run, be medically unfit, crazy, everything – except commit suicide – to make my way home. I lie awake night upon night trying to imagine what you are doing, tasting the food you eat, smelling you, running my hand across your flesh; and finally, I'm here… I'm never going back, Bridge. They'll have ta carry me back in me coffin, bejesus.'

She nods. He makes a pretend grab at young Joseph, separated from his mum when she moves to the shelves for an ingredient, but the lad avoids him. Bridget fronts Larry, face stern, points to the lad.

'It's easy for us to think the opposite. That you don't want to be here. That it's easier for you to be in prison getting three meals a day, while we live hand-to-mouth, without a husband, without a father. That's what it boils down to.'

'Well, it's not my choice.'

How can he ever explain?

They hover with the silence; swig occasionally. Later while they dine Larry notices young Joseph's eyes linger longer on his as the meal progresses. The parents chat. Well, she, mostly, in answer to his numerous questions about the local folk and gossip.

After the meal, she prepares a bed for Joseph and sits with him for an age, while Larry stares into the fire. He wonders how he will bridge the distance between them. The grog builds his confidence. He speaks into the fire but loud enough for her to hear.

'If we are to meet over the next few years it will need to be in secret, or I will be taken away again. We need to leave notes at the riverbend, and meet at family places, for safety. I won't be able to stay here.'

'I've never heard you worry about being *safe* before.'

'I've never been in that stinkin' gaol before. Fifteen years would'a killed me, I tell ya. Four has almost done me in.'

He pauses and appears to reflect.

'It will only be for a while, then they will forget me… Will they send an army and stake out the Abercrombie's for three years, just to trap one poor Irish-bred cornstalk, convicted of stealin' a saddlebag? They'd have to be looney to do so.'

Silence reigns. Larry removes his long boots; stands. Joseph asleep, Bridget covers the pots and secures the corn-beef in the meat-safe. When she returns, she notices him smiling. It's the first real smile since his return.

'Come ere girl,'

He grabs her arm and pulls her to him. Hugs her close. She pushes away to arm's length.

'Not so hard.'

'I'm always hard for you, girl.'

'Take time for chrissake. I'm just getting used to having you here.'

His hands roam freely over her body. They do not kiss. They move to the bed; make love with their clothes on. He notices that her eyes remain open as he closes his.

There's something different. She appears distant, critical. He feels her eyes upon him as he walks to the window to check his surrounds. What does she see? It's as if she expects him to go crazy; break out in a foreign language; commit a crime. She's harder. Or has he changed; suspects danger from all he meets; lost his confidence; wears his shame; is a hollow man?

Twenty-four years of age but older, far older.

Behind bars, alone in his tiny shelf of a bed, he imagined that whenever, if ever, he got home he would make love to Bridget continuously, for a week, before rising for air; imagined he would not need food.

In the morning, Joseph wakes before they do and joins them in bed. Half awake, Larry reaches out to the naked mother asleep on her back and feels the fullness of her breast and the curve of her hip, as he has dreamt. He trails his hand across her round, ripe, belly to her pubic patch. She grunts in disquiet, turns her sleeping back. He plays his hands along her ample hips and slides them clumsily between the junction of buttocks and thighs, and in her half-awakened state, she repels him like a cow shakes flies from its flesh. On his fingers he smells the fruits of their previous evening's love. It will have to sustain him.

He rolls away, leaves the bed and dresses, except for his spurs. He throws pieces of hardwood on the fire, waits a few moments warming his hands over the coals to see if the logs catch with flame, grabs his hat, spurs, and empty saddlebag, then joins the morning gloom, just as the flames erupt along the ironbark kindling.

Bridget won't hear him cross the paddock. He's a bushman, nearly as comfortable in the landscape as are the indigenous people surviving in the margins along the Abercrombie. He has the feeling she was not asleep; was happy for him to leave. Wonders if she is hiding something.

Larry's breath labours by the time he reaches the gorge rim, and he pauses to notice the effect of the sunrise. The golden morning-light bathes the landscape and highlights the trains of fog dispersed like smoke along the gullies, the golden grass-flats, and the vibrant greens of the river gums staggered like moss-pats across the canvas. While he had been able to recall this country when he needed to in prison, he sucks the view in, now, like a dry saddlecloth draws sweat. If captured, he'd have to sip, yet again, upon this well-spring. You never know?

He untethers and saddles the mare, mounts, and following a final check for camp fires, gives the mare her head down the long-side of the ridge towards town.

Later in the day he meets up with mates and they bail up three different groups of travellers returning from the goldfields, yet earn barely enough for drink and a meal. They learn the police patrol regularly, but haven't in recent weeks.

The next day they run horses into a bush brumby-trap Larry and young Jack had built as youngsters. Larry picks the alpha stallion for his own mount, releases the stolen brown mare to join the mob. The stallion was a local champion, bushed for bad behaviour, so Larry, now, is assured of real speed beneath him.

He returns alone, upriver towards his ma's place. The Government has passed laws to make it harder for locals to hide him, which he needs to understand. He gives the new horse its head and gallops at three-quarter-pace for two miles. The horse is strong but not fit, and its breathing could be heard from half-a-mile away. He needs to harden it.

He watches mother Mary's place from a distant hill. When confident there isn't police activity, he moves to her hut and enters, unannounced.

'How are ya, Ma?'

She jumps at the sound of his voice, then squeals upon sighting him.

'It's true. You're free!'

Her face is as he remembers, her smile as quick as ever. He feels her tiny bones as she envelops him in a bear-hug.

'Free as a bird Ma, and I'm never goin' back. They'll have to burn me out of here.'

'I can't believe they locked ya up in the first place, boy. What for? Stealin' some saddlery? Gave ya fifteen years. Where's the justice in that?'

She moves the kettle over the flames and reloads the teapot.

'True Ma. There is none, but I'm fine.'

Her face grows serious.

'They've placed a reward for ya capture, Larry. They're knockin' on the door of all who knew you. The new *Dangerous Felons Act* passed by Parliament means they can imprison anyone who assists you. Anyone can kill you with no questions asked! There's a lot of support for you around here, Son, so don't go and mess in your own nest and tempt someone.'

'I won't, Ma… Here, I've bought ya something nice.'

He hands her a small parcel.

'That's lovely, dear.'

'I made it. I'm doin' leatherwork and carving in the prison.'

She unwraps the package, raises it aloft and examines a carved leather amulet on a plaited necklace, then places it in her lap.

'Thanks Larry. It's beautiful. You make sure ya learn some readin' and writin' if it ever comes available. It can change ya life. At least you'll know what ya are signin' when the police put it in front of ya.'

He sleeps there that night and the next, then rides to Crookwell to meet with some other larrikins including teenager, Foran, a troublemaker and aspiring bushranger, mesmerised by Larry, as Jack and Larry years earlier were mesmerised by Ben Hall, Lowry, Morgan and others. Foran is known to be brave, having been shot by Lowry for standing up to him over a drunken stir at a race meeting, but is skittish.

Midday Christmas Eve, the lads hold up Joseph Hadfield's store in Crookwell and secure cash and forty pounds' worth of goods from the shelves, heavily stocked for the festivities.

Larry splits from the group soon after, then grogs-on in one of the smaller shanties, closer to home. Having slaked his thirst, he hands over pound notes and asks the shanty owner to supply him with three bottles of his finest. By day's end he's left with but twenty-seven pounds and eight shillings of his ill-gotten bounty.

He returns the creek-way, in the late sunlight of a washed-blue, cloudless summer afternoon. He witnesses a Willy Wagtail – a wren-like black and white bird – attack a larger, dull-brown predator, a bird unfamiliar to Larry.

The wagtail attacks the brown bird's head, chirps loudly, stressed, insistent. Larry is impressed with the small attacker's courage. The larger bird, having endured persistent attacks and acting as if they were ineffective, suddenly flees, with the victorious wagtail in hot pursuit.

The wagtail peels off to follow Larry along the river, all the while flicking its cocky little tail-feathers and chirping merrily.

'Aye, to be as plucky and free as you, little chappie,' Larry tells the bird, which he'd once believed was an innocuous sideshow in nature's grand opera; now a hero of a grander scale.

Two hours riding he's back to Myanga Creek and on the hill overlooking his ma's place. The family is together for Christmas. For a wild young man, and someone who'd, once, do anything for a dare, he's cautious and patient.

He observes horses grazing loose around the house, with some tied to a fence at the rear. Women and children in bonnets, with pale blouses and long skirts, bustle about, while men with broad-brimmed hats converse along the veranda. Occasional rounds of laughter waft across the paddock. Already obvious is that the freedom afforded to him as an escapee, is but a pale shadow: a lifetime of which, will take its toll; erode his fragile sanity. The contrast of his life with those partygoers is so stark it strips the bark off his young soul. Too long he's been denied laughter, freedom of association, and the comfort of a settled home, and feels the tug of its absence.

When it's safe, he approaches the hut from the rear, like a drover's kelpie slinks in to meet the mob. He tethers his horse, and laden with goods, rounds a large granite boulder to be exposed to the veranda. A cousin notices; shouts.

'It's Larry!'

Ma pushes to the front of the party, wipes her hands on a grey cloth, and smiles widely.

'Nollaig Shona Dhuit, Larry.'

'Nollaig Shona Dhuit, Ma.'

The traditional Gaelic Christmas greeting.

Soon family members, and a man paying Ma a lot of attention when he believes others aren't watching, grace the table. The children play hand-games and the adults ply grog. Mother Mary offers a Gaelic prayer to the saints and recalls the Christmases in Tipperary: where, in contrast to New South Wales' dry heat, the snow was often round about, if not across, their lands. And where, on St Stephen's Day morning, the boys would secure a wren and attach it to a long pole (for the wren was the king of the birds and a tribute to Christ on high). The 'Wren Boys' would parade down the streets; make a hellish racket.

'It were the first time I set eyes upon your da, "Irish" Joseph, with those pale blue eyes of his. Yes, St Stephen's Day and he a Wren Boy. His whitewashed pole was struck beautifully with holly and garlands, and he positively shone he was so proud of it.'

Ma's peaceful face glowed as she relived it.

'God bless his soul,' she says.

All present raise their glasses and drink to Irish Joseph's health. Tears spill down her cheek.

'Then we'd all sing the Wren's Song.'

With that, she sings in the sweetest Irish lilt to the haunting strains of McAllister's fiddle and O'Lachlan's tin whistle.

'The wren, the wren, the king of all birds.'

'On St Stephen's Day was caught in the furze.'

The song stops, abruptly. Silence! All follow Ma's teary gaze to Larry, who stands awkwardly, trapped, bottle in hand, against one of the roof uprights.

'To you, Larry… It's lovely to have ya with us today. I wish Young Jack, along wit' ya da, Joseph, were here, but… at least we have you.'

Larry is awkward. Doesn't want Ma to get emotional about the prospect of his capture; being "caught in the furze".

'Ah, thanks Ma… Drink up, folks.' He raises his glass. 'There's more where this come from.'

He laughs, and the fiddler fires up a happier tune. Ma grabs a youngster and jigs about the tiny room with the energy of a willy wagtail: the youngster follows as if enticed by joy.

The same children who were the Wren Boys, not many years later, became members of the violent "ribbon men" gangs – sectarian terrorists to the English establishment – spreading terror and fear with fires and fighting sticks. The violence led Ma to convince Joseph to emigrate to Australia, their first-born already punching away in her tiny belly as they embarked on *The Portland*.

With spurs jingling at each step, Larry crosses to Bridget, in close conversation with a stranger who disappears as he approaches. Larry raises a tin mug to salute her; takes a swig.

'To you, m'love.'

'To you, Larry. Drink up while ya can.'

'What do ya mean by that?'

'You know what I mean. The troopers'll soon be afta ya, when they've recovered from their Xmas. Where did all this food and grog come from?'

He flicks a cheeky smile.

'The rich. Only the rich and those who can afford it.'

He sees a lecture hover upon her lips. He jettisons his mug and drags her to dance, his spurs jangling to the rhythm, and the couple whirl until he feels her back soften, and her body press a little closer to his.

'How old are ya now, girl?'

'Twenty-one.'

'Twenty-one are ya? … and I'm the only boy you've ever known?'

She laughs.

'You know the answer to that.'

Larry watches her face flutter, as if she is about to comment further. Sees it shut down. She pulls him closer and steps out to dance, her pace much faster.

Later that night they sleep on the floor, on sheepskin rugs, young Joseph between them.

~

After lunch on St Stephen's Day, or Boxing Day as the protestant poms call it, the family heads home; Larry and young Joseph on one horse, Bridget another. Both horses sweat profusely in the unyielding humidity of the summer heat.

'You know, Ma hasn't given up on me,' he says, as if genuinely surprised.

She doesn't reply. Perhaps assumes silence will act as acknowledgement.

'She tells me that every year since I've been in jail, she has paid someone to write and protest my case. Right through to the Government, no less. I heard nothing. I thought she would never forgive me for harming our Jack.'

'You killed him, Larry.'

'Alright, for killing Jack. Don't you think I know that? That I don't remind myself every fuckin' day? Like I have just now – in my happiest moments.'

'Well, you have to face up to your actions and the hurt you've brought upon others.'

'I'm not a fuckin' animal, Bridge. Regardless of what the government thinks.'

'No, you're not. That's why ya are loved around here.'

She backs off. Young Joseph tugs on Larry's shoulder and points ahead.

'Horsemen, Dad.'

'Shit, traps!'

Larry alerts Bridget.

'Follow me.'

Larry spurs his horse and jumps it into the scrub beside the road.

Bridget follows and they clatter up the fringing ridge. Larry stops a few hundred yards in, checks the road, visible through a small gap in the vegetation. The horsemen amble past in conversation, obviously hadn't seen them. Bridget glares at him, face angry.

'They're not traps.'

'Luckily, no. Not in uniform, at least.'

They relax, ease down the slope and onto the track home.

They arrive home just on dusk. Larry chops firewood to store up for when he is not present. He swings the axe until the sweat runs and the odour of the previous day's grog exudes from his pores. He places the split pieces under the small bark-shingled log-house, close to the kitchen door. He can't believe how more satisfying it is to swing the hammer, voluntarily, for family, than to swing for the prison whip.

When he retires, Joseph is in bed and the large bucket used for bathing and washing clothes, bubbles merrily on the open fire.

Bridget stands before a rough bench; undoes ribbons from her hair.

'I'm for an early night. I'm exhausted. You probably are too. Have a bath, ya stink. The water's there. The traps should all be home havin' Xmas with their families, so we can relax, at least, for one night.'

He realises the wisdom of this, and removes his knee-length boots, while his foot rests upon one of the stumps used for a kitchen chair. He unbuttons his cord pants, all sweat-hardened and stained white on the inside of each leg from riding, and they collapse around his feet. He hangs his rough-weave shirt and grey cotton undershirt on a door-hook. Light, from the penny ha'penny candles placed around the tub, licks at his naked body. Bridget stands, points to the cicatrices etched obscenely across his once beautiful back.

'Jasus, Larry, I didn't know.'

'What?'

'Ya back. It's hacked ta pieces.'

'Tis the prison cat,' he says. 'The pussy no man craves… Are the scars ugly? There is no mirror in the gaol for a man to see.'

She nods her head.

'Jasus, how could ya stand it? The pain.'

'Humpf, ya either do, or ya don't… Most men do.'

He tops the tin bath with hot water and immerses himself. Her face softens thinking of the torture he's endured, and she tenderly washes his back, runs the rough eucalypt-scented cloth over the numerous, corrugated scars.

They don't speak. She leaves him to soak. He submerges his head to remove the suds, then rests it on the bath-edge with eyes closed. He hears Bridget undress in the corner of the room but is too polite to peek.

He steps from the bath onto the rough hessian mat she has placed there; dries himself, then springs into bed. He glimpses her slipping a night gown over her head, and for a moment, admires her plump arse and thick thighs flexing in the flickering firelight. Again, he stores the image.

She joins him beneath the knitted rug and when he wakes the next morning, is not sure if he has merely dreamed that they made love, off-and-on, during the night, or if, indeed, their passion had been rekindled at all. The lack of any movement from his groin area, usually alive at this time of day, reassures him they had.

At first light, without waking mother or child, he leaves the house for the shadowland of bush spread before him, not knowing when, or if, he will return.

~

Early one rain-drizzling February morning, Bridget hears a horse jog up the rutted track. Her heart skips a beat. She is not expecting anyone. She wipes her hands and pokes young Joseph under the pantry-shelf, pulling the hessian-cloth door across, to hide him. She hears swearing and a rough dismount. Listens to the jingle of spurs as the rider walks across the small muddy house-yard to the door, then a long silence. The door creeps open. A pistol barrel protrudes into Bridget's line of sight, followed by Larry's bloodied head.

'Christ, Bridget, why didn't ya come to the door?'

'I didn't know who it was.'

'Ah, I guess not. Fuck, I thought the traps might be layin' in wait fa me.'

'Not in this house they wouldn't. At least not while I'm here. You'd hear me cursin' from a mile away.'

She intakes breath, bites her lip, hard.

'Ah Jesus, Mother Mary and the Saints, what's happened to ya, Larry? You're covered in blood.'

She stands, flaps her arms.

'I've been shot.'

'Oh yes, I can see that and shit, look at yer shoulder. It's a mess. Here, remove ya shirt and sit down… No, lie down, over here.'

When she has him settled, she cleans the flesh around the wound with hot water from the blackened kettle that simmers beside the fire.

'Oh, Christ, steady on girl, ya goin' ta kill me.'

'You shut up Lawrence Cummins. If I don't clean the blessed thing, it will be worse for ya. Umm, it's a deep one, and its left quite a flap of flesh at ya shoulder, there. I'll have to bathe it to remove all that sticky blood and gore.'

'Have you still got that bag needle? Perhaps ya can sew the flap back into place.'

She turns aside to deflect the notion. He nods, lips grim.

'It's all we can do. I've done it with horses, which have staked themselves.'

She lifts the flap with her free hand. He grimaces.

'Shite, it hurt when it first happened, but it's sorta numb now – until ya touch it.'

Bridget washes the wound until the blood flows. She hunts for the needle and discovers young Joseph hiding in the shelf where she'd put him, drags him out, stands him up, and whispers into his ear.

'Go speak with your dad.'

Joseph heads off to the other end of the room towards Larry; sees the pistol glowing in the firelight; grabs it by the blood-stained butt, and holds it against the back of his father's head. Out of it, semi-delirious, the feel of cold metal pressed against his skin, ejects Larry bolt upright and swills water across the room.

'Gooday, Dad.'

Larry grabs the pistol.

'Joseph, you little bastard.'

'Don't speak to ya son like that.'

'He nearly shot me.'

'He doesn't know any better. You've never been here to teach him.'

'Exactly. That's why I reacted.'

Bridget notices a saddled horse, black with a white blaze, wander around the garden, reins dangling.

'Joseph, grab ya father's horse, if ya can, and take it over to the yards, and slip the reins over that wooden pin where uncle ties his horse.'

Larry wonders what uncle? Notices Bridget's face redden. Loses attention once her bag-needle strikes.

Joseph pads into the misty drizzle to secure the horse. Bridget applies fine needlework to Larry's shoulder, attempts to gain an understanding of the state-of-play.

'What in God's name happened to ya, Larry, for ya to be shot up like this? What did ya do, for Chissake?'

'A few of us boys…Tom Hogan… Foran… Johnson, was takin' a drink at McAlister's pub over at Strathaird, when we was recognised and had to draw our pistols. McAlister were nice enough at the time, but later, the two-faced bastard musta put the Taralga traps – bloody Wyles and Chalker – onto us.

'We'd left all pleasant, having borrowed merely a sovereign or two, split up, and only been gone an hour down the track, when we hears horses galloping behind us. It takes a moment to realise it's three troopers chasing us. Then they shoot at us from a distance, the pricks. Winged us and shot a horse out from under young Johnson who was riding with me.

'Poor young Johnson was hurt bad. I thought it better to scarper… I got away, but only just. I haven't stopped riding since the day before yesterday. Chalker trailed me for hours, but I slipped him at the diggings. They will know for sure it's me, so it won't be long till they're down here.'

'Did ya shoot at them, or return fire, Larry? Tell me ya didn't. It's a no-win game against the traps.'

'No, I didn't shoot back. That bloody McAlister will pay for this – the lagger.'

Before daybreak, with a piece of cooked mutton wrapped in oilcloth, and some of Bridget's fresh damper in the saddlebag, Larry, wounded arm strapped by his side, heads into the rain drenched darkness, to remain one step ahead of the traps.

~

On the twelfth of April, Larry again appears unannounced at the door. Bridget can't believe the apparition standing before her. He's covered head-to-foot with blood, as is his horse behind him. His face is swollen and blood has congealed around numerous shot-wounds on his cheek, neck, and shoulder. He is barely recognisable.

'The bloody Webbs from the store shot me,' he mumbles through a bloodied mouth by way of introduction. 'We was lookin' for some food. Young Robert came round the corner as I was walking down the corridor and he unloaded a barrel of shot into my face.'

He points to his swollen jaw, and a large gash where the flesh of his jaw was torn away by the pellets.

'It wasn't as if we was intending to do any blighty harm.'

She appears unconvinced, her mouth tight.

'Well, that's obviously not the way the Webbs saw it.'

'We was drop-bear drunk after spending the day at Locke's, over at Dirty Swamp.'

Larry leans sideways to spit more blood and discharges gobs of it.

'I don't know what is happening to the country at the moment, but everyone seems on a short fuse. The publican, Locke, wanted to fight me rather than follow instructions to act calm, so we traded blows at one point to show 'im I was man enough not ta hide behind guns, as he falsely charged. I was too pissed to make much of a show of it. That was young Jack's thing, fist fighting.'

He takes the chair by the table and flops into it.

'Stupid bloody John Foran wants to boss everyone, including me, but doesn't have what it takes. Imagine the 'prentice tryin' to order the boss around. He woulda shot Locke had I not stopped him. I merely pistol-whipped Locke to show him his position, and that he needed to be punished for laggin' some good men: the upstart. He just won't learn.'

'You're so stupid ta be stealin' around 'ere. It's you who won't learn… Those new laws!'

'What else can I do to survive, woman? The traps took Southgate last month, so they haven't given up on huntin' me.'

'Go and run some brumbies. Stay off the grog. Anything! I don't want you a bloodied corpse like ya mates: Priestley, Morgan, Lowrey.'

'Ah, they was all too arrogant, or mad, or both. I'll be okay. I'm lucky – Lucky Larry.'

She appears partly convinced; her hand and washcloth poised over his wounds.

'How did ya end up at the Webb's, given you had all this trouble at Dirty Swamp?'

'Well, we had to pass Fish River, and Webb's store, on our way back to the hideout. We thought we'd bail 'em up for provisions. The boy's shotgun knocked me arse over and blood everywhere. From the floor I heard young Robert shouting he'd shot me, but hadn't realised it was me.'

Larry lashes out with both legs, in pain.

'Ahh, Christ girl, watch where ya pokin' that thing.'

For a moment she stops scrubbing. He draws a breath.

'Then young Hannah Webb fired pistols at us from the front counter. I staggered to me feet and we were lucky to make it out to the horses. Couldn't even pick up the carry-bag, which held Locke's whisky. Had ta get outa there... Jesus, as bad as they make me out ta be, I could never shoot someone in cold blood like that lad shot me.'

He shakes his hoary head in disbelief. She proceeds with the cleaning.

'You obviously frightened them, poor folk. What were they supposed to do? Did anyone see you coming here? I don't want anything ta happen in front of tha child. No guns. I couldn't handle that.'

'No, we headed in the opposite direction. Even bumped into a couple of roo skinners out that way, so they'll believe we kept going. Ah, Jesus, my jaw pains.'

'I imagine it will ache for a while.'

She patches him as best she can. He has a restless night. He doesn't share her bed, but continues drinking, falls asleep for a few hours at the table, without realising it.

He leaves before the family wakes, meets up with Foran, who'd stayed at a friend's place, and they head for the hideout.

~

It is a stinking hot day and Bridget is resting in the cool of the hut, when she hears a horse jog to the door. It's three weeks since Larry's visit and she's heard nothing. When she steps out, a skinny youth from Strathaird has a message for her to meet Larry at the hideout. She is to ride towards town but when she reaches Kindale rock, is to divert over the ridgetop. If not followed, she is to start a small campfire on the riverbank. Someone will meet her.

Bridget follows directions and after an hour by the fire, notices a fox slink past. Its yellow eyes examine her, then it scurries away. An hour later she hears a disturbance in the brush. She peers into the gloom expecting the fox, only to see Foran, mounted, rolling a durry.

'Shite, ya coulda warned me. Coulda called out or something,' she says, distressed.

'Yeah, I guess so. Wanted ta see what you were up to, though,' he says, with a slight leer in his voice.

'Oh, where's Larry? I was expecting him.'

'Back at the hideout.'

'Is he hurt?'

'Sorta. Better he lays low; he's had hell to pay with those face wounds.'

'The newspaper said he was mortally wounded.'

Foran doesn't reply, lights his rollie with a wax match, struck off his saddle's pommel. His hairless face and the rim of his cabbage-tree hat glow from its yellow flare.

'Is it far, the hideout… it's quite dark?'

He picks shreds of tobacco from his lips with his grubby fingers.

'No, not far. Douse the fire, and we'll get outta here.'

Puffs of tobacco smoke punctuate each word.

They ride east for an hour, all the while moving higher, and whenever they reach a prominent point the Abercrombie plains appear in the moonlight and the stars spew out like fireflies on a swirling pond from the darkness of the far horizon. She believes she could touch those stars, which sizzle directly above her.

They reach a mountain creek and squeeze between small gorges; their sandstone cliffs flush up against its moss-lined banks. Foran halts and indicates they've arrived. They hitch their horses within a tight, rock-lined amphitheatre, and with saddlebags in hand, she follows him uphill into a sandstone overhang.

They stand on the lip of a massive cave, its entrance-nave larger than any man-made edifice she has ever witnessed. Foran leads her around a large rock pile; perhaps collapsed roof material. A woman's chant and the distinctive wooden click of indigenous clap-sticks echo around her like worrisome crickets.

Foran points ahead. His voice echoes into the darkness.

'Stick close to the wall by the path and head towards the light, where you'll find Larry. I'll take care of the horses.'

She shuffles forward. Her eyes adjust to the pitch blackness after the mock-twilight outside. She rounds the corner, brushes against the cave's moist wall as others must have done over the millennia, to find the path lit by a few mutton-oil lamps sited along the corridor wall. The air is crisp compared to outside.

A young Aboriginal woman, naked except for a possum-skin coat draped over her shoulders and long curly hair hanging loose, approaches her in the opposite direction. Both women enquire with their eyes but unable to verbally communicate, pass.

Larry, naked to the waist, sits on a log, placed against the cavern's rear wall.

'You. What's been going on?' she demands.

She searches wildly. Points at places at random. The hideout resembles a caveman's camp… bones and rubbish everywhere; the bushrangers forced to live from hand-to-mouth to avoid the traps. Larry's beard is wild: bushy on one side and bare the other; his hair lank and frizzed.

'What do ya mean, "what's going on?"'

'With that woman.'

'Nothin' is going on. She's my healer.'

'Is that so? I can imagine what she heals.'

'Yes… it is so. I passed out – fell off me friggin' horse – on the way here and the local blacks have cared for me.'

'Larry, it's bad enough having to worry about ya lying with men in the prison, without having to deal with you lying with her.'

'What do ya mean lying with men?'

'You know what I mean. Buggery.'

'Where did ya get that from?'

'The welfare officer from the prison. Said we'd have ta get used to the fact that you would need to get release with other men.'

'Why, those lyin' bastards.'

'He said prisoners knock their front teeth out to be able to suck other men. You've lost yours.'

'That's a load of horse shit, Bridget. I'm not interested in any o' that. The screws knocked my teeth out. It's in the record.'

'What about the newspaper sayin' you was captured in bed with Lowry.'

'Everybody has to share a bed at that shanty. We all do. Jeezus you're an idjit, Bridget!'

'As fer lyin' with women here, I've been far too sick to even imagine that.'

Bridget's mouth opens and closes like a Bolong River guppie.

'She brings me herbs and medicines, poultices and soup to ward off puss and the evil spirits.'

'I don't mind anymore what ya do, I'm over it, and you! Just don't flaunt it, Larry – ya mongrel bastard. Don't bring me, or the child, into further ill repute, or shame me, as a woman.'

She appears shocked at his confession of loyalty. He wonders if there's something she is not telling him? Wonders if he's lost her; lost the child.

~

That night they make love in the corner on the silky, possum-skin rug upon the cow-hide stretcher. Her flesh feels like molten quicksilver to his touch, her smell divine, her shape as malleable as the flames leaping in shadows upon the wall. He is her at times: so much of her is he attempting to absorb, to store in his memory against the times when she would not be there. He realises his jaw has healed and even the pain subsides, momentarily.

They must be quiet, because Foran camps in the same chamber, but Larry notices a shadow move across the flames. One of the Aboriginal women has slipped into Foran's bed. He'll not be interested in other's affairs.

They leave on the fourth day to return to young Joseph at Myanga Creek. After a half-day riding, Foran scouting ahead, they approach the Abercrombie area, and skirt wide of Ma's place for fear traps have it staked out. They are tired and crave a hot cuppa, a steaming stew, and perhaps a bath. As they approach the wagon-trail leading past their hut to the settlers' properties, Larry notices fresh horse tracks, so Bridget continues alone.

Larry and Foran proceed to Bridget's brother-in-law, Josiah Cramp's, hut. Foran rides into town to check on police movements with their "cockatoos" and secure supplies. Unlike Larry, he's unknown in these parts. Larry, too tired from the ride and his injuries, spends the night with the Cramps.

Next day, Foran returns and informs Larry that the police have been patrolling between the Little and Abercrombie Rivers, but have returned to Bathurst to replenish supplies. Larry sends Foran to tell Bridget to join him at the Cramps and then asks him to lie low, elsewhere, until the heat settles.

That night, Larry, Bridget, and the Cramps, drink Larry's whisky, and laugh at childhood stories: missing school, chasing horses, swimming in water holes, dancing, and attending mass, where, as children, they would run crazy. Their laughter leaps through the windows and rumbles free across the starlit plain. Larry can't believe he laughs again.

Young Joseph sleeps on a cowhide at the foot of the bed. Bridget and Larry comfortably make love. Their bodies are re-familiarising, if their minds are not.

The first flush of morning light peeps through the surrounding fog. Larry, already on the bed-edge, a pistol in each hand, wakes Bridget.

She places her hand where his elbow bends – as a question.

'I'm sure I heard something,' he whispers.

'No. Josiah would have heard it also, if it were something to worry about.'

'It were the clink of iron; I tell ya. Stirrup-iron, or carbine up against brass bullets of the trooper's bandolier. A way off, though!' he whispers, forcefully.

'You're imagining it.'

'Foran told me the bastard traps had a black tracker with them.'

'He also said they'd gone home… Relax. They won't leave the warmth of their homes so soon. It could be anything... a possum.'

She pulls him backwards into the bed as if she needs him. She takes his hand and shows him where she needs him. He relaxes. Perhaps she's correct. He searches for her with his lips. If only this could continue, forever.

He hears a willy wagtail's strident twitter – so close. Then he hears a reply, not quite a replication.

Ah, fuck, he thinks. *Black tracker!*

The whistle is a signal. He wonders if the tracker is here to sneak a bullet into his temple while he sleeps, as they did to his mate, Ben Hall?

A voice bellows through the mud-daubed walls.

'This is Sergeant Grainger of the Bathurst police. Those of you inside the house, come out with your hands up.'

Dogs bark fiercely. Bridget and Mrs Cramp squeal, and the children scream and cry in fright at their mothers' responses.

Larry, in desperation, dashes, naked, to the kitchen and back to the bedroom. He sees armed, khaki-clad traps at every corner. His stomach spasms. His mind races but the hangover slows it.

'Oh fuck. Me apprentice didn't cover his tracks. He was followed. Foran, you arrogant, lazy little prick,' he says, as much to himself as to anybody.

The trooper yells from the yard in his loudest parade-ground bellow.

'We're armed and we've got you surrounded.'

Bridget shouts.

'For God's sake don't fire, he'll give himself up.'

Larry has his pistols raised.

Bridget grabs his arm and utters two words, 'The children!'

He flops on the bed. They look into each other's eyes; silent. It could be love. It could be hatred. Larry draws his moleskins to his waist. Turns to the open window.

'What's ya name, Trap? Who are you?'

'Grainger… Senior Sergeant Grainger, from Bathurst… I have four men and a tracker. Give yourself up.'

'Not Chalker? Not that murderin' bastard?'

'No, he's on leave… He's not with us.'

'I'll surrender if you treat me like men.'

'You'll not be harmed if you surrender to me,' says Grainger.

Larry's shoulders slump. He kisses Bridget, just a peck. Lays aside his pistols and moves slowly through the door into the sunlight and down the stairs, hands raised.

He calls quietly to the waiting traps.

'You can lower ya guns. Women and children inside.'

'Nobody else? Not Foran?'

'No, only the Cramps, my wife, and the children. The Cramps didn't know I was here. I snuck in during the night to see me wife.'

Grainger draws his cuffs from inside his coat, stretched tight across his fat belly, and handcuffs Larry. Delight registers on the trap's grubby dial. His hands shake from fear of what might have occurred from a shoot-out. They'd obviously lived rough like the bushrangers they hunted because Grainger was grubby, clothes muddied, pieces of sleep still lodged in the corner of his eyes. Two constables, flies crawling over their sweaty backs, cautiously check the house, while another saddles Larry's horse and assists him to mount.

Bridget and young Joseph watch from the top step as Grainger leads Larry, arms handcuffed behind his back, head slumped forward, away. He appears a broken man. He takes a long look back. No farewell smile for little Joseph. Nothing but abject glumness.

It is the last time he sets eyes upon them, and knows, by the time he and the troop of toy soldiers rounds the bend in the wagon track on their way to reach Rockly by nightfall, then Bathurst Courthouse by the next, that it is, also, a promise. April 1867 (Reported in *Bathurst Times* May 2).

RESTITUTION: GAOL II
1867 - 1876

IF you close your eyes you can see through walls. You can see the highland's far horizons. Thank Christ!

You're dragged back to the hole after months free. Your heart has roamed. The wild country scents still stir in your nostrils if a stray breath of wind finds its way to you, but you fear the moment those scents might escape. The monotony and control quickly intimidate you into conformity, into an awkward comfort, and the company of others eager for news of outside exploits can convince you that you have a community. At some point you recall vowing to shoot yourself rather than ever return. Yet, here you are.

How many years to serve? Thirty in the company of those you'd recently escaped. Will they love you?

What about those outside who love you? How do they fare? Do you get an opportunity to redeem yourself in their eyes?

No way. Even outside the walls the system pervades your life. If institutional representatives do contact family, it's only to excrete in the sanctity of your only nest, the security of your imagination, of a life away from this hell. Their skill at perfecting this, this excrement, is sublime.

'Hey Cummins, guess where we've been?'

No reply.

'We've been delivering family Christmas packages.'

'What, playin' little elves now are we?'

'Welfare… visited, what was 'er name now, Harold?

'Bridget.'

'That's right, Bridget. I visited Bridget.'

'Sure, ya lyin' bastard.'

'Nice little filly, that one. She made a lovely little hack. So good, I had to go back for seconds.'

'Ya talkin' through ya arse, Stevens.'

'No… all for the price of two, family parcels. You can rest easy Larry; the kids will eat for Christmas.'

'She wouldn't go fa anyone as fat as you, ya big useless bullock. Someone else; I might worry.'

'Bit easy, Larry! Hadn't seen a stallion for a long time. A long time.'

During family visits it's suggested that if the wife does the officer favours, then life will be made easier for the lag behind bars. The power in the story is often in what is not said. The implied, the impressed, the threat of what will happen if she does not comply.

'How is my family, Father?'

'I still haven't seen them, Lawrence.'

'The screws are goin' on about visiting them. About their moral danger.'

'It's all talk, Lawrence.'

'I'm not so sure, Father. Smokey Dawsett told us last time he was in here, a screw had visited his family and forced the wife put him up for the night – a long trip. The screw told Smokey's old lady that Smokey was being lashed each day because of a misdemeanour. Told her if she fucked him, he could make it stop. Help her husband.'

'Did she?'

'He reckons she did.'

'I wouldn't be worrying about Bridget, my boy; she's of sterner stuff.'

Here is the role delusion plays. You can delude yourself that your partner was resilient, or delude yourself that they weren't. Whatever way, it places a wedge in the split-rail that pried you free of all that was once good, fair, sweet, and played a role in that dream – a real life! By the time you get home the slip-rails are down, or broken, and one of you has moved on. Agh God, Bridget ya poor thing.

You learn from some taunting screw that the family has visited. That you have a new daughter, Catherine, to meet. That they'd waited outside for hours, unable to enter. Told you're not allowed visitors. For many days, you can't stomach the bile of the anger rotting in your belly, festering in your rock-hard gut, from not being allowed to set eyes upon them. It takes weeks to settle; manage the wobble.

It's strange, but since being recaptured, and learning to write, you find you don't contact the family; don't even send a message due to abject despondency, so ya lose connection, and the children follow any stranger who wanders into the yard; impressed with any man who comes to woo their mother.

You wonder if she'll be able to fight them, those sugar-lipped poets, alone; able to explain how important it is for the children to be present when their father is released; when you slip in quietly through the mist, over the split-log doorsill and lean like a stranger against the slab-timber wall, to reunite; cross-ankled and feeling awkward, about where to put your few shoddy possessions, where to sit, what to say. Should you freeze in silence and say nothing, a preferred choice, or glow like a coal in the hearth and exaggerate, bluster and fake about being comfortable amidst strangers, even if they are of your blood and in your fuckin' house?

One night you dream you are high on a hill, the wind tears at your face, makes your eyes water and you hear a faint sound. Is it a distant voice: a challenging voice. Are the traps onto you?

All day, to avoid capture, you have ridden wide of civilisation, of settlements. You stop and turn in the saddle. You see a tiny pony at the foot of the hill – a brown pony with short hairy legs – and sitting upon it is a child.

'Dad ... Dad ...' a tiny voice shouts above the wind. It's Joseph, hundreds of yards distant. 'You forgot to say goodbye to me!' the boy says to the man – you – high on the mountain.

'Goodbye lad,' the dream-man replies into the wind.

'Bye Dad,' says the tiny child with the breeze-thin voice, then turns his pony's head towards home some twenty miles away, and jogs off.

In the dream you sit askew on that saddle, on that horse, on that hill, for a long, long time. The wind fairly cuts the water from your eyes, and you require a big gulp of air to face the ride ahead. To face the life outside the dream.

~

'The punishment schedule lists yet another two attempts to escape Parramatta which resulted in him receiving twenty-five lashes. The other was at Berrima (three years later), when the punishment was limited to three weeks on bread and water.' P91. It's a Long Way to Tipperary.

In gaol, pain – of body, mind, or heart – is ever your companion and you need it to define your life like the artist needs a black line to define the tree trunk from the landscape; white points to set the clouds alight from the sky, object from field, ground from foreground, drama from story, friend from foe. Don't be mistaken, pain is not something you would seek unless you had some dysfunction. It stalks you. You show one moment of weakness, it will be in there like a goanna up a dead roo.

Gaol and pain are interchangeable: the cat-o-nine sometimes a welcome relief to the pain of loneliness, the pain of depression oozing across every decision, even those decisions you don't get to make. The cat's claws harvest white pain, searing, cracking, soaring pain – Jesus it hurts. It awakens with each breath, each movement you attempt, from the first swish and crack across your back until the final time, weeks later, long after the rotten-mutton smell of your own suppurating flesh has left your body. Finally, you realise that if you persist, you can probably lean your body lightly against a post, or lie a moment on the crackling scabs growing like limpets upon your sorry back, without the pain attacking ya.

The pain in your head, your heart, is black pain. It suffocates you, chokes you, cloys in your innards making you want to gag, or chuck. In its own way, it's just as awful, just as painful. But you are not sure there ever will be a time where you will lean your suppurating self against a wall and realise it has ceased. You grow to believe it will only stop at the end of a noose. Only stop with the gentle swing where your toes no longer touch this sweet earth.

'I'm sorry, Father. I'm not sure I can go on.'

Father Lanigan clucks his tongue a moment.

'You have to, Lawrence. For your family.'

'What family? I've killed one member and shamed the rest.'

'This is your penance, my boy.'

It's as simple as that. Pain it is that you can use to feed your narrative.

A certain amount of pain can break you, yet too little, or too much, can steel your resolve to remain true to yourself, to grasp firm to your bearings. In turn, this angers your betters, or those opposed to you, and having chosen that path, the nettles will forever be there. You learn to defend yourself through emotional distance from yourself and your tormentors, through using your brain and attempting to use the system like you use the tail of the python to choke itself. You learn to read and write better, in the hope ya can make a case to seek justice.

~

'One of the prisoners, Lawrence Cummings, complained of having been flogged in Berrima by the Gaoler and the Chief Warder, while handcuffed behind his back to a ring bolt. He also complained of having had teeth knocked out.' P 840 of the enquiry p71 It's a Long Way to Tipperary...

You believe that blood, common to all men, is a single colour – red. The red you see on the prisoner's back draining along the cicatrices of flailed flesh. You may never have seen the blue blood fresh from the heart, or the black blood you cough up when the blood drains internally and coagulates in your stomach.

You learn different when shot in the jaw, and need to keep running, keep moving, keep ahead of those who wish you dead, those who have just shot you. You find yourself on your horse galloping, drowning in your own blood; speechless despite the pain; gurgling and hissing, and blowing pink bubbles of spit, so much so your horse's shoulder is bloodied pink like the troubadour's horse in a Spanish bull-ring. Only it's your blood, not the horse's; not a dressed-up bull. And, in the morning, you wake and vomit black blood, haggis nurtured in ya own gut. You remember this from when they knocked your front teeth in with the whip handle, and you are handcuffed and can't wipe, nor drain, the bastard stuff.

Oh yes, blood is a many coloured, many splendored, thing. It's blood that stains your soul. It runs thicker than water. It scares the pants off you when you see it, bright as roses, bursting from your brother's head like crimson parrots flashing from a melaleuca. You're not brave enough to watch its fatal trajectory; it's supposed to be the blood of those bastard traps. Even years later you can't stand to trace the bright spray's fatal curve in your memory: The sixteen-year-old's bold body, our Jack, cartwheeling idiot-like over the front of the horse, chasing his own blood.

'Don't worry, Jack. You're safe here. See, we're only five feet apart. We can sit and chat here in the cell and recall those trips along Myanga Creek; speak of wild horses who became our closest friends; relive wild nights, which we thought wouldn't end.'

'Yeah, I know it's you, mate. I see you squatting there in the corner. There's no need to hold up your finger stumps. I recognise you. You shouldn't have dared me with the axe.'

'What? I know you'll never leave me: never let me go. Your hoary face stares me down in my dreams, in the same manner the bloodless battalions of dead soldiers haunt the ageing generals. What could we have done different?'

'Hush now, sit over there, young Jack, so ya can keep close.'

It is family blood that sticks, that lays out your characters' tales as if you have no control, no say in their role. Blood don't take blood. It's as simple as that.

~

You know… you get to believe most of us have no hold over our story. The scene is set long before we're born. If you're lucky enough to be born posh your voice will match that of those who judge you. If you are born amidst the illiterate and the poor, and those who scratch the soil, or hew the wood for a living, you're marked down before you start.

That's it! The ending is visible from the commencement of the arc. The plot rolls out. Your God-given gifts are blunted by lack of expectation and honed on worthless challenges, and regardless of your efforts, the tone of your voice, the accent of your beginnings intersect your tale, to pull the plot in strange and awkward directions. Those agin' you fall in behind, in a long line and overwhelm your will, and the options to become hero diminish, and to turn villain, increase.

You wake one morning in here and you hear only one voice, you are surrounded by the ugly bloody thing. Whilst you have a voice it is not heard outside these sandstone walls, and if it is ever heard, it is considered valueless. As worthless as the copper pennies they put on your eyes after the executioner has set you to swing and you rest in your coffin. Pointless writing your tale: no one will listen.

~

At another point, you wake and realise that there are only two ways to survive. First, you must escape, so your voice is not one among many, but is a lone voice hiding out like a dingo amidst the forests of anonymity. You try with all your will to make that happen, make escape happen, because escape means you don't have to surrender your identity, you can prove the system wrong, you can survive.

'Back in ya cell.'

'It wont be fa long, ya stinkin' bastards, and I'll be out again.'

'We'll see about that. See how sure ya are after a month in the black hole.'

'I've smelt freedom, I tell you, and will take it to the hole with me.'

'All you'll smell is ya own shit down there, and for many a year.'

'Still sweet by your standards, screw.'

It's there, on the record, the number of escape attempts – the number that succeed. What does a chap do? You learn their reach, the law's reach, is further than you imagine: far longer than your own. Despite this, you escape four more times to regain your identity. Once from the escape-proof gaol.

Second, you realise if you are unable to escape then you need to change your voice, along with its story. Few achieve the second: get to have your voice spread like loose pages across the landscape. Why? Because of the steel-cold trap of our cursed voice.

It's funny, strange even, but to find another voice you need to be literate in your own. You need to be able to break it down, to understand its pulse and form, and how it works, and hear it in the poetry of other men, and critique its worth. If, however, you are unable to reflect, to see your patterns, to dream of better things, you end up back in the hole – simple as that. That's the tipping point: realising the system, like water dripping on rock, can grind you down, or you can decide to view it differently and allow it to put a sharp point to the pencil, refine your attitude.

Here's the rub. That single decision, to try and learn from your predicament; learn how to read and write, could mean a difference to you and your spawn: help you find a good woman, keep your nose clean, find fair employment, learn to defend yourself and your family through paperwork, learning, and using the law against itself. This can help set the kids down a different cow-pad, a different groove towards gentler pastures.

How, you ask, do you come to that realisation when the odds are against it?

~

Drip, drip, drip, drip, drip away.

How did you read that line? Yes, you! Did you rush? Did you get the timing, put the pauses in the correct place, allow the following beat, drip *pause, pause*; drip *pause, pause*; or did you just race through it? Drip, drip, drip.

Go back. Do it again. Do it again! Get the monotonous pace right. You can't jump over the pain; you've got to go through it. Didn't we discuss that? Go on.

Drip, … drip, … drip, … drip, … drip away.

Ha, ha!

See, you worry! You're a little shaken. Concern creeps upon your brow. What will you be asked to do next? Is he crazy?

'What right have you to control me that way?' you ask yourself.

That's the institution: the place where you are always watched, where even your thoughts are subject to interrogation, where you are forced to do the mundane their way, the gaoler's way, to a point where you no longer believe you can command your own will, where you ask yourself what is the point? And, like a drip, fall away.

You feign sickness. They are forced to act in a certain manner to reduce your hard labour. You hear them discuss it. They talk behind, above, about, to, but never with, you.

'What are you laughing about, Smithers?'

'At Cummins, Doctor.'

'What? Is he shamming sickness again? It's the fifth time this month. Is it raining?'

'Yes, shamming.'

'What's wrong with him this time?'

'He's learnt to write and the note he's written says he believes he has Kneemonia.'

'What's funny about that?'

'He's spelt it knee…'

'Funn eeee. Next, he'll have dicktheria.'

'You're about as funny as he is, Doc.'

'Not as funny, but we'll get a laugh when I tell him what the cure is. Tell him we'll look at him tomorrow, if it persists.'

You act crazy, so that what they do learn about you is worthless. The institutional pushback is massive.

You get clever. Raise concerns about the injustice, about the inhumane treatment you receive at the hands of His Majesty's institution. Questions are raised in Parliament, a department-led review of the conditions is conducted in 1878, but unless you all – each decaying inmate – corroborates, what gets discussed doesn't get written; and if you all corroborate, then what gets written, generally, doesn't get action. You can't expect to win. As unfair as that is, you guess it is a democratic warning to the corrupt. Let that be a warning to you Chief Warden, Mr damned Small, Mr Comptroller of Prisons, Mr Minister for Justice. Let that be a warning to you all. Questions will be asked!

You notice that outcome yourself. Not a rush, or waterfall, of reform; no acceptance of the role they play in diminishing the life of the aggrieved; but a slow corrosion of their immutable right to violate your humanity. Perhaps they tiptoe more carefully around you, knowing that the Minister is aware of your presence. That, and your ability to be slightly out of control – a little crazy – gives you a slight advantage. This is your identity now.

The interminable space between the drips requires attention. The timing between the words. The place where nothing is being recorded. The pause for reflection, for emphasis. The moment between when enlightened thought about the injustice of your imprisonment leads to an offer of freedom, and the attempt to keep you incarcerated beyond many life sentences. The interjection of a commission of enquiry. The look at the face of another soul. The space where the life you had planned for yourself is kept on hold until you reappear in civilisation.

Drip... drip... drip, is the point. Each artistic effort starts as a point. Tip of a pen on a page, point of a story, tip of a ballerina's toe on the floor, a musical note struck short, the place where a painter first makes their mark, an identifier.

You learn Frank Gardiner, the bushranger, has been pardoned.

'Hey, Larry?'

A voice, through the darkness, from the corridor's far end.

'Yeah?'

'Gardiner got releathed.'

'How do you know?'

'Thweet lipth', the thcrew told me. Never could keep a thecret, old thweetlipth. Thez Gardiner got a pardon.'

'Oh, Jesus, how did he manage that?'

'Maybe they're going thoft on buthrangerth?'

'I bloody hope so.'

A drip is an extended point, trapped. A place under pressure, but not a line; an opportunity for change; a hiatus for a crescendo... or a whimper. You are potential – kinetic potential. This nocturnal drip is so important it keeps the desperate monotony at bay. It creates an interval, a timeline, an audible reminder that you can leave and re-emerge, that you will not simply disappear, you exist in this point in time. Exist at this point of time.

If they've pardoned Frank Gardiner, you half dare, in your delusional madness, to believe they might pardon you; you who has committed lesser offences.

Drip.

Should you agitate for a similar treatment for all bushrangers?

Drip.

You advise your ma, the only trustworthy person you know. It's your twelfth consecutive year behind bars.

Drip.

And Ma, God bless her soul, still believes in you.

Drip.

You promise her that if you are released you will never commit an offence against His Majesty again.

Away.

MOTHER MARY'S STORY
1865 - 1876

YOU'D be sad in the head if you didn't think newlyweds with the names Mary and Joseph weren't destined to have a saintly child. I said so, myself, to Joseph, when I married him, right proper in our village's Catholic Church.

Maybe I did bear a saint. Maybe the foul world into which we introduced him was too much for the poor wee babe. But I hung on to that belief even when it would appear the fates had other plans. That's not so bad, is it? Not so bad for a mother?

I said to Joseph we must leave Ireland and the "troubles", and all his shenanigans with the Faction Gangs, and move to the Colonies, if we were to have any chance of a good life.

At the time, I was wiping the blood off his battered face and bathing his badly burned hands after he'd had a nasty stoush as a Whiteboy. I began thinking, I would, for sure, be doing this one day to dress him for his final march to the sound of the tin whistle, tears and rattle drum, courtesy of his hated Majesty. I'd be kissing his generous lips with a farewell prayer afore they closed the coffin lid, if I didn't do something. I could see no way out of it, fa be he terrorist, or freedom fighter, dead, he was no good to himself or his family. It was like the little people were drawing me a picture plain as day.

'We've got to run me darlin'. We really do… afore it's too late,' I whispered.

Oh, he argued for a tad… months… but, eventually, came around to my way of seeing things. By that time, I could feel a little 'un lodged deep inside me, before it showed physical signs, before I vomited the first time, before me belly started to spread. It was as if the poor child knew he had to burrow in, be determined, if he were ever to survive.

On the ship out here I should have died, so sick I was. I vomited from morning ta night. I would gladly have swum to New South Wales than remain locked on board *The Portland*. At one point, I dragged myself onto the railing all prepared to jump, but a ship's hand saw me and dragged me off and held me down until I settled. Oh, Mother Mary, how I swore at that black-faced fella. Rotten thanks for saving a life. But we rode it out for one-hundred-and-eighty days and crossed that wretched ocean, which had taken the lives of many hoping for a better life in the colonies, and had left me with barely a thread of me own life. Our second wee one, young Joseph, was born not long after arrival, but like his brother, born in the old country, lasted only a few days before he, too, died.

It was four more years until we had another, and when Larry was ready to arrive, he wasted no time. He tore my pelt with utter disregard, and I wondered if it would ever repair, there was so much bleeding.

Oh, in disbelief that he had survived, I scooped him up from the hessian bed and held him in my arms for the first time and felt blessed. It was short-lived, for at that very moment, he stopped breathing. I felt his wee chest stop – I did. I thought we'd lost him too, afore we had a chance to get to know him. So, I held him at arm's length to see what were wrong, and without a lie I tell you, as bold as brass with focused eye, he stared right back at me. Like a creature lost in a strange land, I could sense him delicately weighing the air what snuck across his wee nostril, getting my measure, realising his separateness then and there, before he took to breathing again, and I brought him in close, where he relaxed into my shoulder.

'Who are ya, wee laddie?' I remember saying at the time. 'Who are ya? What will ya make o yourself?'

From then on, I knew he was here to stay, and I loved him for it.

Look... he never gave us no trouble, did Larry. He seemed quite self-contained and made few demands. When his brother, Jack, arrived not long after, he took to that wee blighter like a lonely dog takes to an orphan chicken, and watched over him in his basket until Jack were old enough to move by his self. Then he followed him daylight to dark, shepherding him from trouble, controlling him, until they walked in step, the best of mates until Jack's passing.

Relatives and teachers said there were something hard about Larry – something uncompromising – but for the life of me, I could never see it. One of his schoolmates believed he were a bully. She said he picked on those weaker than his self, but I don't think so. He plain could not stand fools and would brook no "wishy washy" arguments they might raise to avoid responsibility for their actions; to find courage when demanded. He wasn't keen to take a backward step, but you give him warning, you be clear about what is required, and my Larry would do whatever was needed: a good lad.

It wasn't long until the mother-bond was stretched, though, and he spent all day, every day, in the bush beside his father and uncles, with horses and cattle. It may have been this which made him hard, for it is a demanding life in those cattle camps, and no excuses were made for a wee child who could not keep up. Oh, Larry was hard on the horses too, but not cruel. He was never one to blame them for his own misjudgment. He was not one to let them get away with any shenanigans either, would demand top effort, and as Irish Joseph would say, could pull more from a horse than any man. But he always made sure at the end of the day, that they were watered, fed and housed, afore he attended to his own needs. Like I say, he were a good lad.

~

1865 – Myanga Creek

Dear Larry,

How are you, my boy?

I write this to remind you, again, that your family still loves you. I am holding up well and have had no bad health for many a year. Your sisters are blossoming into lovely, young women, and they cheerfully help around the farm and are as handy as young William, who has taken on the role of the "man of the house" since you, your father, and our Jack, have been absent.

Your roan pony has had a foal, a right little champion filly. It is a bay and has few points to remind you of her dam. I intend to have her broken so we can teach your young Catherine to ride when she visits.

It would have been better were you to teach her yourself, but given your circumstances, being in gaol and all, that is not possible.

We don't see young Catherine so often these days unless her mother drops her off. We worry a mite about her mother too, your Bridget, who has less to do with us as time passes, and more to do with her side of the family, the Crumps. Our girls say it's the shame, of you being in gaol, that's driven her away. Not that you are to worry your head about such matters.

Please have someone write in reply if you get to read this letter, because I crave for your news. If there is anything you need, include your request in your letter.

May the Saints protect you.

Your loving mother.

~

What do you do when things start spinning out of control for your spawn? What do ya do? Maybe ya shoulda rode them with a tight rein? Maybe they had too much freedom and it becomes impossible to reign themselves in when circumstances don't suit? But when you've been raised, yourself, in the strangling arms of mother Ireland, and confined by the church and them who believes they are your landlords and betters, then there can never be enough freedom, can there?

Aye, I could blame myself. Maybe I should ha' taught the boys to have a wee more respect for other people's property. Yet, how did them squatters get their property but stole it off the blacks, or claimed it as "finder's keepers"? Who are they to be so high-an'-mighty, and get the law squarely on their side?

Yeah, maybe I could ha' got the boys to see the need to keep their hands off other's goods, but I never imagined we would have any ourselves, so the idea never entered me head. It were said I be light-fingered myself; that I got my boys to lift some silverware off a fancy government surveyor – ya see that serving dish and carving-set up there on the shelf, and, ah, that crystal lamp – but in those days, it were fair game, when a tin plate would have suited the man's rough travelling much better. They were on my land, and I'd bet Dublin-to-a-brick that survey group weren't eating meat they brought in with them, but mine, they'd butchered nearby.

Maybe ya can keep the youngsters away from other bad influences, but those boys loved their da, just idolised him, and ya wouldn't stop them having adventures for all the gold sent to China. And, it must be admitted, Joseph loved them too, and loved having them learn their trade at his feet.

Perhaps it all started there, because back then, there was so much money to be made in moving wild cattle off other's land and selling them to hungry miners. The boys would be with their da, not fully aware of the danger, nor the crimes they were committing.

~

1868 – Myanga Creek

Dear Comptroller of Prisons

Your humble servant, Mary Cummins, writes to seek your assistance in determining the welfare of her son, Lawrence Cummins, formerly residing within Bathurst Gaol, now in Pentridge.

I, respectfully, remind you that my son was put into your care when but a teenager and should be protected from the older criminal types residing within those gaol walls. Surely it makes no sense to have a boy, committed for stealing a mere bridle, exposed to such an unhealthy environment, when his soul could yet be rescued?

Would you please determine, also, if his mail is being delivered to him, for despite my corresponding all these years, we hear nothing from him.

Yours,

Mrs Joseph Cummins.

~

Oh, I did write to him, and still do, but he never got the letters. I didn't want him to forget us, the family, what's left of it. It's his identity. It keeps him firm like love of country and flag keeps you firm in battle, when it appears everything is against you.

And to give Larry his due, he has fought tooth-and-nail to return to us. Each time he escaped he were on his way back here – to us. He said it weren't so much the being free, but returning to country, to where he fit, that drove him. It put all the puzzle-pieces in shape for him.

The letters, if someone were to read them to him, would have been a great comfort to the poor lad, but it was not to be.

We'd heard of the great bushranger, Gardiner's, release, even up here at Myanga Creek. There were so many families affected by bushrangers in our local and wider district. Families like ours, whose sons had joined the game, and families whose lives had been rudely skittled by their shenanigans.

To Sydneysiders, and normal folks, the terror of the bushranger days was over, but it hovered very much on our lips around here. When a big note like Gardiner is set free, it raises some hackles, and news of it travels faster than bushfires across the hills and ridges. We'd probably heard about the move to shift Gardiner well before the newspapers, through some screw whispering in the ear of a prisoner's woman he was extorting.

'Here's my chance,' I said to myself, and next morning made young William harness my sulky, and by daybreak I was on Mr Thompson's doorstep to see what could be done.

~

'You're a good and loyal mother, Mary. How many years have you been petitioning on Larry's behalf, now? Six?'

'Um, six, seven. It's now 1867, isn't it? You lose sight of time when you live out where we do.'

'There would be many a son in that hole, whose family would have abandoned him long ago.'

'Ah, 'tis likely so. But we look after our own in the Abercrombies.'

'Still, you're a good woman.'

'Aye, and you be a good man, also, Mr Thompson, to prepare the letters to the authorities on my behalf. I wish we were better prepared ta defend his good name when the poor boy faced the beak all those years ago. Who would have imagined he would have been dealt with so harshly?'

'Umm, maybe. But it's impossible to read the hearts and minds of other men, I'm afraid. Good chance we may not have been able to help, when all is said and done.'

'But his life is so shit. Since listening to his stories about prison life, which he told me during his escape, I still barely understand what he endures in there. I'm determined to keep him safe so he can return home to his family.'

'Well, the findings of the Enquiry into his mistreatment, has demonstrated the inhumanity of that place, for all to witness.'

'But despite its finding, my Larry still rots in gaol! It has amounted to naught!'

'Well, we'll make another appeal to the Government.'

~

We made numerous appeals and some coincided with the enquiry Larry started. Each time, I'm sure, the government men believed they could refuse his release and that would be the last of us. Year after year we would try a new angle, and "apply influence", I think Mr Thompson called it, but with little effect.

~

1873

'Well, Mr Thompson, I'm here before you yet again.'

'Another letter to your Larry? A Xmas message, perhaps?'

'Aye, not a bad idea at that.'

'Will you be wanting to petition the Government this year?'

'I don't know. For all our efforts and the findings of the Enquiry, we seem to have had no luck, and our Larry wallows inside.'

'True, little has changed for the lad. The Government has shown no remorse, and there has been no public remonstrance of those officers who perpetrated the injustice.'

'Aye, and while we complain, Gardiner goes free as a bird. Why?… Because he comes from the upper class, is why.'

'Yes, you're probably right, yet it may not be all bad. His release shows a pathway, a precedent we can follow to secure Larry's release.'

'But so far they're not interested in seeing a similarity in the case.'

'Well, let's not give up, just yet. There are other avenues we can try.'

'I'm tired Mr Thompson, tired, and I can't see anything changing while this Government is in power. I think they are as crooked as a Tipperary laneway.'

'Hmm. Perhaps we can use their greed to our advantage. I suggest we invest in some influence with both sides of government because the election looms… We need to raise another petition, get voters to back us, but this time we'll bypass the Council and petition the Governor, based on the fact that Gardiner, whose crimes are far worse than Larry's, has been released, while Larry languishes in gaol. There may be clemency based on this fact.'

'Aye, I shall happily pay if you are of a mind it has a chance, and I shall take the sulky from house to house to gather the signatures needed for the petition, myself, to ensure it's done and gets to the Governor early. I'll see the boy be free – as God be my judge.'

It was then the blessed angels sent me a sign. Yes, sent a sign to a wretch such as I. It was a letter from my boy and written in his own hand. I could not believe it. After all this time it were a miracle.

Berrima Prison Jan 1874

Dear Ma,

I had no idea you have been writing to me these years past. So costly you arranging the solicitor to pen ideas on your behalf, for worthless me.

Mr Small, the Gaol Governor, has passed on your letter. I was surprised and angered to learn that there have been others not passed on.

I have been teaching his son how to care for and ride his pony, and the Governor's view of me has changed these past months, because the lad and I get on famously. I wish it were my young Joseph I was helping but, perhaps, the universe is generous and returns such favors as you hand out, and in return, someone will watch over him.

My surprise for you is that, with the help of Father Lanigan, I have learned to read and write. The Warden has respected my achievement and passed your letter on to me in the understanding that I can, now, make sense of it.

Yes, we all heard that Gardiner had been freed, the lucky toff, and argue amongst ourselves whether we would accept being returned to the old country, or even to the United States of America, as a condition of our freedom. I couldn't. I was born here, Ma. Why would they exile me if they were to consider my release? I'd rather try and stay alive, see out my time at Berrima, in order to return to the highlands.

Your Son,

Larry.

~

I drove that sulky from farm to farm to gather signatures to back the petition. I faced abuse at several doorsteps, some saying I was an unfit mother, or a disgrace to the mother church, and refused to sign. But I gave as good as I got. There were many who forgave, and many who realised it were but wild boys and wild country living, and perhaps of no real concern to the law: my Larry a wild horse who chafes at the mere thought of bit and harness, but in time, will tame and use that energy for the community good.

In the end, we secured enough signatures.

Aye, as I said during church confession, I had hope, even after all this time. I had love for my boy, who carried a huge burden over the death of young Jack. But did I have faith? No, I must confess, I had lost faith in the Government and its Justice system, and perhaps even our Lord, but I wasn't going to go down without swinging.

~

(ACTUAL) **Petition of Mary Cummins, 6.6.1874**

To his Excellency Sir Hercules George Robert Robinson, Knight Commander of the Most Distinguished Order of Saint Michael and Saint George, Governor and Commander-in-Chief of the Colony of New South Wales and its dependencies, and Vice Admiral of the same.

The humble petition of Mary Cummins of Myanga Creek, New South Wales, and others, on behalf of her son, Lawrence Cummins, a prisoner in Her Majesty's Gaol, at Berrima, who was (at Bathurst) tried and found guilty of several charges of bushranging, and was sentenced to undergo accumulative sentences, amounting in all to thirty years.

Your Petitioner showeth that at the time of her son's first apprehension he was a lad of but nineteen years of age; that he had been led into the companionship of those who were guilty of breaking the laws of their country: that he was in consequence ultimately arrested, and charged with the commission of a certain offence, and found guilty of the same on the unsustained evidence of one man (which crime it is now known he did not commit), and was sentenced, in September, 1863, to an imprisonment with hard labour for fifteen years, first in irons.

Whilst undergoing this sentence, being in daily communication with old offenders and men of confirmed criminality, he became hardened to crime, until he, with others, planned and succeeded in making their escape; not being able to leave the Colony or to obtain honest employment, your Petitioner regrets having to acknowledge his joining in acts of crime for which he is now suffering.

Such being a brief record of the circumstances which have led to your Petitioner's son being in his present position, your Petitioner respectfully and humbly desires to draw your Excellency's attention to the extreme youth of her son at the time of his first conviction, and also the subsequent knowledge in references thereto; also to the disturbed state of the Colony at that period, together with the repeated success attending the unlawful acts of many engaged in bushranging, which greatly tended to the leading of young men astray and taking them entirely from parental control.

In reference to his escape and subsequent crime, your Petitioner, whilst not at all excusing her son of his errors, cannot but think such was much (if not entirely) accelerated by the indiscriminate mixing of young and unmatured minds with some of the worst of men – men of known cunning and badness, men who deliberately study to lead young men astray, seeming, as it were, jealous that any should be different to themselves.

Being so situated, her son imbibed some of their principles, till he eventually committed those acts which have led to the most serious results.

From correspondence your Petitioner learns that her son's conduct during the time (now nearly eleven years) he has been in gaol has at all times been good, otherwise than his attempts to regain his liberty by escaping.

Your Petitioner is able to state positively that her son, acknowledging his faults, is altogether reformed, and is confirmed in his desires to live by honest means – vowing never again to violate the laws of his country. He has also of late years used his leisure hours, with such assistance as has been from time to time given him, in mental culture and general self-improvement, so as to fit himself for useful employment. Seeing that his industry and attention has been so directed, together with other grounds advanced, your Petitioner humbly prays that your Excellency will, in the exercise of mercy, see fit to grant the prayer of an aged mother on behalf of an erring but repentant son, and permit her declining years to have some comfort in knowing her loved son has an opportunity granted him of retrieving his character and showing his repentance sincere by his being restored to society, and doing his duty thereto as a member of the same.

Your Petitioner cannot venture to hope your Excellency could in any case grant her son's release to this country; she therefore prays that by an act of grace he may be permitted to exile, and thus find the door of mercy not entirely closed against him. All necessary means and expenses attending such can and will be readily supplied.

Your Petitioner humbly leaves her case in the hands of your Excellency, praying most earnestly that your Excellency will be moved to pity her, and give her cause for joy and hope, by granting the prayer of her petition.

And your Petitioner, as in duty bound will ever pray, etc etc.

~

I made sure the petition got to the Governor, but I tell you, I received no reply. I was beside myself. There had been a change of government and I was uncertain in Larry's case, if this was for the better. I had given a lot of money to Mr Thompson to distribute, as needed, to support Larry's cause. We'd heard money had helped secure Gardiner's release, but much of my money went to key members of the outgoing government. I was comforted by the fact that the public officials responsible for the day-to-day system, responsible for authorising the release of prisoners, remained unchanged.

~

Government House Sydney, Feb 1875

'It appears quite clear to me, dear Secretary, that the Colony is on quite shaky grounds if it is to continue to deny the liberty of Prisoner Cummins on the grounds upon which he was sentenced.'

'Is that so, your Excellency?'

'I find it quite impossible to believe that the Government, or its officials, have missed this glaring anomaly for so long. The man should never have been exposed to such treatment. This fact, alone, would be ample grounds for his release. His release submission does not mention it, by the way. It is based on quite different grounds, altogether. Even Cummins' sentencing Judge, Hargrave, in his supporting letter, does not mention the injustice.'

'Mention what injustice, exactly, your Excellency?'

'The poor fellow was sentenced to thirty years hard labour on the roads.'

'That's correct your Excellency.'

'Yet, he's spent twelve doing hard labour within the Prison walls.'

'Umm, that's because the Works' Prison was never constructed as was promised by the Government at the time of sentencing.'

'Well, by default, and I must add, illegally, he has been sentenced to six times the allowable time for a similar crime of "imprisonment with hard labour" than would ever be allowable under British Law, and both the inhumanity, and illegality, of the matter should be addressed forthwith. Contact the Colonial Secretary and advise him of my thinking.'

'Yes, when described that way, it does sound quite improper. I shall note your concern and correspond today with both the Minister, and the Cabinet.'

'Good. Advise them that Cummins, if he continues to behave and does not bring ill-repute to his reputation in the meantime, is to be released a free man into the community, on January, 1876.'

~

I knew that the information I had been sent by the Comptroller of Prisons was as precious as the holy water hidden in the local cathedral at Bathurst.

'Our Larry is to be freed!' I said to our wee William. 'Free.'

He couldn't believe I be crying, but it wasn't from pain, but disbelief and happiness.

'We must tell Larry immediately so he be prevented from doing something foolhardy in the meantime.'

'I'll take the letter to him myself, Ma.'

'You can't ride all that way yourself.'

'Yes, I can. I can ride across country to Berrima, or at worst, get the letter on the day-coach from Goulburn to Berrima. You forget I am a Cummins – a horseman.'

Aye, and true to his word, he pushed across the range like a native, delivered the letter, and returned just after dark. It was a ride to equal any of Larry's, and I could see my wee William had all the makings of men like our Jack (God bless his soul), and Larry.

~

'You wanted to see me, Mr Small?'

Mr Small, the Prison Governor, stands corralled by his massive English oak desk, hands behind his back, staring over the institution's wall at Berrima township, when Larry enters. The room is dark except for the spluttering gas wall-lamp behind Small. Larry has been paraded before this desk on numerous occasions and the room has never appeared light and airy, its sombreness, perhaps, a reflection of the business conducted therein, or a reflection of the hard bastard who inhabits it.

'Umm, yes, Cummins. Read this.'

He hands Larry a letter from a large official envelope, addressed to the prisoner, but with the wax seal broken, meaning Small has read the letter.

Larry scans the contents, subvocalises each word.

It is a letter from his mother dated 12 March, 1875. He reads it again, and returns it to Small.

'Oh shite, does this mean what I think it means?'

'Yes, it does. You are to be released in January – nine months from now… It's official.'

Larry's hands, rough and calloused from years of prison labour, busting rocks, twist and squeeze the tattered hat he holds before him, while his whole being attempts to accept something he has spent the past twelve years expunging as a possibility.

'Um, your mother's Petition has drawn favour with the NSW Governor.'

Larry does not allow himself to show any emotion in front of this cur.

'You're sure, Guv?'

'Absolutely. It is signed on behalf of Minister Plunkett, himself.'

'Agh, Christ. I cannot believe it. Thank you, Guv, Mr Small… January, eh? Agh, Jesus.'

With that, Larry about-turns and walks mechanically out the door, strides the twenty-three paces along the hall until he reaches the exit, stumbles on the sandstone top-step then, like a sleepwalker, slowly descends the remaining four. He part-runs, staggers, for he is not used to running, to the centre of the prison's grass-quadrangle, then throws his hat in the air, shouts, 'I'm free,' falls to his knees, and sobs uncontrollably.

~

Oh, we are supposed to be of the criminal classes, but Irish Joseph would say there were more criminals in the House of Lords than on the streets of Dublin.

I wanted my boy home, by Christ I did.

I didn't realise how much I wanted that, and with the news of his release I worried about the fates and the run of bad luck with losing my men (husband Joseph, young Jack). I couldn't afford to lose another. I was scared witless that Larry would take umbrage at some mean comment "inside" and do something to mess up his release.

I never, in my wildest dreams, imagined that the Government would be so unpredictable, so spiteful.

~

NSW Legislature

'Gentlemen, welcome to this meeting of 26 February, 1875. We have a problem.'

The newly elected politicians, most in waistcoats and sleeves, some smoking, others shuffling papers, look intently towards Colonial Secretary, Robertson's, end of the table.

'It's the bushranger-prisoner, Cummins,' he adds.

'The Braidwood Bushranger. He hasn't escaped, again, has he?' asks the Bathurst representative.

'No, but nearly as problematic. His mother, based on Gardiner's amnesty, has petitioned the Governor yet again, and the Ministry of Justice and Public Instruction have recommended this time that, due to his changed disposition, he be released. His Excellency the Governor, on this advice, has approved his release for next year.'

'Release? To be exiled?'

'No! Not exiled. Free as a bird… into New South Wales.'

'How could that be? Gardiner was released on the condition of exile.'

'The outgoing Government leaving us a farewell present, perhaps? Something sour to chew, while we celebrate the sweets of victory. Remember, Gardiner wasn't born here, so it makes sense to exile him. Cummins is local. Also, we can't rule out that Governor Robinson may have merely forgotten to attach that condition to Cummins' order.'

'Lucky Larry – that bounder has caused us so much grief and expense through his escapes, public enquiries, and bad press. He is the last person to whom we should be showing clemency.'

Another member vies for attention.

'How could His Excellency get it so wrong?'

'Err, His Excellency believes Cummins has been held illegally and we could face serious legal issues if the public were made aware of this miscarriage of justice. He believes we simply can't sentence citizens to such inhumane orders.'

The Colonial Secretary clasps his chin with his right hand while he thinks.

'Well, no one has been aware of it until now and no one has made a fuss. I suggest we ask the Governor if, on the grounds that we are a new Council, he could reconsider his decision and not release the bounder.'

A clamour of comments, all uncomplimentary of Larry, continue until it is obvious the group agree.

'I'll put it to the vote, shall I?... All those in favour, say aye... The ayes have it.'

~

The law is the law, they say. But some can alter it to suit themselves.

As you know, I wasn't above greasing a few palms to enjoy favours myself. That paid off in ensuring officials within the system backed Larry's release, but not the politicians.

~

Government House, Sydney:

'The Colonial Secretary, Robertson, is not happy your Excellency, regarding Cummins' release.'

'Yes, so I hear. It appears the Government believes it has been cheated by the previous members of the legislature. There may have been bribes to important people during their term, to progress the case.'

'Well, it's not true that you shouldn't have ruled on the matter, Your Excellency, the present Minister, Docker, was the one who put the matter before you.'

'I had questions about the legality of the sentence. It's outrageous. Damned Colonials.'

'And rightly so, but they are more concerned about the appearance of their being soft on crime by releasing such a notorious prisoner as Cummins. Releasing him so early in their term, they believe, sends a dangerous message.'

'Umm. Okay, for the sake of harmony with this new Council, if the prisoner, or his mother, have not been advised of the release, then I will agree to revoke the order. On the other hand, if they are privy to the release order, the outcry in the Upper Lachlan will be heard here in Sydney and my credibility will be sorely tested, so the order, then, must stand.'

'Understood, Your Excellency. I'll advise the Colonial Secretary, forthwith.'

~

The Honourable Mr Joseph Docker
Minister Justice and Public Instruction

I have been advised by His Excellency, the Honourable Hercules Robinson, Governor of NSW, that further to his consideration of the Lawrence Cummins matter, and contrary to recent advice to release him, you are advised, herewith, that his excellency has revoked his order until further notice.

This is conditional on the prisoner's mother, or the prisoner, not having been advised of the previous order to free him.

Colonial Secretary
John Robertson Esq.

~

Had young William's marathon ride allowed the letter to get to Larry in time? Lucky for me I did not know that we had lost the petition and Larry's freedom, at that moment, or I would have died from frustration, or fear.

~

Following morning parade, the Berrima Prison Governor, Small, pulls Larry aside.

'Hey Cummins, I really am sorry, but forget what I told you about your release, the Government has changed its mind. I am, of this morning, in receipt of a letter from Sydney head-office, notifying me the Governor has revoked his decision, and asking if I had informed you, yet, of your release.'

'Ah shit. Revoked? Are ya fa real, sir? What did you tell them?'

'That I'd passed on the news of your freedom.'

'Why? Weren't you supposed to do that?'

'No. Appears, I overstepped the mark, informing you, and consequently, can expect a dressing down.'

'Ah shit sir, how could they? How the fuck could they take that away from me – my freedom?'

A red glow spread like a fever across Larry's face. The disappointment and anger followed. It was all he could do to return to his cell, and throughout the day he wanted to run riot amongst the guards, with hammer and rock. Earlier, the younger Larry might have, but if he were honest with himself, a part of him never really believed he was to be released, and he could see that Small had believed in his release, so didn't feel betrayed at that level. It took him a couple of days to reconstruct the impervious wall around his heart and return to the confines of prison life. Accepting further confinement was nearly more difficult than accepting the death of young Jack.

~

NSW Legislature

'It appears, Mr Secretary, that Minister Plunkett and Prison Governor, Small, have exceeded their authority and already have advised the petitioner, and the prisoner, of the impending release date.'

'How could they do that? They don't have the authority. Who the hell do they think they are?' the secretary's voice louder with each question.

'In addition, the sentencing judge, Hargraves, also has been advised of the pending release. This being the case, I believe we cannot revoke the pardon.'

The secretary draws an audible breath, his face reddens. He spins away.

'Ah, Jesus, what a mess.'

''Tis that, indeed.'

'Get Plunkett in here, this minute, the bloody idiot.'

~

I'd written another letter to Larry soon after the one William had delivered. Larry said it was comforting that I was still looking after him, although he said he had promised me, much earlier, he would offer no further problems to either gaolers or government. The poor lad was so down. The black pain of despondency gripped as the reality of having to spend more years in that hole snuck in. I didn't know of his disappointment at the time, of course.

~

Myanga Creek

Dear Larry,

Make sure you continue to behave in all ways, my darling boy, to ensure you do not raise the wrath of the guards and those in charge. Your release is only a few short months now, and if you are of good temperament, you will be free. Do what you have done so wonderfully these past few years; behave.

Please do not spoil this chance, for there are some who would be pleased to do you ill-will and see you remain behind bars. I would not be able to live should your release be denied for any reason and you were unable to return to our warm arms.

I am sad to warn you that you will have to steel yourself for some bad news, when you get here. Your Bridget has another man, who she's been on with for years; is with child; and has left the Colony for North Queensland. I didn't want to trouble you earlier to add more misery to your sorry life, but as you have a long life to look forward to, I thought it better to give you some warning before you arrive.

The family, however, will be so pleased to have you nearby again. Not long now.

Your loving Mother.

~

I wasn't aware he'd entered the house until I heard spurs jingle close behind me. I guess that part is not so strange, as he was always like that, sneaking in. But I imagined him arriving to a big crowd of us, whooping, cheering, and drinking grog.

He arrived a day sooner. I'd forgotten he travelled over bushranger and Aboriginal highways and could be guided by the stars. He was part of the landscape. He didn't have to die like Burke and Wills had, some fourteen years earlier, to become at one with the country, he was born into it – was a part of it.

I hugged and hugged him and would have wept were he the type to join in, but he wasn't. He'd changed. He was lean and strong like an axeman, or a man used to heavy toil, and the missing teeth removed any resemblance of his boyish smile. He was a man now, while the picture in my head was of a teenager. He was a man: totally self-sufficient. One who knew he needed nobody, not even a mother.

He wasn't keen to mix with locals, although they were keen to catch up with him. He was kind enough to his ma to attend the party I'd organised for those who had supported me and his quest for freedom. Some of his old cronies were there, but he wasn't so interested to take up with them. He didn't comment upon losing Bridget or the children.

Soon, he noticed there were some who had been caught up in the controversy of his release and would walk out of the shanty whenever he entered, and there were his nephews and nieces, who my sister-in-law had poisoned agin him, despite my allowing them to remain rent free, in the house she had lived in with Irish John, so many years earlier. Larry was regarded as a bad influence and a lowering of the social shit she would go on about, which was far, far, above her station.

Some locals, like McAllister, feared Larry's revenge for having lagged him to the traps, and we were told, slept fitfully with a loaded rifle, but Larry seemed to pay no mind, nor actions, towards seeking revenge.

It was just when I thought he were settled again that he tells me, over breakfast, 'I think I'll leave the district to seek work and see if I can't begin another life somewhere else. Start over. My past will always dog me here.'

I'd be lying if I said my heart didn't snap then, for it did. The idea he would be absent from our lives, again, after being returned so recently, was hard to believe. But I could see the virtue in it and would not object. I thought it was, perhaps, but a passing thought, one that he'd mull over for some time, years maybe. I really didn't know him anymore, did I?

By mid-morning he was gone. He'd yarded and saddled his favourite horse, and with corned beef and flour in his saddlebag, a handful of tea in his quart-pot, and a hug from me, mounted, and headed bush.

He promised he would keep in touch, but we never saw him again.

FREE AS A BIRD: JAMES LONG'S STORY. 1876 - 1880

HE stands quietly and watches: doesn't take his eyes off the unlocked gate, nor move towards it. It's unbelievable that anyone can succumb so readily to captivity. Many a time Larry has looked through bars and convinced himself that regardless of the incentive, negative or positive, he should never succumb. This fellow is different. He's bluffed. Stuck to the spot like a snail on a damp rock in front of a hungry crow.

The door to the prison is open but he dares not believe so. Will not race through it. Continues to act as if he's trapped. His intelligence pits itself against his desire: his ability to learn transforms him into his own gaoler.

Rather than use brute force, Larry prefers to use the power of the animal's intelligence to tame him. Cole, the property owner, hired Larry to run brumbies off his block. They'd bred too prolifically and become pests, damaging waterholes, busting fences, stealing stockfeed from the cattle. He wanted them trapped and tamed, and had promised his daughter, Ellen, she could have her pick of one for her seventeenth birthday. She chose the noblest, an alpha bay colt, who stood apart from the herd, the morning he'd been trapped.

Ellen, closely watching the first day's proceedings had asked, 'Do you want me to close the gate?'

'No. No need,' Larry had responded. 'Just stand there for a while if you don't mind, in case he makes a dash.'

At that stage, the horse danced with a long rope. Only once had it panicked and run to the rope's end, to outpull Larry, only to be met with a hard-stop as the rope twanged against a solid yard-post where it was tied.

He's surprised Ellen is here. The girl rarely visits the yards. After three weeks, and try as he might, he's been unable to extract even a hello, let alone a sentence, or a smile from her. He'd wondered if the stuck-up bitch would show any interest in her horse, if not in him.

Larry uses the horse's energy to teach it right from wrong. Once learnt, such values, good or bad, are difficult to erase. He knows it's important to ensure it stands – faces you – in order to allow itself to be harnessed and fed, and the rider kept safe from its striking hind legs. Each time the young horse faces Larry, he rewards it with a carrot. If the horse is inclined to move in a particular direction, Larry positions himself to stand in that direction in order to reward him for facing him. Because Larry stands between the horse and the open gate, it is inclined to move in that direction, so learns quickly, and without need to be chastised, or jagged about with a rope, or have its confidence broken. The principle of the double-bind is close to Larry's heart. The horse is of two minds. In moving to be free, it becomes deeper involved in its submission.

If the horse reacts suddenly, in fear or surprise, Larry reacts much later, to promote calmness. Horses learn from the alpha, the brave one. Poor treatment, equally, can teach attitudes that will not serve the horse well. A calm horse learns faster. A confident horse accepts challenges and acts bravely.

Lesson over, they lead the colt to the tackle shed, where Larry brushes, then releases him for the night. He and Ellen part, without ceremony, she to the house, and he to his hut.

He is convinced no woman will ever want to be with him once she knows his history. No woman of substance that is. Ellen, least of all. He's sure his past fifteen years is tattooed on him, obvious to all.

The next day, he drapes a cloth over the colt's eyes, and for ages, rubs its head, ears, and face, while quietly talking to it. Then he rubs it all over with a loose cloth, flapping it occasionally, until the animal is so confused it stands, quietly, awaiting the next ignominy. Larry rewards him after each session of steadiness. Mostly with a carrot, sometimes a break, to recover its wits, or more often, a heartfelt pat and a soft word.

During the afternoon, when the shadows stretch across the yard and up the rails like paper, cut-out figures, Larry lunges him on a long, greenhide rope. When the horse circles competently, he works a halter over its head and uses long driving reins to accustom it to having pressure placed on its mouth through the bit.

'Careful lad, steady – I know what a blasted bit is like.'

Later, he lunges it with a bridle.

Ellen hasn't shown at the yards today. He is disappointed. While not daring to dream, he believed he had made progress with her.

Sometimes, he surprises himself by wishing to be back behind gaol's comforting walls, because there, at least, he had no expectations; knew what to expect. Sure, out here he has what's left of his life ahead of him, but he is so different to those he associates with, that he feels alien, and must appear so, to anyone whose enjoyed a sheltered life. He is fearful that, unable to fit in, he'll live alone. No wife. No family. A busted drover.

Next morning, he repeats the blindfold exercise. This time he concentrates upon flagging the colt's buttocks and hocks where it can lash out with its hind legs if it needs to, but doesn't. With growing confidence, it stands motionless for the whole exercise.

Later, he saddles it with the girth lightly hitched, but tight enough not to slip. The colt humps for a moment, objecting to its burden. Larry moves quietly with it, encouraging it to relax and stand still.

Once it settles, he hitches it to the rails beneath shade. He'll let it stand for a while, to get used to the unfamiliar weight on its back and the girth's restraint.

Larry slips through the yard's split-rails as easily as the magpies do and walks across to the crooked tank-stand by the house to quench his thirst with a tin pannikin of cool water.

'Would you like a cup of tea, James? I'm having one,' says Mrs Cole, Ellen's mother, from the shade of the house veranda, where she's partially hidden.

He shades his eyes with a hand, locates her, and smiles in recognition.

'Oh, thank you, Missus, that would be wonderful.'

Larry had changed his name to James Long. He'd heard his father speak of the Longs from Tipperary, and the name came to him the first time he was asked to provide his identity after leaving the Bolong.

It isn't unusual for Cole, the owner, to invite Larry for morning tea when working near the house. His wife merely follows tradition. The woman, fair-haired with long-sleeved dress billowing and work boots without laces drawn, places a teapot, two cups, and a fresh damper on a sideboard, as Larry arrives.

'Mr Cole has gone to Melbourne on business, James, and he asked me to check if you would mind staying on for a few more weeks – it could turn out even longer.'

'Oh, fair enough. Sure.'

'He says he has a few horses out the back paddock for you to work, as well.'

'Great.'

She pours tea.

'You seem to relate well with horses?'

'Yeah. Better than I relate with humans, I reckon, if the truth be told.'

She laughs, but checks to see if he is serious.

'Can you stay on?'

'Yeah, sure. I can slip anything I have teed-up, back a few weeks… until he returns.'

'Ah, good. He's quite concerned about that Kelly scoundrel, the bushranger, and us women being here alone. Says it would be safer if you were here to keep an eye on us.'

Sweat bubbles across his forehead and beneath his armpits at the mention of bushrangers. Has she tweaked to his identity?

'Oh, them – the Kellies – yeah, I read about them,' he says, casually. 'They seem to be running a few hundred miles further North and West of here. Closer to Albury. I figure they're just a mob of wild boys playin' with the police until they grow up. I'm sure there's nothing to be afraid of.'

'My husband says they are animals, James. The papers say they ambushed and shot police – Fitzpatrick – and robbed his corpse. Left him naked and stiff for the crows. What sort of creatures do that?'

'Do you believe everything you read, Missus? I'm sure they wouldn't bother bush ladies like yourselves, except perhaps, for a meal on a wet night. Sometimes, it's police who can be out of control depending on your rank in life, you know. They're all for the landholders who don't give a fig how they subdue the miners, or the poor sharecroppers. I heard the police violated Mrs Kelly and Ned's sister, which started the whole Kelly vendetta… So, who are we to believe?'

He sips his tea to calm his nerves, cool his desire to chat further. The mother doesn't answer. She argues over the comment like stream water over a stone ledge.

'The sooner they're trapped… or killed, I'm sure the better off we'll be. Apparently, this new Felons Apprehension Act is making life ever more difficult for them to get shelter, or support, and the Police predict they'll have them soon – dead or alive. But my husband argues that this desperation may encourage them to pop up anywhere. Even here.'

She slides into a chair across from Larry.

There's much he wants to say, but can't. He's surprised how disinterested he is in this all-too-common, petty story of the victimised Catholic Irish. He just wants to move along. He knows how it will end – the State will crush them and march on.

'I'm happy to stay, but I'm sure there is nothing to worry about.'

'Only if it doesn't disrupt your life, James.'

'No, there is nothing to disrupt, so I'll be pleased for the distraction.'

'I've noticed that you stick to yourself. You don't go to town. Are there no friends?'

'No. No real friends around here. Though, if the truth be told, I haven't quite been anywhere social to make friends.'

'How long have you been in the district?'

'Nearly three years now, since I moved down from near Albury way. I'd brought a mob of bullocks down from near the border, and decided I'd like to stay awhile after someone offered me a mob of horses to break.'

'Did you bring them all that way on your own?'

'No, I had a team, but I sent them back with my gear.'

He didn't know how much to disclose, but decided she deserved more.

'It's easier to find work alone, and if I stay out on the properties I keep out of trouble. There were times, when I was younger, I would get too much drink on board… so stay away from it now. I use the time to do leatherwork, and you know, I can earn a bit extra from that.'

'We will have to get Ellen to introduce you to some of the young people in the district. How old are you, James? It's hard to tell under that beard of yours.'

She pours a full pannikin of tea and hands it to him.

Then and there, he knocks ten years off his age.

'I'm twenty-seven.'

He'd lost more than ten years in prison; he got some back in one statement. He had another reason. He wants to be young, like young

Ellen. Wants to have some of the things she has: to go to town without looking over his shoulder, to be a little carefree. Also, it will help explain why he has no possessions, and perhaps deter people doing the sums if they partially recognise him: 'Oh it couldn't be Larry, he is ten years older.'

Mrs Cole returns her cup to its saucer.

'Oh, twenty-seven…Ten years older than Ellen?'

'Agh. Is that her age? I thought she was older. She acts older… beyond her years.'

'Yes, only sixteen and she's a good girl. Has many friends… did well at school and has taken confirmation at the church.'

James nods, sips his tea as delicately as he can, while Mrs Cole continues.

'What about family? Where are they?'

He liked it when the boss, Cole, was around; fewer questions. Since gaol, he abhors questions.

'My da and my brother are dead – an accident. My old ma lives near Windsor, where we come from. I don't speak to her… Ma, since her new man moved into the house a few years ago and he and I… disagreed,' he lies, implying that his was a righteous response to violence, hurt, and mistreatment.

Her face suggests she's satisfied with his answers; she reaches across and offers him the plate.

'Have some damper… it's still warm.'

Larry rises and butters a piece at the side-table.

She notices how he holds the knife like a hammer, how he sparingly uses the butter as if such a luxury is scarce, how he holds his mouth slightly to the side as he manoeuvres the butter across the damper like a young boy unused to such delicate activity. She smiles at his awkwardness. He places the knife aside and collects his plate.

'You should try some honey – it's much nicer.'

He looks up, selfconscious, surprised that she has observed him so closely.

She is smiling.

'We have a hive, in a gum, down near the river. We rob it every so often. It's wonderful to have something sweet. The bees can't be so happy that we keep stealing their hoard. We're real bushrangers.'

There she goes again. Does she know something? Is she aware he is an ex-con? Is the grime of his grubby life smeared across his face?

He glances across and she is still smiling, her kind eyes whisper to him, *it's okay, I like you.*

She continues. 'Ellen said to me… she says, "I think James has endured a lot of hurt, or pain, in his life, mother. He appears rather sad".'

'Did she?'

'Yes, she watches people rather closely, does our Ellen. I guess in your case, losing members of your family in accidents like that can make you sad?'

He checks himself. He was going to say something like 'losing your liberty makes you sad'. He was going to agree he was sad. But he doesn't. Can't. He is not used to talking about softer feelings, and struggles to read them in other people, except perhaps children.

'Oh, I'll have to cheer myself up when Miss Ellen is around then, won't I?'

'Yes, you… you'll have to. We can't have her being sad, now, can we?'

They smile.

Larry, having applied the pale honey, sits and enjoys the damper, surprised how comfortable he feels around this woman, despite the interrogation.

Since leaving prison and the high country he has failed to find comfort in women. He is uneasy and too ready to retreat, rather than make their acquaintance. He has difficulty knowing who, in either gender, can be trusted. Gaol was easy. You knew no one could be trusted and the alliances only lasted until self-interest determined they should be broken. Outside, he applies that same formula to relationships, but knows he shouldn't.

Once, on a binge, soon after release, he spent a rough night with a woman, a shanty whore, drunker than he, and got the dirty prison-water off his chest. Not easily. He felt he had to draw his seed from a place that didn't exist, and they nearly knocked the bedhead through the shanty wall. Even then, he found she wanted more than he was ever able to provide. He could not extend himself even to look at her when they parted next morning.

Mrs Cole changes tack.

'With Mr Cole away, join us, Ellen and I, for dinner tonight, James. It will only cost you an armload of split firewood, and we could all benefit from the company.'

He pauses, thinks for a moment too long.

'Well, if you'd prefer not to.'

'No… all good, good, I will at that. If your cooking is as fine as your damper, then I'm sure to be spoilt.'

If he is honest, he is more interested in spending time with Ellen. That excites him. Living in the working-man's hut, the food has been supplied but he must cook it. He usually doesn't enjoy sharing social niceties, but the idea, this time, appeals.

All these years without a woman has tested his patience. He has a yearning for the flesh, unable to describe, and barely tolerable, bubbling inside and he believes it inconceivable that he will ever quench it without amazing luck.

'Well, I best be getting back to work, or the boss will get cranky. You can tell him Ellen's colt is coming along well. We should have her on it in a day or two, then, after a few more days mustering, I'll hand him over.'

Larry returns to the colt, standing calm in the shade. He converses with it from a distance.

'Here I am young fella. Steady now, nothing to worry yourself about.'

He slips between the rails, retrieves the reins then spends more time gentling him. After a half-hour he gathers the reins around the colt's neck and from the nearside, as if mounting, applies weight on a lengthened stirrup, leaving the ground, and a moment later, dropping back. The horse retreats and Larry doesn't react; merely follows it and repeats the process a few times. When he has the horse standing still, through numerous repeated drills, he stops.

'Aren't you going to ride him?' says Ellen.

She'd appeared quietly behind him, but earlier he'd noticed her arrival reflected in the colt's eyes. He doesn't face her.

'Perhaps tomorrow.'

'Why? Are you nervous?'

'No, he is… I don't wish to rush him.'

'Ah. Thought you might be worried he'd buck you.'

He removes the saddle and brushes him down with the saddle cloth, this time without blindfold, and the colt behaves.

Larry then bends to lift its front leg. The colt resists. Larry leans into his shoulder, pinches behind the nearside fetlock and applies weight to the shoulder, forcing the horse to move his leg, which Larry grasps and raises, then rewards him. He swings it out front and draws it back as might be required for shoeing. Puts it down, repeats the process many times, and before the colt is bored, moves to the off-side, and continues the routine. He repeats the process across all four legs.

'Do they always do what you want, like that?' she asks.

'Mostly. Sometimes I put a rope, a sideline, on them. I prefer they choose to do it with only a little assistance from me, though.'

'The gate is open,' she says.

'Yes, that's fine. I don't like imprisoning him. No creature deserves that, unless they're very dangerous.'

'You have strong views on this.'

'Yeah! I hate fences myself – she's a free country, or is supposed to be.'

That evening, Larry bathes beneath the tall tank-stand, dons a clean shirt, and tames his hair, and beard. The meal, though plain – lamb chops, vegetables, gravy, mint sauce – is posher than Larry has experienced. The silver tableware, as fine as any in the colony, with candles in silver holders, and wildflowers in cut-glass vases, adorns a table covered in the finest Irish lace. It transports him from the dreary reality of his day to a world more romantic.

In the sepia lamplight Ellen appears more mature, and everything about her has an untouched, delicate air. Her lips flutter above perfect white teeth. The soft pale flesh of her unblemished face, framed by her auburn hair, shines. If he had any doubts about the desirability of this girl, they are washed away. He must stop staring.

'What is Mr Cole doing in Melbourne?'

Mrs Cole takes a moment to swallow.

'He's sorting out a dispute with the Land's Department… While he's there he's going to a meeting about the Australian Federation, with the Free Traders.'

Larry makes a mental note to learn about the Federation movement. Having spent so long in prison it is as if a piece of his memory has been erased, because life outside had moved on, while his, stood still. Whole gaps exist and it surprises others that he is unaware of some inventions, or signal events, which they take for granted, like new rail routes, the introduction of telegraph, public rendition of patriotic songs like *Advance Australia Fair*, and the organisation of inter-colonial cricket matches. Gaps, also, are obvious in his social skills from living with gaol's base, selfish, and insane. He needs to tread carefully.

'Daddy is going to bring us cloth, imported from Ireland or England: something beautiful. Mother and I are going to sew dresses for the Picnic Races. Aren't we, mother?'

'What? Are they run soon?'

'Yes, the Wadelock Races are a major event as far as races go around here. You should come.'

Larry chances his arm.

'Only if I can join you two.'

Is this what normalcy is like?

Sometimes, he dreams he is in prison locked in with brother Jack's bloody body roped to his. Everywhere he goes the body accompanies him, as a reminder. In the dream, Larry is not identified, kept hidden, because of Jack. The guards believe he has escaped, and he waves his arms and shouts his name as they pass, to reassure them he has not escaped, but no one responds. He's convinced it's only Jack's body they see.

Other times, he stands in a wet courtyard watching lines of prisoners file through the gate on their way to be released, and he is not included. His heart races. He is so desperate not to be abandoned. Each time he attempts to join the line it alters direction and prisoners spill everywhere, rejecting him. Sometimes, they wear the faces of people he has socialised with on the outside. The dreams happen too often, strung together in series, night after night, as real as if he was back in the hole.

When first released and the nightmares persisted, he would visit the shanty and drink his pay until they faded. Prison was ingrained; could not be washed from him.

He is less vigilant today than a year ago. Something, perhaps time itself, changed him. He no longer needs to obsessively check outside his window or wonder who breathes through his keyhole. He attempts to circulate even if he never speaks to anyone while out. Twelve months ago, and sober, he noticed his round-shouldered prison shuffle reflected in a shop window, so now pokes his chest out and his shoulders back in an exaggerated attempt to correct it. All this, he imagines, is the path to normalcy.

At the appropriate moment, he excuses himself from the table and returns to his hut. He enjoyed his time with the two women even if his anxiety rose when Ned Kelly was raised, but pleased he'd responded without an angry voice. Perhaps, with time, he will heal here?

The next morning, he rises early to yard the colt. As he pushes it towards the gate, his heart skips when Ellen appears through the mist. She wears a long coat and, upon her head, a red beanie. She breathes smoke as she walks.

'I heard your door shut and thought you might like help to yard him.'

He smiles.

'I'm always grateful for help to run horses. They have their own wild mind. Rather than curse them as they gallop away with their tails flicking high, I just want to join them.'

She laughs briefly; understands. They walk a parallel course, a cricket pitch apart, each with hands in pockets, each barely concentrating on the task.

'I enjoyed last night,' he says, after the colt is yarded and a rope thrown around its neck.

'Yeah, Mum's a good cook.'

'Umm, she is, but not just the meal,' he adds. 'The company. It was wonderful.'

She blushes. Raises her eyes to find his. Their gaze holds a moment too long. What the hell is that? He hopes she got his meaning; slaps the colt's rump.

'I'll give him a ride today. I reckon he's ready.'

'Today? That's good. How do you tell when he's ready?'

He smiles and it garnishes his tone.

'He's looking for that next piece of adventure.'

She nods, and blushes.

'We'll come back when the sun is higher in the sky, and he and I are a little warmer. In the meantime, I'll milk the cow for your mother to test my cold hands and thank her for last night's meal. You best get some breakfast.'

Mid-morning and following more lunging, he saddles the colt. Ellen has returned only minutes before, asking questions, talking about the mundane, telling him about her friends and their challenges, babbling-on like the waters of Myanga Creek. How he'd love to take this girl to the Creek, to meet Ma. To show her off, to let Ma see how happy he is.

'Righto, time to give him a ride.'

She squeals and claps her hands.

'If I fall off and break my neck, give my saddle and gear to the church,' he says in mock seriousness.

The smile wipes from her face.

'You're not going to fall off, are you? Is he going to buck? Oh my gosh.'

Her concern is genuine, and he feels guilty for raising the drama.

'He may.'

He positions the colt's off-side closer to the rail, so if it panics while Larry mounts, it is more likely to move back under the rider, and lever him into the saddle earlier. He rolls upon him like a warm breeze, surprising Ellen with his agility, and the colt with his weight. The colt reacts and crow-hops until he realises nothing bad is happening – absolutely nothing. Larry, feet still forward in the stirrups, rubs the colt's shoulder, neck, and mane, up and down. Then he sways about on the saddle to give the colt the feel of girth and surcingle, against its sensitive chest and ribs. He faces Ellen with a mighty grin.

'He's a beauty.'

She smiles, delighted in his happiness, and pleased for her colt effortlessly passing its latest test.

He then urges it forward, drives it with his thighs, clicks his tongue; on guard in case the colt takes flight. They circle the small yard clockwise, then counter-clockwise. The horse steps tentative, despite his training, strung-out like a cat with spilt milk upon its back. Larry soon urges him more forcefully; swings the gates wide open while mounted. The colt is wary but remains calm as the gates bounce and rattle when they hit the rails at the end of their swing. Will he cope?

In the larger yard, Larry ensures the colt is gathered beneath him, to be balanced for action and of good posture, to bear the burden of a rider on his extended back. From atop, it feels like riding a snake until the colt learns to move in a coordinated manner. It is off-putting. Instead of turning in a single motion – pivoting off the hind legs – the colt attempts to move in series, starting at the head, then neck, forequarters and finally, hindquarters. Larry exercises him in a manner to ensure improved co-ordination. To do so, the colt must learn a host of rider aids, better applied in the open paddocks.

Larry approaches Ellen, using a long and relaxed rein, confident the colt will behave. He longs for such confidence in himself.

'There you go – a little beauty. Do you want a ride?'

'Not now.'

'Ha, ha, smart girl. You'd have to brush and stable him for the evening, something I don't enjoy. I'll take him out bush tomorrow, and perhaps you can ride him when we return. I think you'll love him. He has a delicate action and sprung step, so won't be hard on your backside.'

He laughs at the thought, and she pats her boyish buttocks, then follows man and horse to the tackle shed.

'You know, James, he looks so cheeky when he walks. His bottom sways. My friend Shona is like that; walks with a sway that the boys tell me is charming from behind, but she couldn't run to save herself. I hope this fellow can run; I'd like him to be very fast. What do you think? Will he be fast?'

He enjoys her ability to chat about the mundane: dogs hungry, chickens not laying, an old saying from her family, something she has read. He feels so comfortable around her, as if they have always been joined, like field and cloud, darkness and moon. It is like having Jack back. If only he didn't have to hide his past life, and betray this wonderful girl.

They split at the saddle shed where she returns to the house, and he grooms the colt before releasing him into the horse paddock.

~

It's Sunday, and instead of riding the colt out to the back-blocks as he had planned, he decides to exercise him closer, then follow the women to Mass in Wavelock, an hour's cart ride. He runs the horse through its paces while Ellen watches. He lunges it, steers it around in long driving reins, rubs it down, picks up all hooves, saddles it and gently, mounts. This time the colt accepts him without fuss. Larry tips his hat to Ellen.

'See you soon.'

He lets himself through several gates until he's free of the yards then attempts a series of gaits – walking, jogging, trotting, cantering, galloping – over the next half-hour through Gippsland's lush bush, which they both relish. They return in time to join the women on their journey to Mass. Freedom is such a privilege.

He joins the spring-cart on the mother's side. Ellen chatters across the mother, so when the colt shies like an idiot at a neighbour's letterbox, he uses it as an excuse to re-join the cart on the daughter's side.

The girl is a hoot, mimics magpie, butcher bird, and crow calls, as if answering them, or engaging them in conversation as she passes. She follows this with an impression of the lady who meets parishioners each week atop the church steps, to hand out hymnbooks. Apparently, the lady never remembers any of the children and asks Ellen each Sunday, 'An who are ye, little one?'

But the funniest impression is of the old priest, who Ellen believes conducts the service drunk on communion wine. She slurs her speech and leans awkwardly over an imaginary lectern to deliver the message. All the time the mother gently chides her.

Larry looks stern.

'God will get you for being disrespectful.'

'Oh, I think he still owes me quite a bit for all I've done for him,' she replies.

'Ugh huh. Like what?'

'Well, I've only missed mass three Sundays in my whole life,' she says, looking his way, seeking approval. 'Surely, I must have a few credits?'

He partly misses his cue, because of the statement's impact, given his background.

'It's true, James,' Mrs Cole adds.

He didn't realise he'd looked at her for confirmation.

What am I doing? Larry thinks. *Wanting to get involved with a good girl like this, after the wild and wilful life I've led?*

He wonders if God has heard his prison prayers seeking a good woman, so he can lead a normal life; sent him someone to soothe his soul? The idea of loving someone, who might be a role model for their children, and assist him to re-enter God's good graces, is nearly more than he can dream.

At the church, Ellen suggests he join them, and to his surprise, he accepts. The two women slide along an empty pew and Larry slips in beside Ellen. As the Mass progresses, her leg rests against his, and despite himself, his flesh hardens as it recognises the softness of hers. Is she conscious of her activity, or unaware of the power her emerging womanhood might have upon him? He can't decide.

The priest rages on about the need to avoid the temptations of flesh, and Larry plots the downfall of the temple. The spirit abides in the house of the Lord but the devil throws the spirit aside, while Larry imagines the ploughing of flesh, here, in the Lord's house.

Does her shoulder rest more fully against his? Should he slide apart to return the space, or slurp up this intimate moment? Should he do something to confirm his suspicion of this beautiful girl's interest in him, or remain polite, and be pleased for the merest hint of intimacy, if only fuelled by his own mind?

Not one to die wondering, he pushes lightly against her leg with his, and recognises a return response. His breath quickens. His hardness increases, with interest.

'Let us stand, to pray.'

Mother and daughter stand and Larry delays, hoping for a subsidence, and is slow to stretch to full height, hoping his protuberance disappears. She leans her shoulder, ever so lightly, against his. It is as if a bull-ant has bitten him, and he sparks away. She looks at him, surprised, then glances down, and blushes.

What have I done?

That afternoon, before he releases the mare, he suggests Ellen take the opportunity to ride the colt, as he'd promised the day before.

'I'll need the side-saddle.'

'No, you don't. It's not smart to ride side-saddle these days,' he argues, with an emphasis on the word 'smart'.

He shortens the stirrups on both sides. He legs her onto the horse with one arm, while he holds the bridle up near the colt's ears with the other. After a moment, both rider and horse are comfortable, so he releases the headstall.

'See, you're a natural.'

The colt responds brilliantly and soon Ellen walks him around the small yard, then jogs him in the large. They make a fine couple, well balanced; her smaller stature less prominent on the colt than his. He's eager to get her opinion.

'What do you think?'

Her face beams.

'Oh, he's marvellous. He moves like a cat beneath you, so light of foot!'

She is excited, and he finds her pleasure a better reward than a paycheque. He assists her to dismount and rather than using the stirrups, she leans forward, and places her arms around his shoulders, her face beside his, and falls forward off the colt, dragging her leg across the saddle. She hangs from him for a moment, until she swings to the ground. The colt shies backwards a few feet but neither notice.

They kiss.

He's convinced she is an angel, but it may be that a relaxed Sunday atmosphere, and church, have seduced him. Up close she smells of lavender, her breath pure, her face shining with excitement. Her flesh is firm yet yielding, her kiss needy, her lips as moist as dew upon a eucalyptus leaf. He's a lost man and she a rescuing angel, he's a broken vessel and she full of all that can heal him. She feels his hardness; the lump she'd viewed in church, and doesn't avoid it, but expels a soft sigh when she brushes against him.

He releases her when they need a breath and stands her slightly apart. He isn't sure what she'll think, once she has a moment to do so.

'Sorry, Miss Ellen, I got carried away.'

'Don't be sorry, James, it wasn't all you.'

She seems far more mature than her years. They walk to the tackle-shed, a yard apart, but he yearns to touch her.

Along the tackle-shed's rear wall hay bags are beds, waiting. Were it Bridget, he would have thrown her upon them and perhaps torn her pants aside, like he had in the shade of the creek bank below her parent's house, only days after they'd acknowledged their relationship. But he feels differently about Ellen. He has the same lust, but his desire is to show respect, to be admired for treasuring her rather than overwhelming her; to be able to look her family in the eye and believe he is worthy of this girl, and willing to protect her. It is more to do with him and his new identity, than his need for physical, material things.

Inside the shed she moves closer, and he doesn't avoid her, but places a finger upon her lips and whispers – 'Let's take it steady.'

They meet again next morning to fetch the horses, as usual, but at the gate they hug.

That afternoon, the mother, looking through the golden sunset dust raised by the yarded horses, watches them leave the yards, holding hands. She's not surprised but is concerned for her daughter being so young.

~

It is November, and returning fresh from working a newly broken mare in the middle paddock, James is surprised to see the boss, Cole, in his going-to-town coat, standing on the homestead steps. Only a year or two older than Larry, he's an average sized, fair-haired man, with a light beard with a ginger, nicotine-stained streak below his nostrils from his ever-stoked briar; and, like Larry, his smile misses a tooth – the gap, to the side of his mouth, only visible when he smiles broadly.

Larry acknowledges from a distance and continues past the tackle-shed, his original destination, through to the closed house-gate.

'Good afternoon, boss.'

'Afternoon, James.'

'Good trip?'

'I think so. Straightened up a problem with my lease on the river block. She's all mine now.'

'Uh huh,' says Larry.

Cole examines the brown mare.

'I see you've broken the big mare. How is she?'

'I like her. She's an honest worker with good cattle-sense. She can cover a surprising lot of ground in a day, too, and doesn't knock up… She got a bit of Shire in her?'

'Wouldn't be surprised. She's out of one of my old man's mares and he did some off-farm carting work, in the early days. Could have been crossbred from one of those horses.'

'Yeah. No. She's going orright.'

Cole nods.

'Come over for a grog when you've cleaned up. I'll catch up with all your doin's.'

Larry, scrubbed up with fresh clothes returns to the homestead just as the sun sinks into the horizon. The two men shake, and Cole passes over the Old Tom, and the sound of spilling spirits echoes off tin pannikin as Larry pours. He drags a heavy, wooden chair beside Cole and salutes his mug. Both men sip in silence for a moment, neither a proponent of small talk. Cole extracts his briar and packs it with a nicotine-stained finger as thick as a pork sausage.

'My wife tells me you've been a great help, James. Not only broke the horses but managed the place and kept my girls safe.'

'All in a day's work.'

'Ellen says the colt is the smartest horse in Gippsland, if not Victoria.'

'Aye, he's smart alright. But Ellen's a good rider and doesn't get in his way.'

'Yes, she's smart but a mere girl, James.'

Larry notices a change in tone, and a chill moves down his backbone. An ambush?

'Aye, but a good girl.'

'Be that as it may, James, Mrs Cole tells me that you two have grown close.'

Larry doesn't want to return Cole's gaze in case he reveals anxiety and his rising anger.

'A lot closer than we were before you left, yes.'

'Her mother says the girl is quite smitten. She's seen you embrace. That is what she knows. What goes on behind our backs is… is another matter, altogether.'

'Well, I…'

'Let me be quite clear, here. She is but a wee child and you are older and more experienced than her. I don't want you sniffin' in a honey pot that don't belong to ya, you hear.'

Larry feels the fighting Irish well inside him, feels the injustice of years of incarceration, the pain of not being allowed to speak back, or to argue, slosh around his mouth, mix acrid with the Old Tom.

'Is that how ya feel? That I'm not good enough for the girl?'

'She's our little girl, James. I can feel as I damn well like.'

Larry stands, his fists balled.

'I know she's my better, it's plain for all to see, but I'd strive always to live up to her. If that's the way you feel, that I'd pull her down, then I'll collect my pay in the morning. Good night to ya.'

With that he storms down the few stairs, across the house lawn, past the shed and the kennel of barking dogs, to his hut. He's devastated. He was so close to having experienced a miracle; the possibility of living a normal life with someone as pure as Myanga Creek headwaters, which, if he was honest, he barely dreamed could happen.

Thirty minutes later he's on his bunk, hands behind his head in prison pose, staring in the dark at the sap-varnished side of the bark-ceiling, trying to keep the rising gall down his gullet. There's a tap on the door.

'James, James.' It is Ellen. He doesn't answer.

'James, open the door.'

'Go away, girl. It's best I don't speak to you.'

'James, I overheard Dad and Mother talking. It's all right… If you leave, I leave – with, or without, you.'

He thinks for a moment. Perhaps he should talk sense into the girl. He opens the door and she rushes to hug him but he holds her at arm's length.

'This is your world, girl. I'm a nobody.'

'No, Mum and I convinced Dad that you are the only person for me. I told him that you've protected me from myself these past weeks. I told him of your plans to better yourself and set me up in a town, when we marry. He can either have me head off tomorrow, as I leave with and marry you, and he never sights me again, or wait as we planned, until I'm seventeen, and he give me away and remain part of my life.'

'I wouldn't be able to look the bastard in the eye.'

'He just gets ahead of himself. He has a short fuse but once his gripe is over, it's over. I'm his little girl – he thought he had longer with me.'

She pushes past his guard, to lean against him and they hug for ages. He gently fingers her hair to expose her ear.

'She's a bloody long wait, if he's cranky.'

ALONG A NEW COW PAD: ELLEN'S STORY 1880

IT happened in a flurry.

All were there: my family and friends, our neighbours, the church choir. We filled the tiny sawn-timber church.

I wore the dress mother and I had sewn for the picnic races from the cloth father brought home from Melbourne. She named it the Ellen Dress, because I'd added yards of lace. She says when she first saw me in it, she knew I was meant to wear it to my wedding. I laughed; I did. She always insists, when something different or spooky happens, that she had pre-knowledge: something predicted in the wind, or through the appearance of a butterfly at the table, or tea-leaf pattern in her cup, at the time it occurs – but never described in advance. Did she see James and I having a happy marriage and family? Were we to be rich? She couldn't predict that, or if she did so, she never shared it.

Father was so cute as he walked me down the aisle. I think the old koala had a little tear. I smiled when I saw James at the altar, all trussed in a flash coat he'd borrowed from Father. He looked so awkward, like a hobbled poddy-calf with large, soppy eyes, but I could tell when he saw me in the doorway, that he was pleased I kept my promise and appeared. He has this thing where he believes he doesn't deserve me. He can't explain why. Has such a low estimate of himself, but compared to other boys around here, he's a rainbow and they a showery day. Ha, I'll convince him over time. You watch!

It seemed to end so soon, the aisle walk, even though I was trying to walk slow and romantic. When I arrived, he whispered, 'I was worried I'd left the gate open and you'd slipped out.'

'Ha, ha. Never.'

He smiled his gap-smile and I forgot any fears I may have had, so endearing it was. It happens every time. We had a cattle dog kicked by a horse, when but a pup, causing him to have a lop-sided smile but his imperfection made us adore him even more. Were James the handsomest man in the country, I don't think I would have felt any prouder of him. It was pure James.

There were twenty or more guests who, after the service, rode back to our home to help us celebrate. I noticed halfway home that James appeared despondent.

'Are you sad, my love?'

He shook his head.

'No, not sad about us, not at all. I wish life had turned up cards which allowed my family to be present, that's all.'

In the rush and excitement, I had completely forgotten that side of his life. I placed my hand over his rein hand and squeezed. He returned a wan smile.

'It is what it is.'

He clicked his tongue and flicked the reins to hasten the pony, and that was the last we spoke of it.

Mother and I had cooked for a week. True to church custom, each guest brought a plate and some, a number, so the tables laboured under the fare of salads, biscuits, cakes, tarts, and plates of homemade sweets like coconut ice, toffee, and fudge. We spit-roasted a leg of lamb, cooked several chickens in camp-ovens, and in the back garden, boiled vegetables in large pots over fires. Mother's vegetable garden, nestled in the corner always damp from the windmill's leaking pump, had been raided ruthlessly. No one went hungry.

Father supplied gallons of grog. All were shickered. Even Mother had a permanent smile on her face as she swirled among the guests, plates high, distributing meals, chatting to rarely seen relatives. Someone poured her a lemonade over many fingers of Old Tom. When it came to Father's speech, he swayed, lurched, and mumbled through a mile-wide smile, words to the effect that he 'wished us well', before Mother attempted to rescue him, only to realise she could do no better. So she raised a toast to the two of us, and all responded.

She laughed a little too loudly, and mentioned the joys that awaited me on the wedding night. I had never seen her hint at matters of the flesh in such a manner, and she gathered further pluck from the crowd's comments. I hissed to my brother to organise the music. He rushed off to motivate the musicians to re-join their instruments, while meantime, mother convinced the crowd about our need to rattle the bed in order to drown out the noise of the tin kettling's ruckus. The crowd responded with lusty cheers and ribald laughter, such as shook the house's cobwebs.

The tea-chest's bass thump, the clicking spoons, the rattle of the washboard, and the fiddle's wail, saved Mother's reputation. A "caller", a chap unknown in the district, rose when the tune finished.

'Ladies and gentlemen. Young and old. Move the chairs aside and let's dance.'

He led a series of Quadrilles, including the Javlins, still popular at bush dances west of the Great Divide. The series engaged both young and old, but by the end of the set, only the young remained dancing, their elders discovering they were either too drunk, or too tired, to continue. The latter moved outside along the veranda, found somewhere to sit, and continued gossiping and drinking.

We decided to leave soon after; did the rounds to say farewell to all and thank guests for attending. I'd known many for my entire life and in some ways, they were as important to my identity as family. Finally, to hide where we were sleeping and to avoid further fuss, we snuck off.

Next day, we lay about but it was sadder than I had imagined. The reality struck me that I would be leaving both home and my family for the first time. I was seventeen. I pushed it aside, so I wouldn't sob all day and upset mother.

Most of the guests who'd stayed were hungover. Not being an experienced drinker, and despite having had only two cups of the local brew, I too was ill, so couldn't imagine how poorly the others must have felt. After the party, James and I had retired to his hut. He'd placed his hand upon my shoulder to restrain me.

'Wait … wait.'

He made me stand outside while he lit some candles.

'Close your eyes!'

He'd lifted me into his arms and carried me across the threshold; kissed my eyelids.

'Thank you for marrying me, my darling. You can open your eyes.'

Before me were bunches of scented wild flowers in Golden Syrup tins, and bunches of golden wattle in corners, vacant shelves, and upon window ledges; my boy's attempt to make the honeymoon suite romantic. The hut was bathed in a yellow candle-glow. It could have been a prince's castle and it would not have been more beautiful.

I shouldn't go into detail about the wedding night, but it was everything I expected… and more. James made certain I wasn't rushed, and I think he thought I was more anxious than I was. I'm pleased we waited, and our union was blessed in the Lord's eyes, though there was many a time I would have weakened without His blessing and James' strength.

I, also, should have woken to the idea that there was mischief afoot, when Mother acted so strangely. We'd gone to bed, and I'd managed to get James settled and become aware of what my body felt as he moved inside me. The bunk rocked and thumped against the wall, when all hell broke.

A voice, as close as if it was in the bed with us, shouted.

'They're doin' it!'

A raft of voices joined in at high pitch and just as close.

'Hurrah!'

They were so loud I believed we were surrounded by the entire wedding party. Rattling stone-filled tins joined together, rained upon the roof; a cavalcade of children whistled, squealed, and bashed tins and pot-lids as they circled the hut; rocks rained on the slab walls; and someone rattled the door as if to enter our bedroom. Then they broke into song and I felt James wilt, and slip from inside me, slide his body onto the bed, although my flesh could feel where his body had been, where his flesh had pressed upon me, and I wanted him to return. I was so sure we were going to be captured and paraded, naked, before the drunken crowd, to confirm that we were making love, that I began to curse in my head, ready to repel boarders.

Then we heard a loud 'three cheers' – Hip, hip, hooray! Hip, hip – then footsteps, as people shuffled away; the voice of our next-door neighbour's son mutter, 'He's a lucky bastard'; dogs bark as revellers filed past their kennels; the rattle of dropped house-yard slip-rails; music restart; and then the hum of conversation and laughter as the party continued down at the house.

'So that's a tin-kettling?' I whispered.

'Aye, that's a tin-kettling. I've heard of them but never been involved. I didn't know what to think. I even thought for a moment it may be the traps calling us out, to arrest us for being so happy. Whew… Now, where were we… before we were interrupted?'

And then he kissed me, did the angel. It didn't take us long to continue, and that's all I'm going to share. I agree with Mother who says what happens between a husband and wife should remain that way.

Oh, one thing… James is allergic to wattle, which he forgot when he chose to decorate his room, and his eyes watered and he snuffled most of the night. On top of the drink he had on board, he was quite fragile. I woke him at one point. He was dreaming and restless and talking in his sleep.

'What did I say?'

'You kept repeating, *Sorry Jack. Sorry Jack...This should be you...* Then, something about... Murphy.'

'Ah.'

'Who's Jack?'

'Me wee brother.'

'And Murphy?'

'No idea. I'll try and settle – it's the drink.'

Midday, I noticed him in corduroy trousers and singlet, high-stepping his bare feet, loading the pack saddles for our trip north to Albury. All our worldly goods fitted into that pack. It was my possessions – clothes, bed-linen, pots and pans – in one side, and horse-breaking and camping gear in the other. James had prospects of a new droving job in Albury. Father argued that we should stay close, but James believed it would be better to make our own way in life. I had brothers and they would inherit the farm. In time we may grow resentful of working with no reward, or ownership. I think, also, that James had never forgiven Father for misjudging him.

We set off early and I have memories of Father, his arm around Mother's shoulders, wave from our front gate, even while we would be, in their view, but three small ants up on the ridgeline, before we fell from their sight.

~

The first week, riding from sun-up to sundown, and sleeping on the solid ground beneath canvas, was taxing and tiring. My honeymoon bed, when the land sloped, or an unseen rock protruded, reminded me of my mother's words "*You made your bed, now you must lie in it*" and I chose never to utter a word of complaint to James. When we made love in the wild, in harmony with the cicadas and frog calls, where time and again, my cries joined theirs, I knew I had chosen wisely.

Each hour we rode further from my home, and family.

One afternoon we bathed beside a large water hole on an inland creek and I was shocked to see the scars inscribed upon James' back.

They were obscene. I was of two minds, like when someone has an obvious disfigurement: should I comment, or not?

'James… your scars?'

He peered over his shoulder, like a dog nipping its back, as if to observe their markings, which he couldn't.

'Them? Accident. Fell into harrow-tines when young. All good, now.'

He knelt to submerge them beneath water. I shook my head and by the time he surfaced, my mind had bubbled on.

Days later, two miles outside the small town of Bright, we camped against another creek, a tributary of the river Ovens. Our fire crackled and was smokeless despite it being a cold, misty morning. The billy buzzed, called for tea leaves to be added. The homely smell of damper baking in the coals wafted tantalisingly around the campsite, teased my taste buds to juice.

Out of the blue, my colt snorted and swung his bottom about, to point his nose into the wind. His nostrils flared and his ears twitched.

The din of galloping horses' hooves on creek-stones swamped the amphitheatre. So noisy. Then four horsemen burst through the mist-brushed bushes to rein-in before us with a clatter and rattle. I curled in shock at the rude intrusion, surprised that the riders were barely older than myself: well-dressed for country youth; two with beards, two clean-shaven; astride excellent mounts.

Then, I thought the worst. I noticed their handguns. Oh my God; we'll be killed.

The heavier, bearded rider on the large white-footed bay, pointed his pistol.

'Bail up! … Ya money or your life.'

Despite the intrusion, James, as cool as ice, remained seated, facing the four with his back inclined against a smooth rock. He could be mistaken for being part of it, covered as he was from chin to ground by his mud-coloured drover's oilskin. The whites of his eyes flashed above his dark beard.

The smaller of the bearded bushrangers swung down from his horse while it slid to a halt. His fancy hat, too small for his handsome head and wavy hair, highlighted the colour of his laughing blue eyes. He approached James; dragged his reluctant horse by the reins.

The bearded lad on the white-footed bay, who had called on us to 'Bail up', cut in.

'Normally, we would not worry simple folks such as yourselves, but the troopers are grinding us down.'

He waved his pistol as a gesture to us to hurry. The young chap on the ground pointed to James.

'Come on – your money.'

The tone and timbre of his voice suggested he was related to the bossy bearded guy.

'Ain't got any.'

'How come you know my name?' the young fellow asked.

James shook his head, wary.

'What name? I don't know you.'

'You called me Danny.'

'I said you won't *get any* money.'

The leader on the bay intervened, impatient; waved his pistol.

'Hand it over.'

James didn't flinch.

'That won't be happening, as we don't have any to hand over. You fellows best move along.'

'Move, me arse!' declared the leader and shot a sideways glance, seeking encouragement from the larger, quiet, unshaven chap mounted on the grey. Laughed loudly.

'Why should we move? He who holds the gun has the power.'

I wouldn't be surprised if the speaker was drunk. He wasn't quite at speed with the events rolled out before him. Perhaps the others were, likewise. James smiled without humour.

'That's why you should move… move, along.'

The four appeared unsettled. James nodded his head towards the unmounted youngster.

'I have a pistol pointed at ya little brother here, and one pointed at your mate, there.'

He nodded his head at the older, unshaven one on the grey, point of a barrel obvious beneath the groundsheet, aimed at Dan.

The leader's face reddened.

'We could blow you apart, stranger.'

Dan, facing James' pistol, point blank, called, 'Yeah, he's bluffing.'

Two clicks, the sound of pistols being cocked beneath the poncho.

'Yeah, maybe blow me apart, but not before your brother dies,' said James, evenly.

The bearded horseman's face changed; his cheeks flushed redder. James watched his comment hit home; stir the rider's anger. He continued.

'His death, my friend, would be on your head... Wouldn't it, Dan? Your grizzly death on your brother's head?'

Turned his gaze, again, to the bearded horseman.

'Blood is thicker than water. A brother is someone you'd dash into a burning building to save. A life you'd put ahead of your own. Your brother's life before your own, eh?'

Dan stood only metres from us, smart enough not to reach for his pistol, which hung cockily from his waist. I couldn't believe James; so ice-cool.

'For the rest of your life the pain of that act – you allowing your brother to be killed – would grind you down, worse than any troopers' actions ever will. It will grind you down like an incurable ulcer, to gnaw greedily, painfully away at your body and soul, young fella. I can assure you.'

The mounted leader checked with his mate, hoping for guidance. The mate's eyes were lustreless, the irises mere pinpricks, his face catatonic. James nodded towards me.

'My wife and I have no gripe with you boys… You move on and nothing will happen. We'll pass through, leave Victoria, pass out of your life forever, and you boys can bail up the next traveller or as many as you like. I don't care. No one will ever know this happened.'

'What if we don't?'

'Then Dan… and I… and your handsome mate, are dead.'

'We'll kill your wife.'

I felt my stomach turn.

'I don't think so,' said James, in a tone as pleasant as if they were chatting at the kitchen table.

He paused for the challenge to sink in, then continued.

'That's why I chose to leave you alive, son. You're smart and a Catholic. You're a man. You don't do that sort of thing – kill women and children.'

'We'll get you as soon as you let us go,' Dan shouted.

'No, you won't.'

'Why not?'

'Because you are men, and you'd have given me your word, before I let you go.'

Dan shared a grimace of disbelief with the clean-shaven, effeminate rider who'd remained uninvolved. That lad raised his hand to adjust his ribboned cabbage-tree hat, as if the circumstances were too difficult to comprehend. But the leader listened, as did his mate. A silent message passed between them – a look of agreement.

'Okay, you're a horse's arse matey, but we're gunna let you go. Mark my words… Don't let us see you around here again, or I'll fookin kill ya.'

'All right. Fair enough – we'll dig out the damper, finish our cuppa, and move along, as soon as you are out of here. Do I have ya word… as men?'

'Aye.'

'Good… Thanks'

'Alright. Come on, Dan, mount up,' said the leader.

'Ya sure, brother? I bet we can take the bastard, there's four of us.'

'What for, stoopid? He says he has no money. Mount up, Dan, ya idjit. Ya always were.'

The lad, angered at his older brother's comments, mounted.

'And one more thing,' said James. 'You shouldn't pick on ya own kind. We Irish have enough trouble in this country, without having to fight our own.'

The leader holstered his pistol. A look of recognition passed between he and James. All gang members spun about and rode from the campsite onto the road, then picked up the pace to a canter as they moved around the bend and out of sight.

Silence.

Neither of us spoke for at least a minute. James stood and flicked the oilskin over to one shoulder and threw a handful of tea into the pot. A fly buzzed close to my lips. James lifted his tea-cup.

'Come on, let's drink up … get out of here. Don't want to push our luck.'

I was shocked by what had happened. I hadn't seen James as a fighter – as a gunman. I really hadn't. No one in our circle had any inkling of how to fight.

'I didn't know you had pistols?'

'Well… I don't have any.'

'I heard a gun cock?'

'Nah, I flicked me enamel pannikin here. It sounded like what they expected to hear.'

He showed me the pannikin and flicked the handle with his thumbnail. I worried even more, wanted to cry, realising the bluff's gravity.

'We could have been killed! We could be dead, all because you were too stubborn to do what they asked of you. Oh, my gosh, what could you have been thinking?'

I wanted to cry but it appeared a wasted emotion.

'We could be wishing we were dead, if we had lost what little money we have… I've met far tougher than they. They just want to be treated fair, and maybe, trusted like men.'

He's a cool head, my husband. Me? Not so cool. I needed to pee so bad I rushed behind a rock and squatted on the side opposite to where the bushrangers had retreated. For the past week I'd needed to do this more frequently. By the time I finished, and the stringent but comforting smell from the sprayed gum leaves had wafted past my nose, I settled.

If it was his gentle manner with the colt that had warmed my heart, his courage under fire inflamed and seared it, for a lifetime.

I stood and arranged my clothing and joined him as he bent at the fire preparing breakfast. I tapped him on the shoulder, and he straightened. I hugged him so tightly it is a wonder I didn't suffocate him. But then, I began to shake as I realised what we had come through, and we stood like this for a long, long time. We were on our own but together, regardless of what life had to throw at us.

It was only weeks later that I read in the newspaper of the siege at the Glenrowan Hotel, and the notorious bushrangers, the Kelly gang, with three members dying beneath a hail of thousands of police bullets. When I saw the photos, I was shocked to learn that it was the same fellows who had bailed us. Such young lads. It didn't seem fair. And, you know what? It reported that Ned, having escaped the police cordon, chose to return to storm the burning inn, to save his trapped brother. As James, prophetically, advised him, it is such a powerful thing – brotherly love.

A week later we were at Albury and settled in a hotel. James left for a few days. Said he had to retrieve some money owed to him for work he'd done before he left for Victoria. Quite a lot of money. Upon his return, we laid down a deposit for our house at Wodonga Flats. The first child was rising like a damper for all to see by the time we took residence.

THE LONG PADDOCK: THE DROVER'S STORY

1884-1896

Oh, may the showers in torrents fall,
And all the tanks flow over;
And may the grass grow green and tall,
In pathways of the drover;
(Andy's Gone with Cattle, Henry Lawson)

IF sheep aren't the dumbest of animals, then they'd be a close candidate. Once one decides to go through the gate, they all must. Like ants they'll pour over man, dog or both, should they attempt to stop them. One in; all in. If one makes a good decision, all follow and reduce the benefit sought by the one who stepped out first. If one makes a poor decision; then again, the rest follow to provoke a disaster like Lemmings over a cliff.

James had built his business on the back of a growing sheep industry. Merino wool was not only the finest in the world, but also possessed a tight crimp suitable for manufacturing high-end fashion cloth. It was a durable export product, able to survive the distances travelled from the isolated stations to the seaboard cities, and over the oceans to the vast British and European woollen mills. In search of their fortunes, cockies across Australia had jumped from what they were growing and poured into the industry. Squatters became rich by selling fleece to the mills and livestock to the punters. Regional centres sprouted behind the golden fleece, and there was money to service individuals, and communities, outside the cities. All thanks to stupid sheep.

The sheep needed to be transported, mustered and their fleece harvested, and James had gained a reputation as a reliable drover. The cheque for the drover at the end of a trip was substantial, based upon the number of sheep moved, so he moved large mobs over vast distances; feats too challenging for many drovers. James and Ellen's bank balance grew, as did the number of their children.

His pa, Irish Joseph, had invested his profit into land – purchased various blocks as security.

'There's no more of it so it has to increase in value,' he'd argued. 'If you look after it; it will look after you. No one can take it away.'

He had never mentioned interest to James, so he had neither heard about, nor experienced, the financial benefits of it. In boom conditions such as existed during the 1880's, a bank could move as much money through loans as it could lay its hands on, and at speculative premiums, while offering interest rates on savings of fifteen and twenty percent. The couple owned their major asset, their house, so there was often a surplus generating passive income from interest.

One evening when checking their savings, he'd smiled at Ellen with a look of awe.

'Interest is an amazing invention. I don't have to rob a bank; they hand money over to me. It's far better than burying it in the back yard.'

'Why do they do that, my love? Hand money over.'

'Interest – money for money.'

'But it's your money, not theirs.'

'Yes, but they pay me so they can use it. I don't have to do anything – just leave it with them. I'm not smart enough to invest it myself. Best I trust them.'

'I don't trust them at all. They don't work for their money. What about the money changers in the temple?'

He tumbled her concern over in his mind like coins in a tin; failed to understand her concern. This was a bank after all.

'That was then. This is now.'

Over time, he'd boosted his savings with money "owed" to him, from a mouldy saddlebag beneath a rock near Myanga Creek. To launder the money, he'd bought sheep with the used banknotes, then sold them months later. The cocky who sold the sheep paid his staff with the notes at the end of the season and they moved the money across various parts of Victoria and New South Wales, without raising suspicions about the notes' validity. Being a substantial client, he was treated like royalty whenever he visited the bank.

James and Ellen had proven to be a good team, which supported their success. After a life in isolation, Ellen enjoyed living in town, but was just as happy to live out of the drover's spring cart; sometimes for many weeks. As the family multiplied it became more difficult, but each year, they spent time on the road.

'It's got that way,' James would joke, 'that I'm afraid to return to town for fear of creating another mouth to feed. There are seven already… Quite a mustering job to ensure they're all at dinner.'

When droving large mobs, James employed a cook, horse-tailer, fence builder, and other stockmen to work the mob. Many lives depended on him. During school holidays, he would use the family – the older girls, Mary, Rose, and Maggie, being capable horse-riders, savvy drovers and horse-tailers, and Ellen, as cook, driving ahead in the wagon with the remaining youngsters, to set up for the evening. Cattle demanded more of men and horses than sheep but are managed similarly on the road. Again, because of his upbringing, he was comfortable droving both. Often, when one species was less popular, the other rose, so his business thrived.

Most nights droving, he would celebrate his freedom by relishing the ability to peer deep into the constellation of stars spiralling out above him, and be thankful he no longer rotted in a gaol-cell's cloying darkness. Other nights, perhaps due to the full moon's pull, if the mob were educated and he had reliable men working with him, he would ride into the closest town and with little enticement, drink heavily. He'd return to camp late the next morning, worse for wear. It was a pattern. The pressure of loneliness and the responsibility of managing mob and crew, would rise, until he had a blow-out.

~

It was the morning of a dry, cold, spring day and the cook had been instructed to drive the wagon far ahead. Travellers reported storms over the range on the near horizon and James, on a punt, had chosen to take his mob in search of green pick that would follow. The trip was estimated to take two days. The terrain demanded that the mob be driven through the night, and possibly the next day, to pass through the scrub to reach water and fresh pastures.

As they'd departed, and the range loomed above them, he wondered if he had made a wise decision. In part the decision had been determined for him by dry waterholes and the carcasses of hundreds of starved sheep abandoned by other drovers on the plains.

The camp's horse-tailer, a dry and wiry old stockman dressed in his only outfit: khaki moleskin pants, a shearer's singlet, a leather hat with its brim turned down square at the front, had nodded his head at the purpling range.

'That looks like smoke, boss.'

The tailer's gammy hip and lopsided gait, a consequence of a riding accident where, trapped by his stirrup, he was dragged for a mile over rough terrain, made him vulnerable on foot but, on horseback, more capable than most. James trusted him.

'Think so?'

A large smoke column hung like a cloud over the horizon.

'Know so.'

'Hmm, might be up where we're heading.'

'Could be.'

'Hopefully, it's miles away and on the plains beyond.'

The tailer drew his lips tight; ambiguously nodded his head, as if in two minds. He rolled a tobacco fig into a skinny cigarette.

'Wouldn't want to be trapped with these little maggots.'

'No, you're right. Wouldn't be a pretty sight… Let's move.'

With that, they left the dry creek-flat and followed a rutted, wagon track up into the forest country.

For hours they pushed the mob across rising countryside at a pace fast for drovers, but murderously slow compared to other travel modes. The dogs and the confinement of the track, plus experienced lead-sheep, had kept the mob intact, and on pace, throughout the night. The track continued to rise through the morning. A whiff of smoke intruded but not regularly enough to cause concern. The sheep were exhausted by mid-morning; unrested.

James wondered, again, if his decision had been a clever one. Bile rose in his throat. It wasn't the whiff of smoke that provoked it, but the terrifying belief he'd botched a critical decision.

The bile taste was too familiar. Most recently, he'd tasted it upon hearing a rumour that his savings bank was in financial difficulty. The implications gripped him, but it took two days to return home to deal with it. He'd appeared at the bank without an appointment, brushed the pleasantries aside, cut to the chase and challenged the manager.

'I hear rumours that the bank can't meet its commitments due to a run of bad debts.'

'Not at all, James. We're travelling fine. Our security is built on the virtue that we are small, with our loans spread across numerous small clients.'

'What about the people you borrow from? Are they secure, and will not call on you?'

'All good – let me assure you.'

He'd dealt with the manager for years and had found him honest.

'I hope so, because I've contracted to re-roof our house, and the wool industry is slowing due to oversupply. We might need our savings.'

He'd left, reassured. Ellen met him at their front gate, eager to know details.

'What did you learn?'

'All good. As I thought… Local bank and local loans.'

'I hope they don't have too much tied up with the land developers.'

'I do too. The manager assures me they're safe.'

The next day the bank doors and those of many others across Victoria and New South Wales were locked shut. Thousands, like James, had heard of problems, poured out of their houses like sheep but unlike James, had withdrawn their money. This led to further rumours and bleating to the press, which caused deposit-holders to jump over others to withdraw their money, created a run, and collapsed the system.

James had been furious. He'd charged to the bank manager's house to find it boarded-up, and the banker, gone. Through no fault of their own, the family was penniless, and for the first time, in debt.

~

On the ridge the sun had risen high above the trees as a blood-red orb. James' eyes smarted, and the misty smoke drifted along the ridge line, the last before the plains, if their informant had been correct.

He jogged across to the drover, riding point; stared at the smoke.

'It's looking a bit closer now. What do you think?'

The drover screwed up his face and squinted his eyes to examine the burgeoning smoke column.

'I hope it's not getting closer, otherwise we're cooked.'

'Yeah, look, jog up to that ridge ahead and check for us, will you? See what it's doing.'

The man cantered off and James, feeling uneasy, clicked his horse a higher notch and suggested to his offsiders that they hasten the mob. The mob, having drunk at mountain streams along the way, was no longer thirsty; had more energy. Even the dogs felt the threat and barked louder, nipped harder at the laggard's heels; pushed them forward. The pace had hastened. The rider returned within the hour; his horse sweaty.

'You were quick.'

'I met the cook returning to warn us that the fire is heading our way. He says it's a monster. From up there the horizon boils with smoke. So much so I nearly didn't return; I tell you, it's so close. It could be every man for himself.'

James peered over his shoulder as if he could sight the entire track.

'Jesus and Mary, we're past the point of no return. We can't turn back.'

The smoke rolled down the track towards them, and despite restricted vision and the oppressive smell, they had no option but to scurry on.

~

He didn't know how to tell Ellen their savings had gone up in smoke with the bank closure. The colony's 1890 banking crisis, stoked by an international depression, had triggered both a general depression, and by 1893, the collapse of the large Australian Federal Bank. Settlers across the colonies were forced to walk off their properties, Ellen's family included. It was desperate times for Ellen and James, and it took desperate measures to survive and ensure their ever-growing herd of children continued to receive their schooling.

James had to go cap-in-hand to the only surviving bank in town to arrange a loan to pay for the renovations they had contracted. Added pressure was placed on the family, hence James, to provide enough income to meet their obligations.

~

After a further two hours on the ridge, the drovers believed they were close to the summit. The wind had been in their faces, so by their estimation, the fire would race up the ridge ahead but, hopefully, skirt them, if it held its direction.

James rallied his men.

'Come on let's jog them for a final push. Any stragglers, we leave behind.'

They hollered, shouted, cracked whips to create panic to urge the mob. The fire roared like a giant tornado in the gully below. James realised the wind had shifted to attack from the fire's direction. Confidence that the fire would bypass them withered on the vine. The smoke blinded the lead sheep putting them of two minds: continue forward or turn and run before the fire. James, also, had to choose to remain with the herd, or abandon it.

~

The new bank loan had paid for the renovations, but the wool industry downturn made it even more difficult to earn droving money to repay it. His rural skills counted for nought when there was no industry.

One night, half-full of Old Tom, he'd joined the dice game at the corner shanty where he sometimes drank. He'd sworn in gaol he would neither drink, nor play dice, upon his release. Even as he sat, he was of two minds but decided to put his meagre pay-packet to the test.

The luck had not left him. He'd won throw after throw, winning enough to meet the month's loan repayment. Unlike previously, though, when ahead, he'd taken his money and quit the game, much to the chagrin of the those who had lost.

~

Smoke thickened windward. The fire crackled, snapped, and sizzled, no longer a background roar. A kangaroo, then her mate, raced from the scrub in panic, barrelled into the mob, hopped, and jumped over, collided through it. The fear of beast and man palpable.

James ordered the horse-tailer to saddle Settler, his favourite horse, son of a famous racehorse, while he gathered the team. He pointed ahead, raised his voice to be heard above the roaring inferno.

'This looks dangerous. You lads race ahead… wait for me past the fire-face. It's not worth all of us getting trapped.' He traded looks with each man to see if his message was understood. Patted Settler. 'If it gets too bad, I'll let the sheep loose and back young Settler, to race faster than the fire and get me safely out of here. None of you has a champion to rely on, so… get going!'

'No way, boss. You can't run faster than a bushfire. Leave the mob.'

'Nah, I'm a lucky chap. I'll back myself. Go!'

The men fled, fell over themselves, tripped like fly-blown sheep in their hurry. The horse-tailer refused to leave the thirty horses and hazed them past the sheep and disappeared into the smoke-covered track ahead. *Gutsy chap*, thought James.

'Just you and I now, fella,' he muttered to Settler, but then the dogs started barking, urging the sheep.

'All right, I'm sorry, I forgot, you fellas are here as well. Let's go!' he shouted.

Despite the seriousness of the situation, he laughed aloud at the commitment of his motley dogs.

He whistled, yipped, and cracked his whip to support them to urge the mob into a trot. Initially, it, like the drovers, was reluctant to move but the dogs, and he, charged the tail to drive it faster. At best, the mob reached a jog. James, looking further ahead through the smoke, noticed embers like Chinese fireworks bombing yellow-and-red sparks upon the sorry sheep, adding further to his concerns.

Understanding wool's fire-retardant properties, he donned his sheepskin jacket and ploughed again into the burgeoning smoke.

The only indication he'd reached the summit was when the track tilted downhill. It may have been false hope, a mere dip before another hump, but the trajectory remained – downhill. Older ewes had lagged, and James had left them. When he looked up, the smoke above had an ominous, red glow.

~

One night of good luck in dice, turned out to be Larry's luck. That one win had stirred James' dice addiction, which Bridget had disliked, and he'd returned… time and again… and lost so much, he'd never recover.

Ellen and the family were oblivious to their plight. How much money he'd owed, how deep in debt he'd taken them, he'd never disclosed. One big win would have solved it. He, like all the drovers, also drank to excess, and being a character, had secured many parasitic bar-mates. It was like the old days revisited, except for one difference – he'd remained straight; never stolen so much as a flint to light his cigarette.

This droving trip, with its large mob, would solve the debt problem, allow him to make enough to repay his gambling debts to the Italian loan sharks, and pay out his mortgage. He was desperate to bring the mob through, it had seemed so straightforward.

He loved his family and feared disappointing them.

~

On the ridge he could hear neither the dogs barking, nor the sheep bleating for the fire's roar. The track, also, scorched. Fear now drove the mob harder than dog or whip. They galloped as best they could. James draped his dry-as-a-bone over Settler's rump, and a groundsheet along his neck, to deflect the radiated heat. The sheep pranced on courageously. He'd misjudged them.

Settler, too, turned skittish in the face of the fire. His ears flicked madly. It was as if his eyes swivelled in their sockets to look back at his rider; initially for confidence, but now, to say, 'Let's go boss.'

James peered ahead through the dark smoke and saw flames flicker above the track. There was no time to delay.

'Come on, boy, let's get out of here.'

He wheeled Settler from the fire-face and took to the bush, which had thinned markedly, and raced beside the mob, parallel to the track. In minutes he'd passed the mob, leaving it to its own devices, and re-entered the track. Above him the tree branches exploded in flame as the plants' natural oils ignited, sending burning leaves and embers to cascade in fiery showers upon them as they galloped.

Unable to see or breathe in the toxic atmosphere, he thought of Ellen and children, not knowing if he, or the other drovers, would survive to tell his tale. Ma's image flashed across his mind, and he prayed for the Myanga's mumbling waters to cool his brow, quench his thirst, replace the fire's cyclonic roar. He believed nothing – neither man nor beast – would survive. He spurred poor Settler once more for luck, not that the majestic beast wasn't travelling faster than any horse he'd ever ridden. Courageous, Settler pounded on.

Then, to his disbelief, he stole a look along the track to find it clear of smoke. A breeze blew up the western slope before him; cool, fresh, delicious like a cold balm over his blistering flesh. He relaxed his seat, tugged lightly on his reins to message the colt that the race had finished. Further on, he stopped, and stared back at the smoke; a curtain pushing in a different direction. The wind had changed. Thank God.

He was safe. Lucky. But he'd lost the mob, and a fortune.

A suffocating sadness throttled the relief and replaced it with a morbid fear. He was old. There were few opportunities in a lifetime to replace a lost fortune, and this one he totally had blown. He trembled so badly the reins fell from his fingers.

As if to distract him from his suffering, each of his dogs appeared in turn, one with a singed coat. He dismounted and patted each. They acted as if nothing untoward had occurred.

'What a bastard, fellas, eh? What a bastard… But we gave it our best.'

He had no idea what the next step would be. Despair? He'd love a beer… or two.

He threw the reins over Settler's head, ready to mount, to search for his drovers, hopefully parked further along the track. Then a dog yelped a warning. James followed its gaze to the track, to witness perhaps twenty sheep stepping along the track as they had done for months. He took a huge breath as the joy that some had survived hit him.

Out of habit he checked around to share his surprise but was alone. Smiled at the dog.

Then another small mob emerged around the corner, followed by another, as smelly, aimless, and careless, as they'd ever been. James mounted and rode back towards the fire, and watched hundreds more emerge.

Some were scalded, but compared to what he had imagined, very few. His sheep and his future were back.

~

His toil is nearly over;
He'll soon enjoy his gains.
Not long he'll be a drover,
And cross the lonely plains.
We'll happy be for ever
When he'll no longer roam,
But by some deep, cool river
Will make us all a home.
(*Andy's Return*, Henry Lawson.)

~

The five-room slab-cut house with a sawn-timber annex; a rusted corrugated-iron roof; and a veranda, front, and back, was home to the Longs. A picket fence and basic garden surrounded the building. The raised, rough-timber floor lifted the house above the flood-line for when the river Murray chose to spill its muddy waters across its Redgum-lined banks. It sat where the town flowed along the railway line, and from a certain rear window, as far as the eye could see, fences separating cottage backyards ranged along the street until it barrelled into Wodonga's main thoroughfare. The country and city had merged.

James was away with sheep, again. None of the nine children had gone, as tempting as it was, because help was difficult to get and the trade unions had jacked up the price of labour, even in the country. Although the Government had resisted the importation of Chinese coolies to boost the labour force, there would be no drovers amongst them had they been available. The new eight-hour-day hardly applied to a drover's trade, so even the union efforts were an impediment rather than a help.

Two scrawny children, the middle ones, if there can be a middle of nine children, William, nine and Sidney, five, rolled like dried leaves on the rough lawn, wrestling, grunting.

Out of the blue William yelled, 'Banker! Mother, here's a banker!"

He had accompanied his mother to the bank; had watched the clerks visit with letters-of-demand often enough to recognise them.

Ellen, now a sun-ravaged drover's wife, dashed from the kitchen, snatched baby Nora onto her hip and reached for the stick she used to chase strays or kill snakes.

'Where is he?'

'Around the back, by the woodheap.'

'Stop there, Mother, I'll deal with him. Stand back.'

'No Rose ... come here, or you'll be hurt. In fact, get inside... Go on, both of you, at once. Inside!'

Rose returned from the side of the house with a shovel, the handle longer than herself.

'Here he comes.'

A man in a dark suit and black hat poked his head around the rear of the house, like a large black snake searching for food, alerted by the rustle of prey.

Ellen spied him. Turned for the front stairs. Shooed the children before her.

'Quickly – run inside.'

They bundled through the door, slammed it shut after them. It was solid timber on steel hinges, able to be locked from the inside; a concession Ellen had won from James to feel safe when he was absent.

Many strange types had wandered into town since the banking collapse, and the Shearer's strike. Men humping their swags across the country in search of work. Men kicked out of home because they could no longer be fed and housed by the family, or could no longer feed and house their family. Men whose community had hunkered down against them, forcing them into opportunism at best. Some even insensitive enough to take advantage of a woman. The dark side of town-life; a lifestyle she had requested of James.

'Bloody snakes they are… bankers.'

Ellen herded the children into the kitchen; made them stand together against the fireplace, while she watched for the banker. The old cattle dog, outside, yapped and its chain stretched and rattled as it strove to attack the intruder.

Footsteps. A flesh-coloured striated face-shape passed across the paling-door's cracks.

A knock.

Another.

Repeated knocks.

'I know you're in there,' a disembodied voice hissed. 'I only want to speak with you.'

They didn't respond.

William raised his club, menacingly.

Ellen restrained him with a hand on his elbow; whispered, 'Hopefully, you'll not need to use that.'

The room was hot, humid, despite the falling light. Dark storm clouds gathered across the far hills. Thunder rolled, rattled the windows.

An hour passed and the door remained shut. The dog barked furiously at small provocations. William searched the veranda.

'He's still out there.'

After two hours of peace, the dog again went berserk. A silhouette of a body passed across the door's cracks; a face reappeared up close; peered inside. An insistent knock. Silence. A hiss through the door.

'We can wait. You'll have to come out sometime.'

'Come back tomorrow when James is here.'

Footsteps padded down the stairs. What would they do next?

The three children crammed into one bed. The complaints about Sidney's stick waxed and waned. Wind whistled and thunder rattled. Lightning illuminated cracks in the slab walls and where the window curtains had not crossed. Upon hearing his mother's shout, William had sat upright with his club ready to strike, should the intruder find a way into the house.

Young Maggie complained.

'Sidney keeps bumping me with the stick.'

'Put the stick down, Sid.'

'No, Mum, what if he breaks through the door? I need to have it close.'

'Stand it up beside the bed.'

Ellen muses. Sunday tomorrow; a day she always dressed as best she could. She dressed the children, and together they would walk the mile-and-a-half past the rows of houses baked silent along the streets, to mass at St Augustine's, which had recently replaced St Francis Chapel, on the site where she had always worshipped.

Across the nation many, like her, had moved from the bush to the town. Houses had sprung up, clustered together. Entrepreneurs circled.

The drover's wife attempted, always, to walk to mass without stopping to address a child's concerns. With coloured umbrella held high to protect her from the heat, she guided her flock.

She'd never managed, once, to make it without a stop, even when she'd delegated the caring responsibility to an older sibling. Sometimes, she'd been determined to be heartless and ignore any request. Just one moment, please, for herself, for God's sake. Let it be granted on the Lord's Day, at least. A moment without the responsibility. To walk on and refuse to turn back; to have what she desires. But she couldn't do it.

The procession, of late, had been more problematic. They must file past groups of dispossessed families, Aborigines, immigrant flotsam from the gold rush. Some of the families, piled upon the detritus of their household goods and swags, begged.

'Tithe for food, lady?'

'Any corn-beef ends at home, missus?'

The drought, the crash, the depression, the banks bit hard, and spat the honest victims onto the street. She could barely feed her own, impossible to feed others.

Swaggies, undesirables, men down on their luck since the banking crash, whistled, licked her with their hungry eyes, made her feel cheap, unclean, as she walked past. Where was James? In the townships it was as if a bushfire had denuded the landscape, removed the stunted, salted shrubs, which had hidden the predators and vermin, and transferred the dangers to town dwellers. She had not felt safe since the changes. *Where was James?*

~

With morning, Ellen decided to confront the threat. If the snake was still here, she'd attack him with the help of the older children and force him to leave her property at least. Keep him at bay.

'Stay inside, youngsters. Come on boys. Grab Sid's stick, William, and your shovel, Rose. If the man…'

William had shaken his shoulder to dislodge her hand. She'd examined it as if it were a venomous object; let it fall to her hip.

'If the man grabs one of us, hit him hard and don't stop hitting until he lets go.'

She'd organised the children behind her and with a thick piece of firewood as a weapon, creaked the door open, peeped out, then rushed across to the old wriggle-tail dog; unleashed him and held tight to his greenhide collar.

The ruckus woke the man on the veranda. Saliva dribbled from the corner of his mouth. He pointed a soft white finger at her.

'Just who I wanted to see.'

The dog unleashed a salvo, barked and growled; pulled Ellen with it as it lunged at the man. Ellen's face boiled corned-beef red.

'Get off my porch,' she shouted.

'I need to tell you that you have one month to pay your loan, or we will foreclose and you will lose everything. One month, ya hear!'

'We hardly owe you anything.'

'You must pay us back as per the contract. It is the law.'

'Dash the law.'

'Wish we could, missus.'

'What? Is it, the bank that stops you?'

'Yes, Ma'am, the bank won't let us.'

'The bank is not a machine. It's flesh and blood… Men. You could choose to relax your rules for good folk like us.'

'No, Missus. The bank has a mind of its own.'

'What? Robs humans like you, of your souls? A bushranger, is it?'

'That's unfair. We have families too. We go to church; have a soul. You chose to re-roof the house.'

'Get off my land or I'll sool the dog onto you.'

'I tell you Missus, I've stopped 'em in Melbourne, kicking you out. They've got lawyers and debt collectors just dying to get at you. You have assets the bank can liquidate to help it survive; others have none. You have a month to pay, or we'll send in the bailiff.'

The dog barked, strained at the leash; slobbered from its straining jaws; responded to the fear in Ellen's voice.

'James will pay it when he gets in. He said he would. He's a man of his word.'

'You said that last month.'

'Well, he must get in this month. There has been no feed on the long paddock to allow him to bring the flock in, but there are patchy, local storms, like last night, and he will follow the pick in. You'll see.'

'Do you know how many drovers the bank has had to foreclose on, Missus? Hundreds. There's no feed; no shearers; no market. It's bleak.'

'He'll be here. Now, get off.'

Young William raised his stick and aped his mother's stance.

'Get off.'

The man retreated.

Ellen, the children, individually and as a group, wanted to cry. They didn't. They'd panted a little like the dog as it flopped on the veranda's hot, bare boards.

~

With pannikins all rusty,
And billy burnt and black,
And clothes all torn and dusty,
That scarcely hide his back;
With sun-cracked saddle-leather,
And knotted greenhide rein,
And face burnt brown with weather,
Our Andy's home again!
(*Andy's Return*, Henry Lawson).

~

Ellen stood on the veranda, at the top of the stairs, wearing a long grey skirt and floral-patterned blouse, with her hair rolled in a side-bun, and upon sighting him, a smile as broad as a frog's. James leant closer to young William when they reached the house-yard gate; whispered, 'How beautiful is she, Will?'

Ellen touched the stair-rail, dropped a step.

'So, William found you?'

'Yeah, I wasn't far out of town but I had to sneak past a couple of squatters' homesteads at night, so they didn't know how far I was travelling, and I was off the stock route, sharing the squatters' grass, so I couldn't send you news.'

James dismounted, pulled the greenhide reins over Settler's ears, and handed them to William.

'Take the horses around the back. I'll be there in a minute to help you unload the pack-horse after I've spoken with your mother.'

William skirted the fenced house-yard with its trim lawn and blooming roses to reach a barn bordering the horse-paddock. James approached Ellen along the stone-flagged pathway. She noticed his bow-legs, their curve perhaps exaggerated by the pale sweat-stains marking his moleskins' inside leg; noticed the click of spurs on the odd flagstone as he stepped. He looked older than his years, weary, grey-haired, stooped, and it shocked her.

'Hi, ducks,' he said, as he hugged her. They pecked lips. 'It's been too long this time. Are the children well?'

The way their eyes joined was all an observer needed to understand that this was a couple in love.

'Yes, all well.'

'Good.'

'Thank heaven you're here, though; the bank has driven me crazy.'

She snuggled in beneath his arm and rested her face upon his chest.

'Umm, so Will said… We'll sort that out tomorrow. I could do with a beer and a home-cooked meal. I've got meat in the pack-saddle. I butchered one of the ewes this morning before I handed the mob over. We'll have to put some of it in the ice-chest.'

He released her, pushed back, and stared at her face for a moment as if checking an inventory.

'I'll help Will with the horses.'

By the time he and Will returned, the house was alive with cooking smells. James guessed stew was on the menu. It could be possum, rabbit, or wallaby; who knows? But the vegetables were home grown, of that you could be assured. Always the optimist, he caught Ellen's eye.

'Who needs money when you can eat like a king? I'll deal with the bank in the morning.'

~

The bank on Townsend St. had not opened, but he waited against its doorframe. He may still be intoxicated, having visited the Irish pub for a celebratory, welcome home drink, and stayed until the early morning. He deserved it. But he'd barely slept, and his head ached.

He ran his experienced eye around the bank's exterior and determined how he could rob it, were he so interested. The two-story building abutted a barber shop, and it was this which would be its weakness. Hop onto the barber's roof, swing over the bank's upstairs porch railing, pop the French doors, and bingo, you'd be in. If you arrived at this time, opening time, while the bankers had the safe open to distribute cash to the tellers, you would surprise them by appearing from the inside; catch them napping; and have ready access to all their cash. Lock them in the safe and disappear out the back door, and… Bob's your uncle.

James had never robbed a bank. His mate Ben Hall, and later, Ned Kelly, were famous for it. Too much could go wrong. Too many people involved to complicate the lift. But he had assisted Hall to stake out possible targets, so seldom passed one without assessing its potential. If things get too bad, and the bank doesn't allow them time to repay the loan, then, perhaps?

The ornate, wooden entrance-door swung open as the town hall clock struck ten and diverted his thinking. As he entered, he hoped his clean shirt and moleskins helped him appear prosperous. His spurs clicked quite eerily on the tiled floor and echoed within the bank's sandstone walls; a sound not unlike the Morse code machine, housed down at the railway station, able to send messages, instantaneously, to Melbourne.

He asked to see the manager and after a short wait, was led inside an office at the end of the tellers' row.

'Mr Talbot, nice of you to see me.'

'We have been searching for you, Mr Long. Your loan payments are well overdue.'

James was not invited to sit.

'Sorry, sir, I couldn't return to town. The drought and the lack of stock-feed had me in a holding pattern, further down the Murray.'

'Be that as it may, you promised us payment a month ago.'

'I can't do the impossible, Mr Talbot.'

'Nor can we. Nor can we… I backed you after you lost your fortune in the 1890 banking collapse, and you repay me this way?'

'All we need is a couple of months.'

'You could sell your horses.'

'I don't think so, I need them for my livelihood; to feed the family.'

'Did you get paid, while you've been in hiding?'

'Droving, Mr Talbot; droving.'

'Well?'

'No. Not yet. Hopefully, by week's end. When the squatter sells his mob.'

'Sheep are worth bugger-all at the moment.'

'Not my problem. Legally, he must pay me.'

'All right, next Monday. You have until then to have your money here. If not, we'll be around to your house to evict you.'

Each identity has a shadow, often an addiction, be it drink, power, or sex. James had numerous – drink, gambling, danger. He wondered what Talbot's might be.

'I hear you've already tried to do that… But, just to let you know, Mr Talbot, if you send anyone around to harm my family again, you'll hear from me.'

'Are you threatening me?'

'No, just letting you know that, by doing so, you would not be free of me, by a long shot.'

The banker pointed to the door.

'Goodbye to you, Mr Long.'

James turned.

'Not free … Not by a long shot,' he shouted over his shoulder as he strode from the office. His spurs clinked on the tiles, each person in the bank heard the rhythm long after his departure and long after the front door slammed.

Later that night, James asked a jockey mate, Jimmy O'Toole, short of stature but long of racing knowledge, a question.

'Does that bank manager, Talbot, still own that champion race horse?'

'The old stallion? Yeah, keeps it over at Stephenson's.'

'Is it still any good?'

'Not bad. Gone off a bit as it's aged… runs a place now and then, at the picnics.'

'Not bad' is high praise in cornstalk's terms.

'Would it have beaten Whistler in his day?'

'No, I don't think so.'

'Ah… Who works it for him?'

'He does.'

~

Early the next morning, James saddled one of the droving horses and rode to the Stephenson's property on the town's edge. Soon, Talbot arrived on a fat, black hack, about fifteen-hands-high and disappeared to the stables behind Stephenson's house. Twenty minutes later, he re-appeared on a well-groomed thoroughbred, and rode it onto the dirt road, where James waited.

As Talbot drew closer, James emerged from the shadows and greeted him from a distance in his most unctuous tone, as if nothing had happened between them.

'Fancy running into you. I didn't know you were a rider, Mr Talbot?'

'A man needs a pastime, Long.'

'Indeed. I wouldn't have put yours as horse riding, but I can see you're quite handy at it. I've got sheep over at the saleyards, thought this road might be a short cut. Not so, though.'

'Ah, I wondered what you were doing out this way.'

'I bet,' James said, then pointed at the stallion. 'A nice horse. Is it the Stephenson's?'

'No, my horse… A champion, Long, a champion.'

James opened his eyes wide, incredulity pasted thick upon his face.

'What… racing?'

'Yes, indeed.'

'Doesn't look like a fast horse. No disrespect intended.'

'So, you're an expert on horse-flesh now, Long?'

'Not really, only know bush horses. I'm not a learned man such as yourself.'

'Indeed.'

'But I'd back one of my droving plodders to beat him over a mile, from what I can see.'

'You'd be joking, of course?'

Talbot's eyes surveyed James' unwashed, woolly-haired gelding; its bones exposed from months on drought-affected stock routes. James continued.

'Maybe. He appears too narrow of chest for my liking. But are you a gambling man, Mr Talbot?'

'I might be.'

'Well, I am… You know that! I'd be willing to go double or nothin' on that bank loan we've been discussing. The deal being that my old work-horse, *Settler*, not this one, could pip that fancy nag of yours over a mile. If I lose, I sell my plant and livestock to pay you double.'

'Would you, now?'

James hoped Talbot knew of his reputation as a poor gambler, and being a greedy banker, would be unwilling to let an easy dollar pass.

'Yes. We could meet at the track in the morning for a lark… no jockeys; just us.'

'Oh, I don't usually ride him myself, to race.'

'Has to be a first time, right? I'll be riding my nag and I'm a much older man. Not agile for riding, am I? On the other hand, you look like a natural, and on a… champion.'

Talbot's head moved this way and that, like a crow inspecting a juicy grub. He chomped on the bait.

'Okay. In the morning… at the track. I'll have the Race Club Secretary there, as witness.'

'Fine. I hope I haven't taken on more than I can chew?' James said, loud enough to ensure Mr Talbot heard.

James departed to meet the agent who had contracted him to drove the sheep, his office a shelter at the saleyard's entrance. His spring cart was parked out front where James fronted him.

'What's the story, do I get paid?'

'When we sell them.'

'That wasn't the deal. I was to be paid on delivery to these yards. I can't afford to wait because my men and the bank are squeezing me. Look, I'll make it easier for you. Give me two hundred in cash so I can pay the crew, and I'll take the balance in sheep, which you assure me are worth absolutely nothing.'

The agent, all beer and belly, tilted his nose, scratched his arse as he contemplated.

'How many head will you take?'

'A hundred.'

'A hundred. That's a bit steep, isn't it?'

'A hundred at nothing, by your estimation, is nothing.'

The agent accepted on behalf of the cocky, and James drafted the hundred-head, and escorted them to the horse paddock behind his house. He would sell them later.

Inside, he hurried to complete the saddle he'd been making for the girls. With less stuffing, it was smaller and weighed half a stock saddle, yet wasn't quite a racing-pad. He'd race in it to ensure Settler carried the lightest load possible. Talbot's champion, because of the banker's size, would have to carry a lot more weight than Settler. It may tip the scales in James' favour.

After dinner, he raided the family cash-tin of twenty pounds then retreated in his usual habit to the pub. There, he backed himself at very good odds with the local SP bookmaker to win against Talbot's champion, risking his droving team's wages, secured earlier from the agent. Most of his drinking mates also placed a bet, with the majority backing Talbot's champion. Most of those who had backed James, backed his horsemanship, because they had no idea of Settler's pedigree: a son of Whistler, and out of a very handy racing mare, a lineage he'd built into his stock horses during his early bushranging days, and part of the Cummins' bush herd.

Next morning, he rose before dawn, fed Settler a light portion of oats, before he saddled and walked him to the racetrack. He imagined he would be the only person at the track at that time, but word had spread. A line of horses were already hitched along the fence beside the finish line. He dismounted two-hundred yards away, behind a brush shed, extracted a tin of Stockholm Tar from his jacket pocket, mixed some with angular pebbles and stuck the goo beneath Settler's hoof, remaining out of sight until Talbot arrived.

Talbot's stylish kit included jodhpurs, tight-white shirt with grey vest, and a green racing cap perched upon his pin head. James joined the banker, now conversing with the racing-club secretary. Settler limped badly; lifted his head high each time he placed weight on his painful hoof.

'Good morning, Long.'

'Mr Talbot.'

The banker appraised Settler's winter coat, unwashed, ungroomed, dishevelled.

'So, this is your challenger?'

'It is.'

'Does he have a name?'

'Settler.'

'Settler?'

James smiled a moment before replying.

'Yeah, Settler… doesn't seem to want to move.'

The banker and the race club secretary exchanged looks and chuckled. Talbot pointed to Settler's leg.

'Appears to be lame?'

'Yeah, walkin' a bit lame at the moment.'

'Did you want to postpone?'

'Thought of it, but decided not to.'

'Why, my good man?'

'A bet is a bet. He'll probably beat your Champion, anyway.'

Talbot's eyes lit up. A smug glance passed between Talbot and the secretary.

'So, you'd be willing to back that statement with a side-bet, I'm sure? You need to learn, my dear man, to be more judicious.'

James nodded in agreement.

'Whatever that means.'

'It's the principle of the thing. You challenged me, and now you need to back it up.'

'Oh, I don't know about that. I only have twenty pounds to my name… the odds would have to be good.'

'I tell you what. You pay me the twenty if you lose, I pay you triple if you win. That's how confident I am in the bluster of your boast.'

'You drive a hard bargain, Mr Talbot. I'll be destitute, as you already know… okay, have it your way… agreed! I need to warm old Settler first, to see if I can reduce the damage the race might incur. I'll join you at the start line.'

'Your reputation will be in tatters after this, Long. You'll wish you'd never been so impertinent.'

The secretary recorded the terms, and the contestants shook hands. Bar mates from the pub, seeing the lame horse, wanted to default on their bets, but the bookie would have none of it. A bet is a bet. Some hollered-out to James and he reassured them with a thumbs-up; that it will be alright. He limped the horse over to the brush-shed and removed the stones from beneath its hoof with his pocket knife. The horse phantom-limped to the start-line.

'Are you ready, riders?' the secretary shouted, loud enough for the people at the finish line across the grass track to hear. 'The race starts at the drop of my arm.'

His arm, hat in hand for flourish, extended above his head, then dropped.

'Go.'

They raced from a standing start, and James, at risk of tiring Settler, pushed to the front early, knowing his only chance was to rely not just on Settler's speed, but also his obdurate personality. Being an alpha male, he resented any horse in front of him, and would die rather than concede. That was why James seldom used him for actual droving, so that he never learnt to follow. He was a bushranger's horse.

From the lead, Settler dug into the contest. At the quarter-mile James slowed slightly and could hear the banker's champion close behind. At the half-mile Settler still retained the lead. Months of hard living on the droving track should stand him in good stead, but he puffed early. James certainly didn't want him to blow, which could be on the cards, this being the colt's maiden race.

At the three-quarter-mile mark, the champion drew alongside and, in response, James raised and flicked his riding whip, as if to urge Settler. In fact, it had been designed to disturb Talbot's champion, swishing around his eyes to disrupt his stride. A regular jockey wouldn't have stood it; would have slapped Settler in turn, but Talbot was not a jockey and may not even have noticed it.

A hundred yards to go and the champion attacked again, Talbot riding courageously, hands and heels, to urge him forward. James gave Settler his head and raked his ribs with spur. The colt flashed his tail and lengthened his stride, leaving the champion further behind with each stride taken, to win by a length.

Talbot was angry. Furious. It was small change to him, but life-or-death for James and his expanding family.

'Cheating… unfair! That horse is a ring-in.'

'Not at all, just a fast horse. As I said, a bet is a bet! I'll settle up at the bank in the morning.'

Which he did.

Talbot didn't manage the transaction himself but delegated it to a clerk. James paid out the loan and received the mortgage-release paperwork. He put the excess in an account for Ellen, which he couldn't touch, and was safe from his addictions. At least the family would always have a roof over their head when he was gone, and the kids able to finish school, if nothing else.

He collected his bets from the bookie and paid his droving team. That left him with a small kitty to sustain him during infrequent droving trips and supplement his leatherwork income.

He went to bed that evening the most relaxed for years.

WHO ARE WE BURYING?
WILLIAM'S SAD STORY.
1909

NINETEEN-year-old William Long reads the local newspaper near the stove. He is lean of limb and long of face, hair is dark, ruffled, morning-scruffy and his fleecy-grey singlet clings to his slim body like lichen to a tree. Beside him, his auburn-haired mother, Ellen, is busy preparing breakfast; places crockery and cutlery on the table; breaks eggs into a bowl; moves the frypan over the open hole in the wood-fired stove to heat the dripping, spitting-hot.

Will glances at her handsome face and admires the agility of her slim middle-aged body, as she moves around the room. He has read the horse-racing section while she organised the breakfast. As soon as the Johnnycakes are fried it will be time to rally his eight siblings to the table.

In the meantime, he scans the front page; a lot of ballyhoo about the establishment of political parties and their role in undermining the wishes of the nation's newly minted constitution and the possibility within five years of a newly minted bush capital being sited just up the road in Canberra. He turns to the second page, rabbit chops the paper-edge straight with his hand to reinstate its crease, then pats it flat on his lap.

He reads intently, bends closer to the print as if he can't believe his eyes, leans back and exhales, looks to the ceiling, pauses for what appears to be an age, then leans forward to re-examine it. His lips move slightly as he sub-vocalises a few lines.

'Good gosh, Mum, listen to this.'

Ellen looks up, testily, her face serious. Recent events have challenged her patience. Dealing with the grief and pain of losing her James, only days earlier, and organising a funeral, among them. She needs to prepare breakfast, clean house, and cook for the afternoon wake. Friends and guests from her church are excellent cooks and even better critics of any catering, so she needs to concentrate. She doesn't have time to listen to William, who loves to read newspaper snippets aloud. Not a strong reader herself, she has learned to forgive this irritating habit because it keeps her informed, but not today, she doesn't have time today.

'You need to listen to this Mum. I can't believe it!' He reads from the *Border Mail*.

'EX-BUSHRANGER'S ROMANTIC CAREER

'Well Known in Albury and Wodonga

'By the death on Monday of James Long a most eventful career was brought to a close. For some years Mr Long resided near the railway line on the Wodonga Flats.

'It is not generally known that James Long was identical with the celebrated Larry Cummins, the bushranger, who caused so much trouble in the 60s. On one occasion Cummins' brother had been arrested for horse stealing and was being conveyed to the Binda lockup by two mounted police.

'Larry determined on his brother's release so a body of desperate men was got together and the police escort, with their captive, was way-laid at a wild place on the track. Cummins fired a shot at a constable, after ordering them to 'bail up'. Instead of hitting the officer, however, his shot hit the prisoner who fell dead off his horse. Larry had shot his brother dead!

'Larry Cummins was tried, found guilty, and sentenced to imprisonment for life at Berrima Gaol. While serving his sentence this intrepid man determined to escape. He managed to secrete himself in an outhouse and worked his way along a

flue till he reached the outside wall. Armed with a piece of bent iron, he worked all night at the mortar between the bricks and made a hole by disloding the latter, of sufficient size, to admit his body.

'This was the last the police saw of Larry Cummins for many a long day. He had to swim across the Wondilly (sic) (it was the Wingecarribee, anyhow) River.

'Free again, Cummins made his way back to his old haunts in the vicinity of Mudgee, Laggaa (sic) (Laggan), Crookwell, Bunda (sic) (Binda). Tuena and other now respectable towns.

'Cummins stuck up the Mudgee mail coach on one occasion and robbed it of 200 pounds. He afterwards made his headquarters at the Limerick Hotel between Peelwood and Laggan. This place was where Lowrie (sic) the bushranger stayed. It was kept by a Mrs Hogan, mother of a lady who subsequently became Mrs Charles Edgehill of Mundawaddera Station.

'The police, who had been watching the hotel for some time, disguised themselves as diggers, and attempted a surprise early one morning. Lowry was sleeping in a bedroom off a veranda. The police called on him to surrender. There was no answer. They there upon fired a volley through the door. Lowry opened the door and was shot, though not fatally.

'The police started to convey their prisoner to Goulburn Gaol, 43 miles away, but the rough journey was too much for the injured bushranger who died on the road.

'Larry Cummins was subsequently arrested and tried at Goulburn. He was convicted and sentenced to a long term of imprisonment in Parramatta Gaol. Being once more inside the walls of a Goal, Cummins determined to again get free. He conceived a bold plan remarkable only for its simplicity...'

He looks at his mother and weeps; can't control it, nor stop his hand shaking, can't determine if it's from fear or rage, or both. How could they (whoever 'they' are) pass on such lies about his father? How could they publish something like this destroying his father's identity and, perhaps, his own? "They" seem so sure. So much for Irish solidarity, the protective sanctity of the bush-brethren, the comforting brotherhood of the Abercrombie small settlers, if this slanderous information be true.

He sidles across to his mother, who weeps, silently. He places his hand upon her small shoulder and feels the horrible tremble of her tiny body, feels her bones brush together like the feathers of a bird's wing. A sadness washes through him. He's never seen his mother weep before; feels compelled to comment.

'How could they?'

'How could he?' she adds.

'What, be a criminal?'

'No, he was not a criminal. How could he not have said something, even a hint to warn us, prepare us, in case his secret identity was ever exposed?'

He has no answer.

'What should we do?'

'What would your father want?'

The pair stare at each other in silence, confounded. The red gum firewood spits and crackles within the cast-iron stove. Will purses his lips as if sifting the right words.

'He used to say "*grab the bull by the tail, and if it turns to attack you, that is its first mistake! You pull on the tail and knock it head-over-heels. Little beast against big.*"'

She pauses, then stands.

'Okay, wake your brother and sisters and we'll have a quick family meeting to prepare them for the news before the funeral begins.'

~

The church is half-full by the time the family arrives. There are familiar faces but many they don't recognise. By the official start time the church overflows. Young Sid sweeps his hand over the pews.

'The bastards are all here to gloat.'

'Shush, Sid,' says Mary, looking prim in her nun's habit. She tucks the back of his shirt into his shorts.

Father Brennan, plump and freckled, with a jungle of ginger hair, commences the service by welcoming all to celebrate the life of James Long, father, drover, horse-breaker, husband of Ellen.

Hymns are sung, prayers invoked in Latin and the congregation responds, '*...and with you*'. The few Protestants in the congregation are unsure when to bob, stand, or kneel, and this entertains the youngsters throughout. Father Brennan invites William to the pulpit to deliver the eulogy. William mounts slowly but deliberately, and looks upon the congregation for a long moment, while he collects his thoughts.

'Thank you.'

The murmuring across the room stops. He pauses, intakes a breath.

'Thank you, folks, for joining with our family today to help us farewell our father, and Mum's husband, James Long, who died in his sleep earlier this week on Tuesday, 18th October, 1909.'

His voice echoes, repeats itself around the tall, wood-lined ceilings.

'For those who don't know me, my name is William Long, and as the oldest surviving male in the family, and the oldest son, the job of speaking about my father on behalf of the family, falls to me. Before I continue, I personally would like to thank Father Brennan and our sister – Sister of Mercy, Mary – for conducting a wonderful ceremony. The Holy Father, the Pope himself, would be proud that a good Catholic family had inspired one of its eleven children (two others of whom have joined our heavenly father) to dedicate themselves to the church, and would recognise the generosity of Father Brennan in welcoming Sister Mary to officiate in his service.

'Our father, James, would have been pleased to see so many friends and associates, customers, and competitors, join us today, to pay your respects. Interestingly, he would be equally pleased to realise that his favourite horse, Settler, is nearby to assist him on his journey from this world to the next. If you look outside, you'll see Settler tied to the church fence. We all understand that as a horseman Dad was as close to his horses as he was to man, (don't laugh). They are a part of his identity. He said often that "*...no horse ever offered me harm, which is more than I can say of my fellow man.*"'

A murmur of understanding washes like a wave across the crowd.

'Dad was raised in country New South Wales and earned his living as a drover, horse-breaker, and leatherworker, and was never happier than when he was away from the confines of the town and surrounded by his beloved bush. But he and Mum were equally keen to ensure we were as familiar with the intellectual and spiritual world as with the natural, and made sure we attended school, and church. If ever we feigned sickness to wag school, we had Dad to deal with, and he always said he was an *'expert at shamming illness and could recognise it in others'*. While he attended a bush school, he failed to attend often enough to learn anything of use. Certainly not enough to do anything other than the horse business.

'Now, I know you would have read yesterday's *Border Mail*, so there is no point in avoiding its allegations. No one could be more shocked than us. Mum has cried all morning. She had no idea of Dad's history, or previous identity. She says it feels as if they've described another person and if he is Lawrence Cummins, the bushranger, then she has lost two people. First, a husband, and second, the basis of a credible memory of him. Sorry, Mum! You didn't deserve this.'

He pauses, struggles to retain his composure. His voice wavers.

'We are not angry at Dad, but at the newspaper besmirching him and hurting our mother. We cannot deny the allegations because we simply don't know. Dad reckoned he was wild when younger, but we never saw any evidence of his wildness, violence, or thieving, for that matter.

'The claim he went to gaol may explain his many scars, especially the cicatrices across his shoulders. But there are other explanations: boyhood larks, busters from falling horses, for example. As for family? We never met any, so it could be true that he hid them: protected them. He told us they were all dead.

'He also said that there was no point visiting Windsor, where he told us he was born, because there would be no one there to remember him. Knowing how much Dad loved us, separating himself from family to ensure they weren't tainted by his reputation, would have been very distressing for him, but you'll have to agree, it was also a caring thing to do.

'If he was a bushranger, and in the view of the press, a successful one, then we must believe that he paid the penalty for his crime in gaol. Fifteen years loss of liberty is a heavy penalty for a crime against property. If, in fact, he killed his brother, then knowing the type of man he was, and how much he loved family, I can't imagine his degree of suffering. It must have been horrendous. I believe he has suffered enough in his lifetime for us to forgive him, now.

'Whatever the truth we only knew him as a loving husband and father. He was certainly a "man's man", but he treated us gently and lovingly, as best he knew how. He worked tirelessly, with no backing or sponsorship, other than his wits, to feed and school us. I'm happy to say, without a shadow of a lie, we had a very secure and happy childhood.

'He felt most alive when he was free of the towns. Perhaps we were happiest too, when, on school holidays, we would join him droving and live for weeks enjoying the "great outdoors" as he called it. We cannot imagine a better childhood.

'My greatest possession remains the green-hide bridle he made for me for my ninth birthday. Not only was it brand new, it was the only one of its kind. You'd have to belong to a large family to appreciate the importance of that. I was the envy of all my friends on that occasion.

'I loved to watch him work with leather. *'Idle hands do the devil's work'* he believed and the leather-work kept him sane in the long paddock tending a herd. As his health faded, I'd sit for hours in the shed and we'd chat while he applied his craft. He had a bucket of patience, and with string and awl would weave great stories of men and beasts into the fine stitching.

'Speaking of gifts, Sid believes Dad's greatest gift to him was that he taught him how to defend himself. Baby Nora said she remembers Dad best for teaching her how to ride her pony the real way – not side-saddle. Mary appreciated the time he spent listening to her read. To each of us, in his own way, he brought forth gifts.

'My parent's relationship was a love story. Mum met Dad as a sixteen-year-old when he visited her property to break a horse that grandfather Cole had given her for her birthday, and she married him at seventeen. She says she has never looked at another man since she laid eyes on him. On Dad's part, he always said it was Mum who "gentled" him: made a real man of him. One admonition from her was enough for him to change whatever it was that displeased her.

'You might laugh, but it's true… As we all know, towards the end of his life he did like a wee drop – a few beers – a little too regularly, perhaps.'

A chuckle runs through the congregation.

'… because the doctors tell us that it was the drink that killed him. He loved to get down to his local on Melbourne Road to meet his mates. He said he liked it because it was run by the Irish. I guess we could have stopped him going there, given he was crook, but Mum said he should be left to enjoy it because he'd worked so hard all his life and it hadn't been an easy one.

'It may appear strange to you, given his history, but Dad believed the greatest feat he ever achieved was to read and write, skills which he learned as an adult. I think it will be quite strange to walk onto our back veranda on a Saturday morning and not find him sitting there, reading *The Bulletin* and swearing about one politician or another. By weeks' end he would have read every one of its articles. It may also surprise some that he had read several classics and could recite verses from Homer and Cicero, which he referred to as a guide. He said there was always a bible to read but he enjoyed the thinking of a wider church – of Aristotle, Plato, and Shakespeare. Where that came from, I do not know, but he was always happy to listen to us read and to ensure we understood what it was we were reading. "*Ideas, good and bad, can change a man*," he would say, "*so be aware of where you get them*."

'Finally, I'd like to say James... Larry, Dad, thank you for being part of our lives. Thank you for protecting us from many of the winds that had buffeted your life. Thank you for your energy, your wisdom, your free spirit, your courage, your sense of family. We love you.'

~

The church organ gasps and wheezes through a well-known hymn; fills the stone church with its sonorous wailing. On the priest's command, six parishioners rise from their pew and move self-consciously along the aisle towards a rough-pine coffin rested on trestles before the altar. The men assemble each side, and after sorting a mix-up in height, for there was no rehearsal, raise the coffin by its straps, and wait. Larry's old leather hat, ringed by sweat and stains, battered by years of use, sits strangely out of place on the coffin's lid.

For the second time that day, Ellen weeps. The tears don't squeeze from her eyelids, they roll forth. She uses the corner of her embroidered-linen headscarf, to dry them. A lifetime of stoicism won't permit wailing. She remains stone silent.

The command is given, and the coffin is carried towards the exit by the somber-faced men, their rough cotton shirts sweat-soaked beneath their armpits and down their backbone. Ellen and the nine children follow, the children's bare feet soundless on the hardwood floor. For a moment, a little too long to be fashionable, no one else joins them. They are a sorry little family group, culled and alienated from the predominant herd.

Larry's body disappears out the door. The family follows. Where will they go? Next, the congregation stand, shuffle along to the centre-aisle, exchange glances, intermingle into single-file to exit. By the time they emerge into the late spring sunlight, the coffin lies on the cemetery cart. Young Sid leads Settler, son of Whistler, over to the dray and ties his reins to the backboard.

The cart moves off without ceremony, while the congregation continues to flow down the stairs. The old priest stands on the porch, wishes each person farewell, pays no attention to Larry's family.

The family treks off. They won't attend the graveside. It is too far, and they can't afford it. They'll wait at home to welcome any well-wishers when it is over.

Larry is placed in a pauper's grave in the Wodonga cemetery to morph into yet another identity. No one can locate it. As Larry, years earlier, said in court when asked why he didn't attend Jack's funeral – 'We let others do the mourning up in the Abercrombie.'

THE WAKE, THE WOKE AND THE AWOKEN – HI-STORY?

LATE afternoon. The Crookwell community hall's chocolate-coloured doors are open. Horses, buggies, sulkies, billygoat-carts are hitched at various spots around the grounds. Some of the buggies are smart indeed; highly polished, city-clean with mere surface dust and splashed mud, their horses groomed shiny. Others are the usual fare, owned and driven by locals. These are workworn, mud-encrusted, with pieces of hay or fencing equipment stuck in various places, their horses dull, ungroomed.

Within the sawn-timber hall, light from the afternoon's fading winter sun barely penetrates or illuminates the space, or warms the dance floor's cold, bare boards, dusty, and un-mopped since last month's ball. Pieces of confetti bustle about where breeze trickles in through the open doors. At one end is a long, undraped table loaded with grog, supplied by who knows who: the historian most likely. On the dance floor, Ellen Long's younger children tow each other around the polished floor; one upright, pulling, the other crouched on their haunches, sliding. They weave in and out of the conversing parties, who stand scattered across the floor like floating algae upon a pond. A sound like a fake bell, a steel spoon bashed against a tin jug, calls for silence. A fellow in a posh suit, with a speaking tone to match, has their attention.

'Ladies and gentlemen, thank you for coming. I'd like to ask you, first, to charge your glasses, and then join me in the meeting area for a conversation.'

The meeting area, rows of chairs facing a small table, is at the opposite end of the hall to the bar. People move in threes and fours to populate it. The posh guy continues.

'I'm the Interrogator for this meeting. I've been asking questions about the life of Lawrence Cummins aka James Long, deceased since 1909. Why, you might ask? Well, time, if it does exist, may be a multilateral, moving phenomenon, where any recording of events is fractured, like light through a crystal, by perspective, intersecting histories, and fashion. We need to capture that. To this point, the record has been written by myself, my cousin Maurice Cummins and a few others, but I know you all played a part in the story, and I wondered if you had anything which should be discussed before we lock it away? Has Larry been treated fairly?'

Mother Mary looks about, appears as if she is about to comment when an elderly man, his waistcoat stretching at the buttons, rises and interrupts.

'You wish to comment, Judge Hargrave?'

'Yes, I do. I can't see what the fuss is about. The man got what he deserved. He was charged, initially, with minor offences but it was well known he'd been stealing horses and cattle for years. These are serious offences. The Police had evidence for those minor offences – stolen saddlery in this case – not the major ones. I did the community a service by removing him and his terrorist activities from the district.'

The interrogator raises his hand to halt the judge.

'Yeah, but what about the lad's human rights?'

'It worked out fine. The lad was rehabilitated and returned to society.'

'But would he have been able to have had a more productive and happier life had he been treated fairly by the law?'

'Who's to say, more productive? He acquired family, a job, friends by the end of his life. More than many who pass through the system… I treated him fairly.'

The interrogator flashes a wry smile.

'How would a Hargrave know what is *fair*, given the privilege you and yours have been raised to expect in your English upbringing? You didn't have to contend with the sort of rock-scrabble childhood of the poor Irish immigrants… You were called the "crazy" Judge, weren't you? What's the chance, someone meeting you at the wrong time of your illness' cycle, would escape unharmed?'

'I'll ignore that remark. I never allowed my health issues to interfere with my judicial responsibilities… The unspoken charge against Larry is, of course, that he murdered his brother, Jack. That's it, isn't it?'

'Yes, but legally, he was never charged with that, and surely should be judged accordingly. Not for murdering young Jack,' asserted the interrogator.

'Well, he should have hanged for that murder. Let that be on his record.'

'Well, did he murder me? I don't think so. There is no evidence,' jumps in young Jack Cummins, to the awe of all attending.

'There was your body,' says the Judge.

'Yeah, but what did that prove? I'd been shot? No witnesses, no horse tracks, no weapon, no cross-examination of the Police Report. You've got to be real. Everyone knows Larry loved me. There's no way he would have killed me.'

'A mistake, an accident?' teases the Judge, a cynical tone to his voice.

Jack points an accusatory finger, grime-encrusted from the grave.

'It was the only thing you could come up with to explain your lack of evidence, wasn't it? What about dying at the hands of the Police for having shot at them earlier? Did they take a rifle from our farm when they arrested me, and shoot me with that? There was motive for them. Did ya think of that?'

'Well, I argued it was Tom Francis, Larry's father-in-law,' interjects historian, Maurice Cummins. 'The evidence is there to see.'

An older man in damp farmer's clothes looking as pale as young "Jack", stands, waving his cup of gin. Spirit sloshes over the lip, falls upon his children, without him being aware of it. He is young Jack's namesake, his uncle, Irish John.

'No, it could ha' been me who shot you, young John. Perhaps it twere nuttin' but a horrible accident. Can anyone tell us why I shot myself on the same day Jack was killed?'

The interrogator's eyes open wide. He appears embarrassed.

'Why don't you tell us?'

'Why should I? It's all settled. Families and history have so many secrets.'

Judge Hargraves rolls his eyes in incredulity.

'So, Larry was "unlucky" to have been the recipient of my loaded sentence?'

Irish John turns serious.

'I would say so. Da family conspired to let Larry take the rap. He did time for all. I guess he blotted his copy book after he escaped t'ough? He shoulda laid low and made dem forget him, but no, not him, the bloody mug-lair.'

Young Jack nods.

'That's the type of lad we like to think our Larry was; loving and all. I loved him even when he chopped my fingers off at the woodheap. Which seems strange, but I did dare him after all.'

'Mr Interrogator,' interjects local publican, Locke, '… I dared him to put the gun aside and fight me at the tavern. I thought he was a thug – I really did. Just an out-of-control bully.'

The interrogator nods.

'But he did, didn't he? He did put the pistol aside and did fistfight you.'

Locke is visibly angry.

'Aye, until I got the upper hand. I'd smacked him so hard with a left hook he went wobbly. I could have messed him up bad but that bloody worm, Foran, stepped in with his pistol and stopped the fight. If Larry was fair, he would have taken a beating at that point, except he pistol-whipped me in front of everybody. In front of me family. Such a biiiig man. A thug!'

Young Jack waves his hand to stop the chatter.

'Hold on a moment. Look at the size of you. You'd have to be half his size again, and sober as a judge. No disrespect, Judge. He still faced you, as drunk as he was.'

'Had it been *Mad Dog*, or Hall, they would have shot you for obstructing them,' adds the Judge.

Young Jack nods his head in enthusiastic agreement.

'Yes, if ya examine the record, Larry never shot at anybody.'

Bushranger, Fred Lowry, pushes his chair back as he rises to speak.

'Doesn't surprise me. When the traps rushed us that foggy morning at the Limerick Hotel after the coach robbery, we were surprised, still grog-soaked and sleepy. I rushed out to defend our honour. Where was he? I was willing to tackle the whole troop, but where was he? The two of us could have made a break – got away. Police report said they found him still in the bed, like a pansy. His pistol still on the sideboard. It were fine to share me bed, but not to fight beside me. At least I died game, not like a piss-ant as he.'

Lowry mimics an effete Larry and prances around with a limp-wrist. '"Oh geeze, Lowry, they had us surrounded, man."'

Laughter pervades the meeting in various quarters.

'What sort of identity is that?' he adds.

Young Jack scrapes his chair aside and charges at Lowry to knock him down. Mother Mary intervenes; blocks him. Jack shakes his fist, pushes Mary aside, but she claws back.

'Come on, Jack, sit down, nutting gained for sharing emotion, now.'

He wants to continue; defend his brother.

'He knew the pain and tragedy that follows shooting someone... That there's a big cost ta taking a life, ya flaming idiot. If you'd lived long enough to have others dependent on ya, you might have come to the same conclusion. Look at Ward, the feared bushranger. When they shot him, they found his pistol wasn't loaded. Just waved it about. That's being a real man.'

Jack sits, his fists balled, the grime of the grave obvious.

'Well, he sure could ride. I can assure you of that,' someone in the crowd offers.

The interrogator searches the audience to determine who spoke but, from the uproar, assumes there is general agreement. Then another voice above the crowd: Larry's old horse-tailer, along to pay respect to his boss, who'd hired him despite his disability.

'Yeah, Chalker, he could ride all right. Cover a lot of distance in a short time and on the most unlikely of horses.'

Trooper Chalker, now identified, rises from the front row and stalks to the table; faces the crowd. A hiss emanates from parts of the room. His khaki uniform is parade-ground clean and his knee-length boots shine in the dim light. He stands at attention, removes his notebook from his shirt-pocket and selects the appropriate page before he speaks.

'I chased the male suspect, Lawrence, *Larry*, Cummins of Taralga over two days and got close enough to shoot him in the shoulder. The blood trail was such it would have killed a roo if it lost that amount of blood, but the deceased kept on. At one point he rode up in the thickest of scrub, in the near dark of night, on the rough side of a mountain range, at the same pace as I, chasing him in the forest country below. When the alleged suspect and I galloped into the diggings I was so close to him I could grab his collar, and drag him off his horse, but he camp-drafted my horse into a bloody mining pit, using only one arm. A super-human feat… I hated Morgan, the mad bastard, but I respected Cummins,' continues Chalker. 'The suspect could have shot me when I was down that shaft. I'd not hesitated to shoot him, earlier. But he were content to make his escape without killing me. Morgan was chicken-shit easy to take, compared to Larry.'

Senior Sergeant Grainger wriggled forward on his chair to sight Chalker.

'He didn't like you though, Constable. When I nabbed him during his big escape in '67, he said had you been present, he wouldn't surrender. Didn't want to die like Hall or Morgan. He called you a "murdering bastard". Would that be correct young Mrs Cummins, you were there?'

Bridget stiffens as if physically touched. Pauses before answering. 'True! But he didn't shoot then because he didn't want our children to be hurt, or for them to be haunted by witnessing the killing of their da. I begged him to go quiet. Police get a set on a man, a family, and the worst can happen.'

'But that's because you wanted him away again, so you could go back to your rutting ways with that blonde "fancy man" warder from down Goulburn way,' shouts mother Mary.

'That's not true, Mary. Nor is it true that Larry were gutless. Family was what was important to him, when it was all said and done.'

Mary, head down, comments as if to her shoes, 'Well, a fat lot you did to help him with that.'

Bridget draws breath, her cheeks redden, her lips draw taught.

'Speak for yerself ya bloody old harpy. Look what's left of ya family? Larry was not all Mr Innocent hisself in that domain, I'm sure.'

Mother Mary ignores the provocation.

'Look, we must be careful to speak about this fairly so the boy has a chance to be judged fairly. Keeping it all in a good light is important, even when things go wrong. The Cummins' name must be protected.'

'Pity the boys didn't think about that before they went rampaging,' Bridget mutters, not quite under her breath.

Mary swivels on her chair as if to attack. 'Well, your father played a large part in that, taking them duffing, if we are to speak the truth. What sort of responsible idiot were he?'

Interrogator. 'But are we denying history by "gilding the lily" to protect families? The historian must be invisible, but perhaps if family chooses not to see what is there by connecting the wrong dots or not seeing the dots, then history is cheated. If Larry died of cirrhosis of the liver and Bright's disease, why don't we describe his drunken incompetence and decay? Because it contrasts with a picture of a religious family, as practiced by his offspring, or plays into the expected trajectory of those who don't fit into the comfortable paradigm?

In the back row, bushranger Foley in crusty moleskins and bloodless face, chuckles.

'Ha ha, I was just thinking when we bailed up the Mudgee Mail Coach Lucky Larry didn't object to being placed as the hilltop watch. He didn't insist on switching roles to be in the thick of things.'

'It was alleged he was there. That someone saw him there. But the person they saw was far away, and they could have been mistaken,' argues Judge Hargraves.

Foley straightens, resentment knots his brow.

'Oh, he was there, alright. He got equal shares of the haul.'

'What happened to all that money, by the way?' asks Constable Chalker, disregarding the current thrust of the discussion. 'It was a King's fortune at the time, right?'

Lawyer Thompson checks with Mary before answering.

'Mary may not wish to say, but I think most of it was spent buying Larry's release. She had her own income from selling farm stock, but it takes a lot of money to buy influence in NSW.'

Sargent O'Malley jumps in.

'The money's not sitting idle in an isolated cave somewhere, waiting for a lucky fortune-seeker to find it, like Ben Halls' millions, is it? That's why I gave up police work early and went prospecting. I was sure I could locate Hall's money. Maybe you found it, Chalker, with your black trackers?'

'I wish!... You could have used the trackers yesself, O'Malley, but you were too arrogant,' says Chalker.

'Greed and informants work better. Ya don't have ta spend as much time wet and cold, and on a hard, bloody saddle,' offers O'Malley, his soft body a testament to avoiding long, starving, uncomfortable, stakeouts.

A young woman in a black-dyed, flour-sack dress, raises her hand to speak.

'I'm Miss Hannah Webb from the store. I'd say Lawrence could have died numerous times, but something saved him. Luck? When my brother headshot him, as he attempted to rob our store, he fell, rose, and staggered around like a rooster with his head ripped off. I thought he was dying, I did. I have no idea how he made it to the horse. My brother said he didn't realise it was Larry until after he pulled the trigger, but I knew who it was when I shot at him with Daddy's pistol.'

Young Robert Webb cut in.

'They ran like rabbits they did… We were so sick of being robbed, we vowed to fight it every time.'

Bridget shakes her head as if to tear the argument with her teeth.

'Larry always said he had no fight with local people. He paid for as much as he took.'

Young Jack studies the Webbs in horror, disgust awash in his words.

'You shot at him, while believing he was about to die?'

Interrogator: 'Another example of terrorism?' hoping to divert young Jack.

Publican Locke rises to defend the young Webbs.

'Like all of these lads, he'd be a nice bloke when he weren't pickled, our Larry. They enjoy getting drunk and fighting too much. Both in equal draughts. Larry was a drunk, as we were told at the funeral.'

Ellen's face beamed a broad smile.

'Ha ha, but he also was very funny when he had the drink in him. He wasn't one to come home and abuse us. For a long, time I'd await dishing up the meal until he'd returned from the pub, then listen to the gossip while we ate, always told in the most dramatic of ways, and then be swept up in his arms, carried into my bed, and be made to feel the most important woman in the world. He had a turn of phrase, did James, if he put his mind to it, and the drink were in him. He weren't an insensitive beast around women, as I understand some men are. Oh no.'

Son, William, pats her hand.

'Settle down, Mum.'

'As witness, nine children?' adds daughter Catherine, with a smile.

Gaoler Small clears his throat, remains seated.

'Umm, don't wish to speak ill of the dead, but for a long time at Berrima I thought he was the most unlikable of characters. I really hated having him on site.'

Mother Mary appears surprised.

'Did he terrorise you?'

'No. He just chipped away with smart-ass backchat. When it was cold or wet, and he didn't want to work, he'd be sick. He was always sick – feigning it at least.'

'A malingerer?' asks Judge Hargraves.

'A malingerer. Yes. His record shows he spent more than 580 days sick. Nearly two years of his twelve years with us,' says Small. 'You saw his record. He led us on a merry chase. He escaped at every chance he got. Even from the new escape-proof Pentridge. You couldn't trust him.'

'Clever?' asks the judge.

The gaoler thinks for a moment before replying.

'Devious.'

'But, Mister Small, your son wrote a book about living at the prison and spoke glowingly of him.'

'Well, two things, Judge. The bastard changed and, second, he loved children. What do you make of that for a fearsome bushranger? Larry never seemed to mind the young fellow playing beneath his feet when he worked. When he'd handle the horses. The boy loved him.'

Interrogator: 'What horses?'

'We needed horses for the work-detail wagons so stabled them in the prison. I also kept horses, and my lad's pony, there. He taught the boy to ride and the lad turned out an able horseman.'

A nere-do-well looking fellow, with a scar down one side of his face rises and addresses Small.

'Isn't it true that Larry stopped a prisoner with a shovel from killing one of you screws?'

Interrogator: 'And who might you be, sir?'

'Rather not say, cobber. Just take it as one who witnessed the event. Small covered it up, to keep quiet how much unrest there were at Berrima. Larry saved his bacon and a bloody brave thing he did too, your Larry, Missus Cummins.'

Interrogator: 'Thank you, sir… So, Mr Small, smart-ass backchat wore you down and led you to invent the gag – to shut him up.'

Small reacts as if he's been slapped.

'How did you learn of that?'

Interrogator: 'From the Commission of Enquiry… It still didn't stop you using it, though, did it? Left fewer bruises for the police to find. Protected your arse.'

'I'm not saying… other than to say there came a point where Larry didn't need it any longer.'

'How come?' asks Judge Hargraves.

'He learned to read and write, and had more important things to think about,' says Small.

'So, he was clever?' urges the Judge, determined to make a point; putting words into the mouth of witnesses, something he despised in the barristers who faced his Court.

'Hmph. Like rat-clever. Observant. Reflective. Problem solver. Photographic memory. Learned to read with minimal assistance, you know.'

'So, if you disliked him so much, why did you agree to his pardon and sign for his release?' asks Colonial Secretary Robertson.

Small sneaks a glance at the Comptroller of Prisons, then the Minister, but they refuse to meet his gaze.

'It was time.'

The Colonial Secretary, following a suspicion of his own about Parole Board corruption, pushes.

'So, you weren't directed to do it?'

'Not told, exactly… there was agreement on the Parole Board, and one felt politically inclined to join the sentiment of the times.' Sweat bubbles across Small's brow, rolls down his backbone, his lips appear drawn tight. 'Look… how come I'm feeling like I'm on trial here? Like I'm the criminal?'

The interrogator: 'We're seeking the facts. Your life, and Larry's, seemed to inexorably cross, like cattle-pads that join or tear apart depending on the terrain. There are many ways to weave a story of someone's life. Is family history too forgiving? Is local history bubbling behind the rock of far wider events? Is the recount merely another coverup of the oppressed, by the oppressed, trying to fit the dominant paradigm, rather than being responsible for defragging that paradigm? Are there national archetypes at play – Irish victims?'

Gaoler Small interrupts.

'Well, government officials… we are trained to write reports which reflect the wishes, or policy, of the government-of-the-day.'

The Colonial Secretary has a wry smile as he asks.

'You didn't receive remuneration for agreeing to Cummins' release?'

'No, not at all.'

'Mrs Cummins, you didn't pay this man to influence the release of your son, Lawrence?'

'No, Mr Secretary, I didn't give no one in the government money for Larry's release.'

The interrogator: 'Come on, Mrs Cummins, it's facts here, surely? Most actors are dead and moved on. No need to protect their identity.'

'I gave Mr Thompson money that he said would make people sympathetic to Larry's case. That's all.'

The Interrogator turns to the lawyer.

'Mr Thompson?'

'I gave money to… agents… of various political persuasions. Some got more than others, but nothing direct. I have no idea where the money-trail ended. I'm part of the Justice system – I couldn't do that… could I, Judge Hargraves?'

'Indeed, Mr Thompson, you could not. You would end up in gaol yourself.'

Interrogator: 'It appears we will never come to the truth of this matter, even in death. We continue to protect an identity even when one is deceased.'

''Tis no extra effort to speak well of the dead, than 'tis to speak badly of them,' Father Lanigan reminds the crowd.

Interrogator: 'Your life also seemed to intertwine with Larry's didn't it, Father?'

'True, it did.'

'You married us – Lawrence and I,' says Bridget.

The priest contemplates, chin in hand.

'Tis true, true – mm how long ago now…? A long time.'

'And you helped Larry learn to read… in Berrima,' adds Small.

'Aye it wasn't much, really. Just made a few books available as I saw fit. He became quite hungry for dem. Quite hungry,' says Father Lanigan.

'Looking after the Irish flock, eh?' says the Judge.

'As best I could, for it were nearly impossible to get clerics to live in some parts of the country. The Church followed the gold like everyone else. It was also an injustice to find the Irish Catholics still taking orders from the "proddy" landholders, even over here. The youngsters rebelled. The cornstalks were raised free and to take their orders from no one. Their identity was not aligned back to the old country, but here. They ranged the bush with allegiance to family and opportunity.'

The Colonial Secretary's lips twist with cynicism.

'Bit romantic?'

'I didn't see Lawrence being like the old "ticket-of-leave" lags, living their criminal lives here in New South Wales exactly as they had before they were transported. He was one of the home-grown bushrangers, with skills that matched the opportunities of the time – good horsemen, bold, daring, brave, bored, spectators to wealth – which helped steer them towards crime. The gold pointed to new opportunities, not only for Catholics and the Irish, but for Australians,' explains the priest.

'That was certainly my summation of the situation at that time,' adds historian, Maurice Cummins.

The Colonial Secretary chortles – in danger of falling off his chair such is his convulsive laughter.

'Next, you're going to tell us he had a political orientation before those Victorians, Ned Kelly and Joe Byrne, in the 1880s. "Lucky Larry's Manifesto". Ha!'

Lanigan maintains his composure.

'No, he was merely wild – one of the early wild colonial boys. He later learned, having become literate, to respect the law and how to use it to improve living conditions for all.'

The Colonial Secretary slaps his knees.

'You're not going to use the Enquiry as an example of his altruistic leanings, are you? That's preposterous for such an opportunist.'

Lawyer Thompson, firmly, without levity, intercedes.

'Well, it could – because, through the enquiry, he brought the eyes of the outside community onto the plight of prisoners.'

The Minister for Justice and Public Instruction, jumps in.

'What a fuss about nothing. Merely a fuss about transparency – something we struggle with even today.'

Thompson's face shows irritation.

'Indeed, transparency… you strip a prisoner of his identity through ensuring you can see his every movement, yet policy-makers like you fail to see the virtue in transparency for your own endeavours. The added virtue of this case is, it's a prisoner driving the enquiry, not an outside advocate touched by God to notice the concerns of the downtrodden.'

There is quiet in the room; all, like a magpie worrying a lawn grub, turn over the proposition – that someone inflicted with a disease can determine its cure. Ted, Larry's pub mate from Albury, stands, and quietly comments.

'Look, I just want to say that as my friend, James seemed content to be a mate, one of the boys and a family man, as best he knew how. Like Mr Small said, he loved children, especially his own. He was happy to be making an honest living and returning home whenever possible to his family. He appeared to have little interest in public crusades, or in any public exposure for that matter, in all the time I knew him.'

'That's because the shady beggar didn't wish to be recognised,' some smart aleck mutters, setting loose a chuckle to wander aimlessly around the room.

The interrogator raises his hand. The room quietens like a receding ocean wave as the sound of numerous boots crunching on granite outside grows louder, intrudes. A child rushes to a window, peers into the gloom.

'Soldiers. There's soldiers coming.'

The rhythmical noise of marching boots dominates the room. Crunch, crunch, crunch.

'Platoon… Halt!'

The crunching sound ceases. A drill voice echoes.

'Soldier number 2247, you're dismissed.'

'Yes, Sergeant.'

Shuffling boots.

'Where's your kit, lad?'

'Don't have it, Sergeant.'

'Why not, boy?'

'Couldn't carry it, Sergeant.'

'Why the fuck not?'

'Don't have an arm to carry both it and the rifle.'

'What happened to your arm?'

'Lost it in Pozières, France, Sergeant. Jerry artie.'

'That's very sloppy, soldier. Could be dereliction of duty… Quartermaster?'

'Sergeant?'

'Bill this man for the loss of one arm, human, general purpose, for-the-use-of…'

'Shirt as well, Sergeant?'

'I was billed for that, and one glove, already, Sergeant.'

'Collect his weapon… Any bullets in the magazine, Private?'

'Ah… three.'

'Why didn't you hand in your ammunition?'

'In case Europe invades us, Sergeant. There are many we left alive.'

'Don't be an idiot, soldier. No one's going to invade Australia.'

'Isn't that why we went over there?'

'No, we went to become Australians, to forge our identity as commanded by the King. ANZACs.'

Mumbling of numerous voices objecting.

'You could'a told us.'

'Quiet that man! Attention! Be off 2247, this is where I was told to deliver ya. Sorry we are late. Wrong grid reference from HQ. You understand, being an arty man… By the left… quiiiick march.'

Gravel crunches to the marcher's beat. The sergeant chants: 'Left… Left… Left, right, left.' His rhythmic voice slowly fades. Silence reigns. Lone footsteps clump up the stairs. All eyes watch the door. A tall, uniformed youth, face pale, gaunt with black-ringed eyes, enters warily; freezes like a child before a ghost.

Ellen stands, peers at the apparition.

'Is it you, Sid?'

'Yes, Mum. It's me. Back from the war: the world war – Egypt, Gallipoli, France.'

Ellen runs to him, hugs him so hard he's breathless.

'What have they done to you, lad?'

'They changed me. They said they had a job for us wild colonial boys. Said it was right up our thieving, fighting, riding, shooting alley. Would suit our nature.'

'The bastards. But you're home now, lad. You're safe.'

'I've been in the army, Mum. It's like a prison as Dad described. An institution. I'm terrified of you all, and the world outside it. Our family is doomed.'

'Shush boy. We'll talk of this when the meeting's over, and I have you home.'

Interrogator: 'So, before we were interrupted, Ellen, you said Larry left his own mother and family to start a new life?'

'Dropped his age by ten years, also,' she adds, now seated with an arm around Sid. 'I thought the age gap between us was too wide anyway, without adding those extra years… Look, I think it showed how much he loved them… his family, that he would sacrifice his happiness for theirs. He didn't know he was going to meet another woman and build a family when he left home, did he?'

Father Lanigan nods and tuts his tongue.

'But hard on his mother, not contacting her again. Especially, given the effort she put into freeing him.'

Larry's Aunt Maggie, scowling, rises.

'Personally, I don't care if the family never hears of him again. What distress and shame he caused! Most likely prompted the death of my poor husband, John, as well... if we are to believe his account. I didn't want the scandal. I didn't want my children mixing with Mary and her tribe after the murder and imprisonment. We came to Australia to free ourselves of this thuggery. We cut ourselves off from Mary's side of the family, never to be mentioned again.'

The interrogator, steering the conversation back to its previous track asks, 'But, Mary, your family was not the struggling tenant family of the usual, Irish Catholic renegade, was it? You had property?'

'Aye, we had a wee bit o land here and dere,' says Mary. 'But it were but the pickin's left after the Squatters took the sweet meat of the best waterholes and most fertile lands. Had the gold not shown its sparklin' face, we never would have been able to afford dat. We managed to get by, and along wit families such as the Hogans, Crokers, and Vardys, who became kin by marriage, we became da heart and soul of our community. Ya hear people conversing about us at Council meetings, still.'

The audience chuckles. The interrogator stands; rubs his hands together.

'Okay, on that positive note, it appears to be a good time to end this meeting.'

'How come Larry's not here?' a journalist from the *Bathurst Times* interjects.

Maurice, the historian, offers an opinion.

'Well, typical of Larry, he's gone-to-ground. He's as hard to locate in death, as he is in life.'

'Why?' asks the journalist, double-dipping where the polite let lie.

'No one can locate his grave in the Wodonga Cemetery.'

'Anyway, it would be cheating,' continues the interrogator.

'What do you mean?'

'None of us get to rewrite our narrative after we are dead.'

'Well, it would answer many questions.'

'It would, indeed, but then it wouldn't fit elusive Larry, would it?'

Whilst the questioner is unhappy with the answer, there is no further comment.

The interrogator raises his hands; attracts attention.

'Thank you, folks. Please feel free to stay and chat. There is more to eat and drink at the supper table. Travel safely. The meeting is over.'

The children report, later, that they saw their dad, James, standing outside in the dusk, listening, but he appears to have been invisible to the adults. Others believe they hear his spurs tinkling on the cold starry nights up in the Abercrombies. But what are you to believe?... after all, they're descended from the Irish and there's always blarney afoot.

THE END

ACKNOWLEDGEMENTS

AN aspiring author has much to learn. I would like to thank Carolyn Martinez and her enthusiastic team at Hawkeye Publishing for editing and husbanding this work from manuscript to printed book, and for taking a punt on me. In addition, I'd like to thank author and creative writing lecturer, Dr. Maria Simms from Laurel Cohn, for her early manuscript assessment and developmental advice. I'll always appreciate her sensitive critique of my unorthodox approach, ongoing support and friendship.

This is a work of the imagination but draws heavily upon Maurice Cummins' family history, *A Long Way from Tipperary*, which I'd commend to those interested in deeper understanding of Laurence Cummins' story. Sadly, it is no longer in print but can be accessed through library archives. I also acknowledge Henry Lawson's poems, *Andy's Gone with Cattle* and *Andy's Return*, and his wonderful short story, *The Drover's Wife*. I used the former to acknowledge our debt to him as a bush advocate, and to alert students of Australian literature that he may feature more centrally in this story. To this end I used the carcass of the latter, his short story, (pp169-175), for artistic purposes, to compare town-based drover's wife, Ellen, with his character.

I would like to acknowledge the assistance of the Australian National Library for providing a copy of *A Long Way from Tipperary*. NSW Corrective Services' Corporate Records and Archives, and NSW State Records, who facilitated a search of their records by first allowing access to files, and second, linking me with Anne Lyon, an accredited researcher.

Various individuals have assisted. Hudson Jefferies, for bringing Larry's story to my attention following a conversation he witnessed at a family reunion. Carolyn Long, for explaining with her husband, Phillip, how the wider Long family was informed about Larry (Chapter 1), and later, assistance in contacting Dominic Cummins, who advised me regarding any sensitivities with the ongoing Cummins' family line that my penchant for intrigue and drama may unconsciously disturb. Kevin Rowles for both an early www.Ancestor.com.au enquiry and for interviewing Maurice Cummins on my behalf. And finally, Carolyn 'Bodge' Long, for permission to use her story (Chapter 1). To those mentioned, thank you very much.

In repayment, I hope my animation of the story will help inform future generations.

Peter Long

BOOK CLUB QUESTIONS

1. What role does identity play in our lives, society, and culture?

2. What role does family identity play in forming personal identity?

3. Where does the author stand on nature versus nurture/environment question?

4. What questions does this story raise about the criminal justice system and rehabilitation?

5. Literacy was important to Larry. Will it remain an important personal and societal requirement? Does diminishing novel readership indicate any trends? What are the implications, if any?

6. Are there parallels with Larry's story and Ned Kelly's?

7. Are there parallels between the Irish migrants and successive waves of migration?

8. Larry was portrayed as a gambler. Why does gambling (and perhaps horse racing) have such a stranglehold over the Australian psyche?

LITERARY DISCUSSION

1. Can readers identify with Larry? Is there a villain in the story?

2. Australia's identity once relied on rural elements. What is the present generator?

3. How realistic is *narrative* a metaphor for identity? What genre would describe your narrative? What themes would repeat? What metaphor might best describe you?

4. The novel has numerous narrators. What are the strengths and weaknesses of such an approach compared to a single narrator?

5. Lawson's short story, *The Drover's Wife*, is a sympathetic view of a woman's lot, and the resilience of country folk. Ellen's is a view of a woman's lot as Australia transitioned to the town. What are the differences, if any? Would it be the same for the modern partner of a fly-in-fly-out worker, in a largely urban-sited population?

6. Why might the author have chosen second person point-of-view in the prison chapters?

7. What might Larry's race against the bushfire represent?

ABOUT THE AUTHOR

Peter Long has worked as a stockman, public servant, consultant, researcher and academic. He studied in Canada and holds degrees from University of Queensland and University of Toronto. His poetry has been highly commended in the McGregor Literary Competition and a long poem published in Paper Children, an anthology from that competition. He has been long-listed and published in The Stringybark and Sydney Hammond short story competitions and his collection of short stories long-listed in the 2020 Hawkeye Manuscript Development Prize.

Peter Long resides in Brisbane (Meanjin, Turrbal-Jagera country) in Queensland, Australia.

Identity: Larry Cummins, Bushranger, is Peter's second novel. His first novel, *Steve Hart: The Last Kelly Standing*, is also published by Hawkeye Publishing.

Book reviews can make or break a book. If you liked what you read today, please do consider posting a review on Goodreads or your favourite forum.

Identity is available at hawkeyebooks.com.au and all good bookstores and libraries.

If you enjoyed this book, you may also like:

Steve Hart: The Last Kelly Standing follows the life of Steve Hart, one of the Kelly gang members, that builds on the legend of Steve Hart escaping the Glennrowan siege and the life he may have had in the aftermath.

Lament is a thrilling rewrite of the Ned Kelly story that reimagines the life he may have lived had he escaped his past.

What if you Fly? is a page-turning WWII adventure that starts in Australia and travels the world through the eyes of Frances Davies, code named Funnel Web.

www.ingramcontent.com/pod-product-compliance
Lightning Source LLC
Chambersburg PA
CBHW011557190726
48287CB00010B/2946

* 9 7 8 1 9 2 3 1 0 5 0 7 2 *